FINAL FONDUE

Val noticed Grandad's drooping eyelids. "Why don't you go to bed? I'll take out the trash and set up the coffee maker."

"Okay." He gave her a peck on the cheek. "Good night."

Val carried the trash bag through a small enclosed porch and opened the back door. With no moonlight, she could barely see across the yard to the shed where the garbage bin was. She waited for her eyes to adjust to the dark and then started toward the shed, focusing on the uneven ground so that she wouldn't stumble.

Halfway across the yard, bulging eyes looked up at her. She jumped back, startled, and dropped the trash bag.

Then she laughed. The plastic eyes sat atop the festival's souvenir crab hat. One of the tourists staying in the house must have dropped the hat in the yard.

Val stooped to pick up the hat and froze.

Two feet away, a woman lay on the ground, a rope around her neck, her eyes open and lifeless as the crab eyes . . .

D0752865

Books by Maya Corrigan

BY COOK OR BY CROOK

SCAM CHOWDER

FINAL FONDUE

Published by Kensington Publishing Corporation

Final Fondue

Maya Corrigan

KENSINGTON PUBLISHING CORP.

http://www.kensingtonbooks.com

KENSINGTON BOOKS are published by

Kensington Publishing Corp.
119 West 40th Street
New York, NY 10018

All Kensington Titles, Imprints, and Distributed Lines are available at special quantity discounts for bulk purchases for sales promotions, premiums, fund-raising, and educational or institutional use. Special book excerpts or customized printings can also be created to fit specific needs. For details, write or phone the office of the Kensington special sales manager: Kensington Publishing Corp., 119 West 40th Street, New York, NY 10018, attn: Special Sales Department, Phone: 1-800-221-2647.

Kensington and the K logo Reg. U.S. Pat & TM Off.

ISBN-13: 978-1-61773-142-6
ISBN-10: 1-61773-142-0
First Kensington Mass Market Edition: July 2016

eISBN-13: 978-1-61773-143-3
eISBN-10: 1-61773-143-9
First Kensington Electronic Edition: July 2016

10 9 8 7 6 5 4 3 2 1

Printed in the United States of America

To Nora, Paul, Kate, Kai, and Oscar
with all my love

"Fondue is a conjurer of the past."
—David Sax

The Tastemakers: Why We're Crazy for Cupcakes but Fed Up with Fondue

Chapter 1

Val Deniston stood aghast at her bedroom door as her grandfather carried out an armload of her clothes on hangers. "What are you doing?"

"Emptying your closet." He looked frazzled, with tufts of his white hair sticking out like wings above his ears. "You gotta move all your stuff. And don't complain, because putting up tourists for the weekend was your idea."

True, she'd urged him to rent his unused rooms during Bayport's Tricentennial Festival, but he'd gone overboard. "Pile the clothes on my bed. I'll deal with them. Last I heard, you had people staying in the spare bedrooms, not *my* room."

Granddad reversed course and laid her clothes on the bed. "Jennifer Brown, the woman who reserved three rooms, called back and said she'd cancel them if I didn't have another bedroom to rent. I couldn't let her cancel, not after I went to all the trouble of fixing up those rooms."

All the trouble for him amounted to rooting

around the attic for some framed Hitchcock posters, leftovers from his defunct video store, and hanging a poster outside each bedroom. Val had scrubbed the bathrooms, made up the beds, and even added decorative touches to match his posters. Seagull decals in the *Birds* room. Baskets made of coiled clothesline in the *Rope* room. Photos of Mount Rushmore and of cornfields in the *North by Northwest* bedroom.

Val moved jackets and skirts from the closet to the bed. "What poster are you going to hang outside this room?"

"*Rear Window.* Don't bother putting any gewgaws in here. You have a window facing the backyard. That's good enough." He pointed to the black suit atop the pile of clothing on her bed. "You might as well get rid of those New York clothes. You don't need them around here."

He was right. She should donate the suit. She'd worn it often as a cookbook publicist in New York, but never in the eight months since she'd moved into Granddad's house on Maryland's Eastern Shore. Now that she was running a café at an athletic club, she could get by with casual clothing. "Where do you want me to put my clothes?"

"The stuff from your dresser can go into the big suitcase in the storage room. Take the clothes on hangers to the closet in my bedroom. Plenty of room there now, though it was full when your grandmother was alive." He turned to look out the window. "She's been gone six years."

Val joined him at the window. "I still miss her too."

He squeezed her hand gently. "I know."

She went back to the closet and unhooked the dresses hanging there. "Now the only question is where *I* go for the weekend."

"I arranged for you to stay with Monique."

Startled, Val nearly dropped the dresses. Why had he suddenly reached out to her cousin? He'd been nursing a rift with Monique's branch of the family for decades, long after everyone else involved in it was dead. "With the traffic this weekend, I don't want to drive back and forth to Monique's house. I'd rather stay with someone in town and walk to the festival."

"I can guess who that someone is." Granddad crossed his arms. "Gunnar Swensen."

Ah. Granddad had chosen Monique as the lesser of two evils, but he'd guessed wrong. Though Val had no problem spending a lot of time with Gunnar or even sharing his bed, she wouldn't stay overnight at his place. Too soon to take that step with him, but high time her grandfather stopped treating her like a teenager. "I'm thirty-two years old, Granddad. I'll sleep where I want."

"Monique dropped this off." Granddad pulled a key from his pocket and gave it to Val. "You'll hurt her feelings if you don't stay with her. There are ways around the traffic. It's a straight shot to town by water from her house. That husband of hers can ferry you."

Val would hate to depend on Maverick Mott for transportation . . . or anything else. "His boatyard is a stop on the Chesapeake Bay History Tour this weekend. He'll be busy demonstrating how to build and restore wood boats." She was resigned to staying with her cousin. "I'll avoid the traffic by driving to Monique's house late and leaving early."

"If you don't need my help here, I'll go down and fix a welcome snack for our guests. They're supposed to arrive around four. That gives me half an hour." He walked toward the door. "With all this festival to-do, I haven't had the time to get on the computer and read this week's lecture. I hate to fall behind in my homework."

"Please don't fall behind." She looked forward to the end of his online course in private investigation. Until he finished it, he'd keep hogging her laptop. His sleuthing a few months ago had given him delusions of becoming a private eye. Why not? After standing over a hot stove once or twice, he'd passed himself off as a food guru, the Codger Cook. He'd used her recipes to snag a job as the local newspaper's recipe columnist. At least this time he was making an effort to learn the basics before claiming to be an expert. "Be glad the money you collect from renting the rooms for three days will cover your tuition."

"That's the only reason I agreed to this."

If hosting tourists proved painless for him this weekend, Val would try to persuade him to rent the spare rooms through Airbnb or another accommodation service. The house would then produce the income needed for its repair and spruce-up. "Maybe you'll enjoy the company."

He put on his bah-humbug face. "I don't need

company. I want them to stay upstairs and not get in my way. I moved the small TV from my bedroom to the alcove off the hall up here. With the window seat and the rocking chair there, they should have plenty of room to sit."

For the first time, Val regretted urging him to open his house to strangers. They would take over the nook where she'd spent countless hours reading. As a child visiting her grandparents, she'd also eavesdropped from that spot, whenever voices drifted up the front staircase. "With the TV there, you'll hear the audio downstairs."

"Not if I take out my hearing aids or turn up the TV in the sitting room. I'll be glad when this festival's over." He went down the back stairs, the maid's route to the kitchen when the Victorian house was built in the nineteenth century.

Val would be glad to have the weekend behind her too. When she volunteered for the Tricentennial Festival committee, she hadn't realized it would eat up all her free time. Except for the usual six hours a day she spent running the Cool Down Café at the racket and fitness club, she'd done nothing but festival preparations for the last few weeks. Besides coordinating the food vendors and producing a pamphlet describing the town's restaurants, she'd also prepared as much food as she could ahead of time for her festival booth promoting the café. She looked forward to next week, when she could go back to playing tennis with her friends and testing recipes for her cookbook.

After clearing out her bedroom, Val packed a

small bag for the weekend and put it in her car. She'd just hung up the last of her clothes in Granddad's closet when the hall phone rang.

She answered it and heard a voice from the past. Her brusque former boss raced through the hello-how-are-yous and then said, "I'm calling to offer you your job back."

For a moment Val was too stunned to speak. A few months ago, she'd have jumped at a chance to go back to the job she once enjoyed. She wouldn't jump now. Yet she felt a flutter of interest, and she couldn't suppress her curiosity. "Has something changed in the department?"

"We're not bringing out any more cookbooks by Chef Henri La Farge."

So the man responsible for her removal as a cookbook publicist was out. But the department head who'd kowtowed to him was still there. "Thank you, but I—"

"We'll give you a fifteen percent increase over your previous salary. Take the weekend to think about it. Call me Monday . . . no, Monday's Columbus Day. Let's talk Tuesday, okay?"

He hung up without waiting for a reply. He hadn't changed.

Val cradled the phone in her hand. She'd decided a few months ago that she belonged here in Bayport, close to Granddad and her cousin. So why would her old job even tempt her? Unfinished business, that's why. She'd pitched her tent here with new ropes and guys, but the old, frayed cords still flapped against the canvas, reminding her of her destroyed career and the colleagues she'd left so abruptly. Should those cords be mended or cut? She'd left friends behind, but made new ones here. She'd also left her cheating fiancé in New York. Now she spent time with Gunnar. After quitting his government job, he could have set up his own accounting practice anywhere. He chose Bayport because she lived here. How would she feel if she left?

She put the phone down and rubbed her temples. Having made a decision, she should stick with it, but she was always second-guessing herself. Her part in solving two recent murders in Bayport had given her ample reason to distrust her first instincts.

Granddad peered into the hall from the sitting room. "I hope that wasn't our guests canceling or demanding another bedroom."

Val couldn't resist a tit for tat. "They needed another room, so I okayed it. I figured you could move out." She pointed to his bedroom at the end of the downstairs hall. "You want some help packing?"

Granddad's eyes turned as round as his wire-rimmed bifocals. "What's the matter with you, Val? Call 'em back and tell 'em no dice. I'm not going to leave my own house."

She grinned. "Just kidding. What snacks are you putting out for our guests?"

"Come to the kitchen and see." He pivoted and crossed the sitting room toward the back of the house.

She followed him, expecting to find chips and dip on the counter. Instead, a sectioned platter held strawberries, banana chunks, and wedges of kiwi fruit. Cubes of angel food cake were in a bowl, and a ceramic pot rested on a stand with a tea light under it.

"That's impressive, Granddad." She managed to keep the surprise out of her voice. "Where did you get that fondue pot?"

"Found it in the attic. Back in the sixties and seventies, we used to have neighborhood fondue parties. Cheese fondue at one house, beef fondue at another, and then chocolate fondue somewhere else." He picked up a dog-eared index card from the counter. "Here's your grandmother's favorite chocolate fondue recipe. I'll try it out on our guests. If they go for it, I'll enter it in the dessert cook-off on Sunday. It's less work than making cookies."

"You can't go wrong with chocolate." Val picked up one of the fondue forks on the counter. Set into its five-inch-long wood handle was a metal piece of equal length, the last two inches of which forked into pointed tines. "These elongated tines are for spearing meat. The forks for cheese and chocolate fondue don't need to be so long and sharp."

"I only found two of those. We have seven of these." The doorbell rang. "That's probably one of our guests." Granddad donned a khaki apron with CODGER COOK printed in red letters on it.

Most people took off an apron when company came, but not Granddad. He didn't mind spilling food on his old clothes, but he kept the Codger Cook regalia spotless to promote his "brand." He lived in hope that someone would snap a picture of him in the apron, post it online, and bring him instant fame.

"You take care of the snack, Granddad. I'll meet the guests at the door."

"And collect the money for the rooms. I said payment was due upfront. They'll probably want to pay by credit card, and I'm not sure how to use that gizmo you have for your phone to swipe the cards."

Val hurried to the front door. A petite woman stood on the porch, dressed for the mild autumn afternoon in rolled-up jeans and a rust-colored corduroy shirt. Despite clogs that added to her height, she stood no taller than Val's five foot three. She looked under thirty, but not by much.

She smiled, revealing dimples in her plump cheeks. "Hello. How are you? I'm Fawn Finchley. If this is Mr. Myer's house, I'm supposed to stay here this weekend."

"I'm Mr. Myer's granddaughter, Val Deniston. Please come in."

Fawn put her overnight bag on the floor in the hall. "This is such a cool house with the round tower and the gables. Is it as old as it looks?"

Val suppressed a smile. "It's 125 years old. Some of the buildings in Bayport's historic district go back to the early eighteenth century, when the town was founded. Would you please sign the guest book?" Val pointed to an open book on the table by the staircase. She caught a whiff of cigarette smoke. The house rules she'd printed and left in each bedroom specified no smoking. Fawn was probably used to smoking outside. If she did it indoors at home, her clothes would have given off more than a whiff.

Fawn took her time signing. "No one else has signed in yet. I must be the first one here."

"Right. I can run your credit card for the three nights you'll be staying."

Fawn's forehead wrinkled. "Didn't Jennifer take care of that? She made the reservations."

"She didn't pay yet. Don't worry about it. We'll deal with it when she gets here."

Granddad appeared in the archway between the sitting room and the hall, looking like a beardless Santa with furry white eyebrows and bifocals slipping down his nose. His Codger Cook apron over a plaid shirt and navy trousers substituted for Santa's red suit. "Come in and make yourself at home." He motioned them toward the sitting room.

Val introduced him to his first guest.

Fawn gave him a high-wattage smile. "Thank you so much for opening your beautiful house to us, Mr. Myer. The woodwork in here is gorgeous. Such a homey room with the fireplace and bookshelves, and what pretty dried flowers."

Val tried to catch Granddad's eye so she could give him an I-told-you-so look. He'd complained about spending money on the flower arrangements for the coffee table and the fireplace mantle. They were worth every penny. They picked up the yellow and muted orange colors of the throw pillows on the sofa and added cheer to a room with worn furniture.

Fawn asked about the Codger Cook apron, giving Granddad a chance to awe her with his celebrity status as the newspaper's food columnist. While he preened and Fawn fawned, a second guest knocked on the door.

Val opened it to a thirtyish man with a pallid face and protruding ears. Noah Hurdly had clearly come straight from work, wearing dark trousers, the matching suit jacket folded on his arm and his off-white dress shirt open at the collar. He carried a leather attaché case and a matching overnight bag. Val asked him to sign the guestbook. He took two seconds to scrawl his name and offered her his credit card.

Granddad was showing Fawn his collection of classic movies on the shelves near the fireplace when Noah went into the sitting room and introduced himself.

Fawn's face lit up like a child's on Christmas morning. "Noah! The best man, right? I'm a bridesmaid, Fawn Finchley."

Noah seemed at a loss for words. He cleared his throat. "Oh. The latest bridesmaid."

His toneless voice gave Val no clue if Fawn had replaced a dropout bridesmaid or had joined a growing line of the bride's attendants.

If the idea that she wasn't the first bridesmaid chosen fazed Fawn, she didn't show it. "I'm so excited to be here this weekend. You're a lawyer like Jennifer's fiancé, right?"

"That's correct. Payton and I are attorneys at the same firm in Washington."

Fawn turned to Granddad. "We're all here to plan a wedding. It will probably be at the big house the groom's parents own on the bay. This weekend we're going to check out locations for the hen party, the welcome party, and the farewell brunch."

"Count me out of that." Noah peered at Granddad's videos. "I see you have all the Hitchcock films, even his early talkies, *Murder!* and *Blackmail.*"

"Hitchcock fan, huh?" At Noah's nod, Granddad continued, "You can borrow any of these and watch them on the TV upstairs. It has a built-in DVD player."

Fawn looked toward the hall. "Here comes the maid of honor. Hi, Sarina."

A woman with an olive complexion and dark hair in a loose braid walked into the sitting room, not having bothered to knock before entering the house. She cut a bohemian figure in a leather vest over a gauzy top, shin-length gaucho pants, and gladiator sandals.

She gave Fawn a curt nod and the best man a big smile. "Nice to see you again, Noah."

"Likewise." He shook hands with her.

She then extended her hand to Val and Granddad. "Sarina Rafael." She had a few inches on Fawn, less meat on her bones, and a face with coarser features.

"Sarina is a painter." Fawn fingered her shoulder-length brown hair, which flipped up at the ends, perky like her personality. "I've been meaning to ask you about your last name, Sarina. Isn't there a famous artist named Rafael? Is he your great-great-great grandfather or something?"

Sarina rolled her eyes. "That artist's *first* name was Raffaello. He was Italian and died five hundred years ago. My last name is Hispanic."

"So you're not related to him," Fawn said. "I'll bet you don't paint like him either."

Before Sarina could respond, Val asked her to sign the guest book in the hall and requested her credit card.

When Sarina returned to the sitting room,

Granddad suggested the guests go with him to look at the bedrooms, decide who would stay where, and get settled.

Sarina put up her hand like a traffic cop. "No. We'll wait for Jennifer. She should get the first choice of a room."

Noah jerked to attention. "Jennifer's staying here?"

Fawn looked equally surprised. "I thought she was spending the weekend with Payton's family and just the three of us would be here."

"She thought so too." Sarina plopped into the armchair near the sofa. "But her future mother-in-law invited old friends for the town's festival."

Val exchanged a look with Granddad. No wonder Jennifer Brown had needed a fourth room at the last minute. If the bride-to-be didn't have a place to stay, the rest of them had no reason to come. Odd that the mother didn't tell her son sooner that she wouldn't have room for his fiancée. Not exactly welcoming. Back when Val was engaged to Tony, his mother had at least been polite to the fiancée she viewed as unworthy of her son. She'd doubtless done a happy dance when Val broke off the engagement.

"Where is Payton staying?" Fawn asked.

Sarina gave her a you-moron look. "At his parents' house. Where else would he stay?"

Granddad excused himself and headed for the kitchen.

Fawn sidled up to Noah and spoke in an undertone to him. The two of them drifted into the dining room, deep in conversation. Sarina glowered at them.

Was she always bad-tempered, Val wondered, or did she have something against the new bridesmaid in particular? Maybe Sarina was jealous of the more attractive Fawn.

Val pointed to the pamphlets and flyers on the coffee table. "There's some information about the festival. The opening ceremonies and fireworks are tonight. I'd be happy to answer any questions you have."

"Thank you." Sarina picked up the pamphlets. "This is all the information I'll need."

Val took the curt words as dismissal. She hurried to the kitchen.

Granddad was pouring melted chocolate into the fondue pot. "Everyone might as well sit down and enjoy this instead of twiddling their thumbs until Jennifer shows up. You're sticking around, aren't you?"

"For a while." Val couldn't pretend enthusiasm. She preferred twiddling her thumbs to sitting at the same table with the odd trio, but Granddad could use some help with them. "Do you mind if I sample the fondue?"

"Go right ahead, but don't tell me it doesn't taste good. I'm serving it anyway. Fondue is a great ice-breaker. People sit around the table and talk."

Val speared a banana chunk with a fork, dipped it into the chocolate, and popped it into her mouth. A mixture of dark chocolate and milk chocolate with a hint of brandy. Pretty good. "It tastes terrific." She dunked a cake cube as he beamed with pride. "Did Jennifer already pay for her room and Fawn's?"

"Nope. I took a credit card number to hold the reservation, but I didn't charge her card."

"Fawn thought Jennifer had paid for both rooms. I'll work it out with them."

Val took the fruit plate and the bowl of cake cubes to the dining room table while Granddad set the fondue pot on a stand with a candle under it. He invited everyone to sit down and suggested they slide the chairs close to the end of the table where he put the chocolate.

Fawn clapped her hands together and said that chocolate fondue was her absolute favorite. Once seated, she pricked a strawberry with her fondue fork, plunged it into the melted chocolate, and promptly lost the fruit. While everyone else watched, she went spearfishing for the berry and succeeded only in coating the metal half of her fondue fork in melted chocolate. Chocolate dripped onto the tablecloth as she moved the fork from the pot to her plate.

Luckily, Granddad had chosen a washable tablecloth. Val jumped up. "I'll get you a new fork."

"I can just lick the chocolate off." Fawn brought the fork to her lips.

"Stop!" Sarina barked. "Nobody wants a fork with your saliva going back into the chocolate." She launched into a lesson in fondue hygiene, ordering the removal of dipped food from fondue forks before eating it.

Meanwhile, Val brought Fawn an unused fork.

Noah, sitting next to Fawn, speared a cake cube, bathed it in chocolate, and gobbled it up as quickly as he could while observing Sarina's sanitary rules.

As he chewed, he impaled his next piece of cake. Fawn shoved her fork into a banana chunk, apparently determined not to lose that piece of fruit in the chocolate.

Val dipped a kiwi wedge in the fondue pot as soon as Fawn's banana emerged from it. "What type of work do you do, Fawn?"

"I'm a gate agent at Reagan National Airport."

Noah's fork stopped halfway to the chocolate. "Do you like that job? Dealing with passengers complaining about delays and demanding different seats?"

"You'd be surprised how many of them smile when you smile at them. If I can change frowny faces into happy faces, I go home feeling like I've made the world a better place."

Granddad beamed at the Pollyanna-on-steroids bridesmaid. "I'm sure you make everyone's day a little brighter."

Sarina stabbed a heart-shaped strawberry and held the fruit up for inspection. "How much money does a gate agent make?"

With that question, she stuck a forkful of reality into the bridesmaid's jar of honey.

Fawn's smile at the maid of honor was forced, showing only a hint of her dimples. "I don't earn much, but I get benefits and travel perks. I love to travel, like you love to paint, Sarina. How much do you make from selling your paintings?"

Touché.

Sarina plunged her strawberry into the fondue and lifted it out. "I work full-time as a computer graphics specialist. That job pays well." While she held her strawberry over the bowl and examined it from various angles, no one could get a fork in edgewise.

Fawn held a strawberry at the ready. "What kind of job do you have, Val?"

"I manage the café at the Bayport Racket and Fitness Club. For the festival, I'll have a booth with salads, sandwiches, and snacks."

"It's healthy food," Granddad said, "but it tastes good anyway."

Sarina put down her fork. "Where's Jennifer? She should be here by now."

Granddad skewered a cake cube. "Traffic's heavy on three-day weekends with good weather. All you need is one fender bender on the Chesapeake Bay Bridge, and you got a mess."

"She usually texts if she's delayed." Sarina fished a phone from the deep pocket in her gaucho pants and pressed buttons. "No messages from her."

Noah dipped his cake cube, beating Granddad to the chocolate bowl. "Texting while driving is illegal in Maryland. She must have read the warning signs on the road."

"As if anyone pays attention to that," Sarina said.

"Jennifer would." Fawn's strawberry fell off the fork on its way to the chocolate pot. "Gosh, I hope she's not involved in an accident."

Much ado about lateness. Val wondered if Jennifer was accident-prone or if her friends had little to say to each other except to dissect her every action.

Chapter 2

The fondue didn't serve as the icebreaker Granddad had expected. Sarina maintained stony silence as Fawn peppered Noah with questions about his favorite movies and his tastes in music.

A wind-chime tune came from Sarina's skirt pocket. She pulled her phone out and stared at the screen. "Jennifer's just getting into Bayport, but traffic's at a standstill with so many streets closed off."

Val had plotted a way around the detours. "I can give her a back route here if you like."

She took the phone Sarina handed her. Jennifer sent a text describing what she could see from the car. Val texted back directions for avoiding the Main Street traffic, read the updates Jennifer sent about her location as she drove along, and then handed the phone back. "She should be here in a few minutes."

Fawn stood up. "Great. I'm going outside for a cigarette. I'll take my plate to the kitchen."

"No need," Granddad said. "We'll clean up."

But Fawn had already disappeared through the butler's pantry.

Val picked up the nearly empty bowl of cake, followed Fawn into the kitchen, and pointed to the back door. "If you'd like, you can go out here and sit in the yard. There's a picnic table."

Fawn finished dumping the strawberry stems from her plate into the trash. "Perfect." She put her plate in the sink and went outside.

Val refilled the bowl of cake cubes. When she returned to the dining room, Noah was scrolling through messages on his phone, and Sarina asked where the bathroom was.

Val decided to send her upstairs rather than to the bathroom outside Granddad's bedroom on the main floor. She didn't want the guests intruding on his personal space. She walked Sarina to the hall and pointed up the staircase. "Turn left in the hall upstairs. It's the third door on the right."

As Sarina climbed the stairs, Val looked out the screen door. Three cars were parked on the street besides her grandfather's big Buick. The Ford that looked as beat up as Val's ten-year-old Saturn probably belonged to Fawn, the shiny black sedan to Noah, and the compact hybrid to Sarina. A gold hatchback slowed down and eased into a spot behind the sedan.

A woman in a tan miniskirt and jacket emerged from the hatchback. She took a large wheeled suitcase from the trunk. Rolling it behind her, she walked on spike heels toward the house. Val still owned shoes like those, left over from her New York life, but she'd never worn them here. Just looking at those heels made her feet hurt. And looking at the woman's cascading tendrils of light brown hair with gold highlights made her envious.

Val tried to smooth down her own curls that spiraled out in all directions. If she highlighted her hair, it would still look like a bad wig, but multicolored. Better to stick with its natural cinnamon color. Less conspicuous.

Jennifer Brown introduced herself and clasped Val's outstretched hand in both of hers. She signed the guest book with a flourish. "Here's my credit card."

"Thank you. Should I put Fawn's room on your card? She'd thought you'd paid for her room already, but my grandfather didn't charge anything on your card yet."

"Fawn said that?" Jennifer's golden brown eyes widened. "Go ahead and put it on my card. I'll straighten it out with her. I don't want you caught in the middle."

"Thank you." Val charged the credit card for both rooms.

When Sarina came down the stairs, Jennifer air-kissed her and then went into the dining room to bestow an air-kiss on Noah.

Granddad welcomed her and suggested she sit next to Sarina, where Val had set another place. "We're having chocolate fondue."

"Thank you." Jennifer plopped down. "I'll have some fruit and skip the chocolate. So which is the tastiest fruit?" She listened to the opinions of her friends, with her fork poised over the platter.

The indecision amused Val. She too was often

undecided, but never about food, only about minor matters like where to live and work.

The doorbell rang, and she got up to answer it. She'd gone halfway through the sitting room when Jennifer brushed past her, zoomed into the hall, and cried, "Payton!"

"Jennifer, baby, I'm so sorry you have to stay in a dump like this."

The man with the husky voice spoke quietly, but Val heard him. Incensed, she clenched her fists and glanced back at the dining room. Granddad, whose hearing was no longer acute, couldn't have overheard the conversation in the hall. Sure, the house's exterior could use a facelift and half the furniture was ready for the dump, but that didn't make the Queen Anne Victorian with its handsome woodwork and stone hearth a dump.

From where she stood she couldn't see Payton's face, only his hands kneading Jennifer's backside as they embraced.

Val's cell phone rang. She hurried to the front room, the former courting parlor now used as a study. She turned her back to the adjacent sitting room and pulled her phone from the pocket of her jeans. Gunnar was calling. His mellow voice warmed her all over, like a smooth wine banishing the burn of Payton's rotgut.

"How are your weekend boarders?" he asked.

"Well, they're everywhere." Some of them possibly within earshot. "I'll tell you more tonight."

"About tonight. I can't meet you for dinner after all. Building the sets for the play is taking longer than we expected. If we keep at it for a few extra hours tonight, we can finish the work tomorrow morning and go to the festival when it's in full swing."

Val stifled a groan. Between her work on the Tricentennial committee and his on a local theater production, they hadn't spent much time together for the past few weeks. She would have more free time when the festival ended, but Gunnar would be tied up with rehearsals for the play opening at the end of October. "I won't see you until tomorrow afternoon." She didn't quite manage to keep the whine out of her voice.

"Sorry. I'll make it up to you. Dinner tomorrow night?"

"I'll hold you to that." She hung up, disappointed. So much for her plan to talk to Gunnar tonight about her job offer. Val didn't want to discuss it with Granddad yet, unsure how he'd react. She couldn't talk to her cousin about it either. Monique would just reiterate what she'd said a few months ago: *You belong in Bayport.*

Val tucked her phone away and joined the guests in the dining room. Jennifer's fiancé had gone.

Granddad came in from the kitchen, carrying something behind his back. "I have gift certificates for a souvenir hat for each of you. Val left her hat in the kitchen. She'll model it for you." He presented her with a red felt object. A pair of plastic eyes protruded from the top of it and long pieces of stuffed felt hung down from either side.

Fawn, back from her tobacco interlude, giggled. "It looks like a frog."

"It's a crab hat," Granddad said. "Crab is king around the Chesapeake Bay."

Val put on the hat, tucking her hair under it. "The things hanging down like floppy ears are supposed to be crab claws."

"Maybe my bridesmaids should all wear crab hats." Jennifer winked at Fawn.

Granddad handed out small envelopes with the certificates inside. "You can redeem these tonight at the festival. Everything in town is an easy walk from here. Turn right and walk five blocks to get to Main Street. Then follow the signs to the festival."

Val filled in details that Granddad's sketchy instructions lacked. "Most of the festival events will take place in the park on the other side of Main Street—the fireworks over the water tonight, concerts, and the cook-offs on Sunday. The municipal parking lot across from the park is where you'll find the food and craft booths, but those don't open until tomorrow. Tonight you might want to eat on Main Street. Several restaurants in the historic district are offering small-plate samples of their signature dishes."

Val would make a meal of those herself tonight, now that dinner with Gunnar had fallen through. Granddad was going out for pizza with a buddy.

He walked around the table to the sitting room. "If you're ready, I'll show you folks the bedrooms."

Val figured she was excused. "I'll clear the table, Granddad, and then head to town myself, if that's okay with you."

"I'll take care of the table. You go ahead."

* * *

Tricentennial banners hung from the lampposts and stretched across Main Street in the historic district. Narrow wood buildings, once the homes of eighteenth and nineteenth century merchants and shipbuilders, now housed boutiques, restaurants, and antiques shops. With the center of town closed to cars, people who would have clogged the brick sidewalks strolled in the middle of the street. Like Val, many of them wore crab hats.

She ran into two members of her tennis group. While talking to them, she spotted Granddad's guests. Jennifer in a black top and a miniscule red skirt tottered on black high-heeled sandals. Sarina and Fawn wore the same outfits they'd arrived in. Noah had changed from business attire to a turtleneck, cargo pants, and boat moccasins.

It was twilight by the time Val had visited three different eateries, cobbling together a meal of oyster stew, crab-cake sliders, and locally made ice cream. On her way to the festival's opening ceremonies, she took a shortcut, turning into a side street with few tourists on it. In her athletic shoes, she moved quickly and soundlessly on the sidewalk. She heard footsteps behind her. She glanced back, but the claw hanging from her crab hat interfered with her peripheral vision. She swept the claw back, looked behind her again, and froze. Chef Henri La Farge! She'd hoped never to see him after she left New York, where he'd waged a vendetta against her. He blamed her for the crash that destroyed his vintage car and landed him in the hospital. Hard to believe, though, that he'd come all the way here to harass her.

His dark mustache, halfway between a handlebar and a Hitler, twitched. "You! I recognized you even under that silly hat. You can't hide from me." Chef Henri's accent suggested he grew up on the left bank of the East River, not of the Seine.

Val took off her crab hat. "I have no reason to hide from you."

"You wrecked my car. You nearly killed me. You ruined my life!" He punctuated each accusation by pointing his index finger in her face. "After months in rehab, I'm still on pain meds. All because of you."

She didn't flinch though she risked getting her eye poked by a fingernail his manicurist had honed into a weapon. "I didn't cause that accident. You grabbed the steering wheel away from me." If he hadn't been drunk, she wouldn't have had to drive his car for him.

"That's not what happened."

"How would you know? You were too soused to remember anything that occurred that night. If you hadn't unbuckled your seatbelt, you would have escaped with minor injuries." His bones had broken in the accident, but his habit of blaming other people for his failures had survived intact. "Did you come here to stalk me? The police chief is a friend of mine. He'll run you out of town if you don't stop following me."

Henri emitted a strangled noise as if choking on

bile. "Follow you? Don't flatter yourself. I came here to judge the cook-off."

He was judging the cook-off? Val had heard that the festival chairman was looking for a replacement judge after the chef who'd agreed to do it backed out a few days ago. But Henri didn't usually venture far from Manhattan. He had nothing to gain by coming here except getting in her face. "You traveled to Bayport just to judge the cook-off?"

"Of course not. I'm opening a new restaurant in Washington and publicizing it here."

Why would he open a new restaurant in the culinary hinterland of D.C.? A second Manhattan location would make more sense, but only if he still had a business at the first location. Ah. Now she understood. His restaurant must have folded. Losing it also meant he'd have trouble finding a publisher for his next cookbook. "So your New York restaurant went under. What a shame." She spotted a family of four, Granddad's neighbors, walking toward the festival.

"It went under because I was in the hospital, thanks to you. It's your fault that—"

She cut off his tirade by zipping across the street and joining the family. Too bad he was judging the cook-off. He was sure to find out that one of the contestants was her grandfather. The chef wouldn't just destroy Granddad's chances of winning the contest, he would make fun of the old man. She'd better prepare Granddad for that. She put her crab hat back on and looked behind her. No, Henri wasn't following her.

When she arrived at the park where the festival's main events would take place, a large crowd had already gathered. She had no hope of finding anyone she knew amid the sea of crab hats. She settled down on a small patch of ground to watch the opening ceremonies and the fireworks that would explode over the creek bordering the park.

Back at the house after the fireworks ended, Val made a berry syrup for tomorrow morning's pancakes while Granddad set the dining-room table for breakfast.

He joined her in the kitchen. "Our tourists are back. They went to the festival together, but they came back separately. While I was in the dining room, I heard the front door slam three times."

Val noticed his eyelids drooping. "Why don't you go to bed? I'll take out the trash and set up the coffee maker."

"Okay." He gave her a peck on the cheek. "Good night."

Val carried the trash bag through a small, enclosed porch and opened the back door. With no moonlight, she could barely see across the yard to the shed where the garbage bin was. She waited for her eyes to adjust to the dark and then started toward the shed, focusing on the uneven ground so that she wouldn't stumble.

Halfway across the yard, bulging eyes looked up at her. She jumped back, startled, and dropped the trash bag.

Then she laughed. The plastic eyes sat atop the festival's souvenir crab hat. One of the tourists staying in the house must have dropped the hat in the yard.

Val stooped to pick up the hat and froze. Two feet away, a woman lay on the ground, a rope around her neck, her eyes open and lifeless as the crab eyes.

Chapter 3

Val raced into the house and bolted the back door behind her. Nausea hit her like a rogue wave, churning up her stomach. She ran to the kitchen sink and took deep breaths.

The queasiness died down. Maybe she hadn't stumbled on a dead body after all. Fawn could be playing a prank, wearing Halloween ghoul contact lenses and white makeup.

Val didn't believe that enough to go back outside. If Fawn really was dead, whoever had put a rope around her neck might still be in the backyard.

She pulled out her cell phone and noted the time. Five after ten. On a Friday night with so many tourists in town, the police would still be busy. She called Bayport Police Chief Earl Yardley. If this was a prank, he would give the prankster a lecture she wouldn't forget. And if it wasn't, he'd know what to do. Before taking over as chief here, he'd worked as a detective in other Maryland jurisdictions.

Val was relieved to reach him in person instead of his voice mail. "Chief, it's Val Deniston. Someone—I think one of the tourists staying here—is lying in our backyard. She looks dead, and she has a rope around her neck."

The chief groaned. "If anyone else in this town said that to me, I'd tell 'em to go sleep it off. With your knack for coming on dead bodies, I take this seriously. Do the other tourists staying at the house know about this?"

"They don't know I found her dead."

"Don't say anything to them. I'll be there shortly with the EMTs. For now, stay inside with the doors locked." He hung up.

Val went to the front hall, saw that a light was on in her grandfather's room, and knocked on the door. "Granddad? I have something important to tell you."

"Come in." Still dressed, he was sitting on the edge of the bed, with one shoe on and one off. He looked up at her. "You're pale. What's wrong?"

She sat down next to him. "Get ready for some bad news. I found one of our guests dead in the backyard—Fawn."

He clutched the edge of the mattress. "Are you sure she's dead? Did you check her breathing and her pulse?"

Val shook her head. "She has a rope around her neck. I think she was strangled."

He reached down for the shoe he'd taken off. "She might still be alive. I'm going to check. You stay inside the house."

Val couldn't talk him out of going to the backyard.

She walked back to the kitchen with him, gave him a flashlight, and watched from the window when he went outside.

He returned a minute later. "She's dead alright. The strangler took the time to make loops at both ends of the rope for a better grip."

Not a spur-of-the-moment crime. "I saw you shining the flashlight around. What else did you see?"

"A crab hat and two cigarette butts on the ground. A couple of strawberries on a plate and a little bowl of chocolate on the table."

"She was having seconds on the fondue." Half an hour ago, Val had wiped fondue drips from the counter near the microwave and wondered who'd melted chocolate tonight. Now she knew.

Granddad stared at a photograph on the wall, a candid shot of himself and Grandma taken a few months before she died. "Over the last few years, I've seen a lot of deaths. Your grandmother, Ned's wife, and a couple of real good friends. They were in their seventies. It's unnatural for a young person to die." He pointed at the ceiling. "Do you think one of them murdered her?"

"Not necessarily. Someone she didn't know could have followed her here after the fireworks. Let's not assume we have a murderer staying here."

Granddad squeezed her hand. "I'm mighty glad you're *not* staying here."

"Me too." She reached into her pocket and fingered her cousin's house key. Good thing Monique wouldn't have to wait up for her. The police might be here for hours, and Val didn't know when they would let her leave. "Be sure to lock your door tonight."

"You forget I have a watchdog. I'll put him in the hall outside my room before I go to bed."

Val smiled. "RoboFido to the rescue again. You've come up with more uses for that barking motion detector than anyone could imag—" She broke off at the sound of knocking on the front door. "That must be the chief. I'll let him in."

"Look out the sidelight first and make sure it's him."

Val went to the hall and peeked through the sidelight. Chief Yardley, a large man in his late fifties, stood on the front porch with a young policeman, Officer Wade. Val remembered the rookie from the last time she'd reported a murder in Bayport. He looked no older than a recent high school graduate, though he was probably in his twenties. She opened the door.

The two men came into the house, followed by a pair of EMTs, a wiry man and a husky one. They'd come without sirens, but the flashing lights on the ambulance would alert anyone who looked out the window of an emergency at the house. Maybe no one would look. Harvey, the neighbor with a driveway adjacent to Granddad's, had left for the weekend to avoid the influx of tourists. Across the street, the couple with a baby and a preschooler usually didn't stay up this late. But dog walkers might come by. Everyone on the street would know something had happened at Granddad's house, by morning if not sooner.

Val led the way to the small enclosed porch at the

back of the house. She pointed to the door leading to the yard. "She's out there, on the ground, halfway between here and the shed."

The chief nodded. "Okay. You and your grand-daddy stay inside."

Relieved at not having to look again at those dead eyes, Val stood at the back door with her grandfather, watching as Officer Wade's powerful flashlight illuminated the yard. The EMTs crouched down. The body language when they stood up confirmed that Fawn was beyond help.

Val left her grandfather on the porch and went into the kitchen.

"Hello? Anybody here?" a man's voice called from the front of the house.

Noah. Val hurried to the dining room to head him off. "Hi. Do you need something?"

"I was in the window seat upstairs, looked out, and saw the ambulance lights flashing. Is your grandfather ill?"

"He's fine. Thank you for asking." Val would have been surprised if that answer satisfied Noah, the lawyer.

"Why is there an ambulance here?" Noah's eyes widened, his curiosity giving way to concern. "Is Jennifer okay? And the others?"

The unnamed *others* sounded like an after-thought. Why would he think Jennifer wasn't okay? Though Val wanted to allay the man's fears, she abided by the chief's request not to tell the guests what was going on. "I have no reason to think there's anything wrong with Jennifer."

Val heard voices in the kitchen. The chief said

something she couldn't catch, but Granddad's voice carried.

"She was the only likable one in the bunch," he said. "Where's Val?"

"I'm in the dining room, Granddad."

The chief came into the dining room with Granddad and showed his badge to Noah. "Earl Yardley, Bayport Police chief. Your name, sir?"

Noah gaped at the big man. "I'm Noah Hurdly, attorney-at-law in Washington, D.C."

"I take it you've reserved a room in Mr. Myer's house for the weekend." Chief Yardley pointed toward the sitting room. "Please have a seat in there. Mr. Myer will join you there."

The chief turned back to the kitchen, motioning Val to follow him. He asked her what she knew about the woman lying in the backyard.

"She registered as Fawn Finchley. She told us she worked as a gate attendant at Reagan National Airport. She and the other guests are here to help plan a wedding for Jennifer Brown, who's also staying here."

"Which room was Ms. Finchley staying in?"

Val shrugged. "Granddad would know. I left here before the guests chose rooms."

"You know the drill from the last time you found a body. The medical examiner and the crime scene unit will be here shortly. Don't talk about what you saw at the crime scene to the media or anyone else.

"I want everyone together in one room, including you. Would you tell your other guests to join your granddaddy and Mr. Hurdly? Don't say why. I'll give them the news."

Val took the staircase that went up from the kitchen. She paused outside the room she'd occupied for the last eight months and knocked softly on the door. No answer. She went down the hall and knocked on the first door to the right. No answer in the *Rope* room either.

Sarina opened the door to the *North by Northwest* room a second after Val's knock. She wore a zippered black caftan that could serve as either a robe or a costume for Morticia in *The Addams Family*. "What is it?"

"There's an emergency. Could you please go downstairs?"

"What kind of emergency?"

Val framed an answer that no one could call a lie. "I don't know all the details. We have to vacate the second floor." She knocked on the nearby door to the *Birds* room.

Jennifer stuck her head out, her hair mussed and her face free of makeup. "What's going on?"

Sarina glared at Val. "She says we have to leave our rooms and go downstairs for some reason. This better not take long." She banged her bedroom door closed and marched down the front staircase.

Jennifer opened her door fractionally wider. "Is this really necessary? I was already in bed." She wore what looked like a red silk scarf hanging from spaghetti straps and ending at her upper thigh. Her black satin pajama bottoms swept the floor.

"I'm sorry. I wouldn't have woken you if it weren't important."

"Okay. Give me a minute to get dressed. Is Fawn downstairs already?"

That would depend on the meaning of *is*. Val tried to come up with a better evasive answer. "I knocked on both doors down the hall and no one answered. I'll try again. Which room was she in?"

Jennifer pointed toward Val's room. "Straight ahead at the end of the hall." She closed her door.

Val retraced her steps and paused outside the bedroom that was usually hers. Would she ever go into it again without thinking about Fawn's death? She took the back stairs down to the kitchen and found Chief Yardley still there, putting his cell phone away.

She pointed at the ceiling. "Fawn had the room right above here, my room except for this weekend. I'm staying at my cousin's house for the next three nights."

"Your room here is off limits until we've had a chance to search it. Is everyone downstairs?"

"All except Jennifer, the bride-to-be. She'll be down shortly." Val headed for the sitting room.

Granddad was in his usual chair facing the fireplace and TV. Instead of leaning back in the recliner, he sat rigid. Val moved an ottoman she often used as a footstool from the study to the sitting room. She set it near Granddad's chair and perched on it.

Jennifer came into the room, wearing jeans and a turquoise T-shirt. At her current rate of wardrobe changes, she'd go through everything in her large suitcase before the weekend was over. She settled down on the sofa next to Sarina.

Noah, in an armchair at a right angle to the sofa, frowned. "Why isn't Fawn here?"

Sarina folded her arms. "She's probably one of those women who keep everyone waiting."

And Sarina was one of those women who belittle other women, Val decided. Fawn's three friends had talked as if she were still alive. A smart murderer would do the same.

"Did you folks wear those crab hats tonight?" Granddad asked with forced joviality.

Jennifer smiled at him. "Fawn and I put them on as soon as we picked them up. Of course, I took mine off when I went to meet Payton for dinner and then put it back on when he left. It was easier than carrying it around."

Noah's mouth turned down at the sides. "Payton left?"

"He couldn't stay for the fireworks," Jennifer said through tight lips.

"Did you pick up a hat, Sarina?" Granddad asked.

"Yes, but I didn't wear it. I'm giving it to my eight-year-old niece. She might want to be a crab for Halloween."

As far as Val could tell, the aunt didn't need a hat to prove she was a crab.

"I'm saving mine too," Noah said, "as a gift for a neighbor's son."

Val covered her mouth to hide a smile as she imagined the staid lawyer in the souvenir hat. The "claws" hanging down like spaniel ears from the hat would hide the big ears that protruded from Noah's small head. He might be the only person in Bayport who'd look better in a crab hat than without it.

Chief Yardley strode into the room, a daunting

presence in his uniform. Both Sarina and Jennifer gaped at him in surprise. Officer Wade followed him, a notebook in hand. The rookie would jot down information for his boss, as he'd done the first time Val had met him.

The chief introduced himself to Jennifer and Sarina. Jennifer gave him her name. Sarina didn't, until he prompted her.

The chief cocked his head toward the dining room. "Bring in two of those chairs for us, Wade."

The officer placed the mahogany dining chairs facing the sofa and sat in one of them.

The chief remained standing. "I understand you're all here as a group to plan a wedding, and I'm sorry I have to give you bad news. Tonight we responded to an emergency call placed from this house. When we arrived, we found Fawn Finchley dead."

Jennifer covered her mouth with her hand. "Fawn's dead?"

Noah's eyes bugged out. "Was it an accident or—?"

"We're treating this as a suspicious death."

Jennifer wiped the corners of her teary eyes. "You mean Fawn was murdered. Why would anyone kill *her?*"

The intonation surprised Val. What did Jennifer's emphasis on *her* mean? That Fawn had been too nice to kill or too insignificant?

Sarina shrugged. "Maybe she was in the wrong place at the wrong time."

"Or with the wrong people," Granddad muttered.

The chief stepped closer to the sofa. "I'd like to know when each of you last saw Fawn Finchley."

Sarina tapped her fingers on the arm of the sofa. "I saw Fawn near the bandstand around eight, just as the opening ceremonies were starting, but I didn't talk to her. There was a crowd between us."

"That was long after I saw her," Jennifer said. "We all walked to the festival from here around five o'clock. We hung around there for a while and stopped to pick up the crab hats. Then we split up. I went to meet my fiancé for dinner at a restaurant on Main Street."

"Is your fiancé from this area?" the chief said.

Jennifer shook her head. "He lives and works in Washington, D.C. His parents have a vacation house on the bay fifteen minutes from here. He's staying there this weekend."

"What's his name and how can we reach him?"

"Payton Grandsire." Jennifer rattled off her fiancé's phone number.

Grandsire. If Payton was the son of the Mrs. Grandsire Val knew from the racket and fitness club, then Jennifer would have a formidable mother-in-law. Penelope Grandsire's bread-and-butter shot, the one she relied on to win points, wasn't a backhand or a lob, but a straight-in-the-kisser bullet at her nearest opponent. Of course, she couldn't intimidate every player with that shot, only those who wanted to keep their own teeth.

"What did you do after dinner, Ms. Brown?" the chief asked.

"Payton went back to his parents' house, and I walked to the festival park for the fireworks. I looked for Fawn and Sarina, but I didn't find either of them. For a second I thought I saw Fawn in the crowd, wearing a crab hat, but it could have been someone else about the same size."

About the same size. Val tensed, remembering the crab hat lying near Fawn's body. Large enough to cover most of the head and part of the face, the hat would make hair color and style hard to discern in dim light. Could the murderer have mistaken Fawn for someone else wearing a crab hat? Fawn and Jennifer were close in height, both of them shorter than average . . . *as was Val.* All three of them had worn a dark top and a crab hat tonight. What's more, Val and Fawn had both worn jeans.

Val flashed back to the moment when she'd sensed someone following her this evening. Chef Henri had seen her in an outfit similar to Fawn's. An image of his face contorted with rage sprang into her mind. Her throat narrowed. She clutched her neck. The strangler might have intended to kill her, not a weekend guest.

Chapter 4

Val grasped the edges of the ottoman to steady herself. The idea that someone hated her enough to want her dead made her feel weak. A few months ago, a murderer had stalked her and, having failed to kill her on the first attempt, kept right on trying. Would she once again have to look over her shoulder at every turn?

The chief left the sitting room to confer with the medical examiner. With Officer Wade still in his seat, everyone in the room remained silent, giving Val a chance to collect her thoughts.

Henri might have tailed Fawn to the house, believing her to be Val. Once here, though, Fawn had gone inside the house to melt chocolate for her fondue snack. It wouldn't have taken long for her to do that in the microwave. Meanwhile, Henri might have crept around the perimeter of the house, checking if others were inside or if his prey was still alone. Then Fawn went out to sit in the backyard.

Chief Yardley returned to his seat next to Officer Wade. "Where were we? Ms. Brown, you couldn't find your friends at the festival. What did you do then?"

"When the fireworks ended, I waited around for a while, hoping to see Sarina or Fawn or Noah. I didn't, so I walked back here alone and went up to my room. While I was reading and sending e-mails, I heard someone in the hall bathroom . . . Sarina, I assumed, because she and I share that bath."

"What time was that?"

"No idea." Jennifer looked at the woman next to her. "Do you know, Sarina?"

"I don't generally check my watch when I use the facilities." Sarina turned toward the chief. "I'm sure you want to know how I spent the evening." She didn't wait for him to confirm that. "After we bought the crab hats at the festival park, I walked back to Main Street to visit the so-called art galleries. I stopped at the wine bar for a light meal and went to the fireworks. When they ended, I waited for the crowd to clear out and then walked back here."

The chief turned to Noah. "And you, Mr. Hurdly? How did you spend the evening?"

"After we all split up, I walked around the festival area for a while and then went to Main Street to eat. While I was waiting for my meal, I got a text from Fawn."

Jennifer leaned forward. "Fawn texted you? About what?"

"She wanted to talk to me and suggested we get together for dinner. I told her no. I'd ordered my meal already and figured I'd be ready to leave by the time she got there. I assumed we'd have another chance to talk this weekend." He rubbed the back of his neck. "If we'd had dinner, maybe we'd have watched the fireworks and walked back here together, and she wouldn't be dead."

Sarina dismissed his concern with a wave of her hand. "You can't blame yourself for what a crazy killer did."

"Did Ms. Finchley text you often, Mr. Hurdly?" the chief asked.

"No! I just met her this afternoon. She must have gotten my phone number from the wedding party contact list Jennifer sent out a few days ago."

"Any idea what she wanted to discuss with you?"

"Her text didn't say. You can read it for yourself." Noah pulled out his phone, poked at the screen, and handed over the phone.

The chief looked at it, frowned, and passed it to Officer Wade. "Copy that text message . . . exactly. Between the abbreviations and misspellings, I can only guess what it means."

For the first time since they'd gathered in the sitting room, Val felt she had something to contribute. "Noah, you had a te—" she stopped herself from saying *tête-à-tête*, though that's what it had been. "You had a talk with Fawn this afternoon. Do you think she wanted to continue that conversation?"

"Possibly. She needed some legal advice."

Sarina's usual frown smoothed out as her eyes

widened. "Fawn asked you for *legal* advice this afternoon?"

She'd doubtless assumed, like Val, that Fawn had been flirting with Noah. He might have thought that too, until Fawn set him straight. No wonder he'd been in no hurry to meet her for another chat.

Jennifer shook her head. "Poor Fawn. She was drowning in debt. She co-signed some loans with her deadbeat husband. When she said she wanted a divorce, he emptied their accounts, took off, and left her to pay off the loans."

Noah nodded. "That's what she told me."

Sarina raised her eyebrows. "She didn't act like someone drowning in debt. Always smiling. Half the time jumping for joy."

"How well did you know her, Ms. Rafael?" the chief asked.

"I met her two weeks ago, when Jennifer invited the bridesmaids to dinner. I already knew the other two, but not Fawn."

Jennifer nodded. "Fawn and I recently reconnected. We went to the same high school, but lost touch for ten years. Then we bumped into each other at the airport last month. We went for a drink . . . well, quite a few drinks. I asked her to be a bridesmaid so I'd have one old friend at the wedding." She sighed. "I won't, after all."

Val felt sorry for Jennifer, who'd instantly drafted someone she hadn't seen for a decade into her wedding party. She also had to put up with a bad-tempered maid of honor.

"Any idea how to reach Ms. Finchley's next of kin?" the chief asked.

Jennifer rubbed her temples. "Her parents, the Schranks, might still be living in Franklin. They didn't like Bo Finchley. Fawn broke off contact with them when she ran off with him. Her mother's first name is Mercy. I don't remember Mr. Schrank's first name, but I can tell you where they used to live."

"Give that information to Officer Wade, please." The chief stood up. "I want to thank you for your cooperation. I hope you'll stay in Bayport, even though this young woman's death will make that hard for you. The first forty-eight hours after a crime are crucial. I can't force you to stay here, but if you don't, you may have to return to provide information. Please contact us if you recall anything that slipped your mind tonight—something Ms. Finchley said, someone you glimpsed her speaking to this evening, or any details about her, even if they seem unimportant."

The chief cautioned them not to talk to the media about the crime or the victim. He would release that information when appropriate.

Once the police and the guests had left the sitting room, Val moved from the ottoman to the sofa. "Why don't you go to bed, Granddad? I'll stay until the police are finished here."

He yawned. "No, get on your way to Monique's house. There's nothing you can do here. But don't oversleep in the morning. You gotta be here to make breakfast."

Ten minutes later, Val was on the road to her

cousin's house. Monique lived on a peninsula with a creek on one side and the bay on the other. Val never drove there at night without remembering the time an SUV driver had followed her from town and forced her off the narrow road, the first of several attempts to get rid of her.

Tonight, when she saw headlights in the rearview mirror, she thought about Chef Henri. What kind of vehicle did he drive now to replace the classic car he blamed her for wrecking? If he'd meant to kill her and realized his mistake after strangling Fawn, would he try again? Possibly, but not tonight. He wouldn't have lurked around the house with the police there.

Still, Val kept an eye on the rearview mirror. She breathed more easily when she turned into Monique's driveway and the car that had been behind hers kept driving toward the end of the peninsula.

The hall light was on, though the rest of the sprawling ranch house was dark. Monique had left a note for Val, telling her to sleep in little Mandy's room. With no one else around, Val was spared from talking about the murder, at least for tonight, but she couldn't stop thinking about it. If only she hadn't suggested Granddad rent his spare rooms—well, she had. And now she would deal with the consequences, one of which might be that Fawn was dead instead of her.

At six thirty in the morning, Val went into her cousin's retro kitchen–family room. The coffee machine sputtered, gurgled, and filled the room with an enticing aroma. Monique stood at the counter, the rest of the family apparently still sleeping. Tall and slim, she looked like a model even in wrinkled pajamas. Her long hair was sleek and shiny enough for a shampoo commercial.

She looked up from scrolling through photos on her fancy camera's display. "Hey, Val. Did you sleep well?"

"Better than I expected. What are you doing up so early?"

"Looking at the photos I took yesterday." Monique filled two mugs with coffee and put them on the counter. "I'll be running around all weekend, taking pictures. They'll be for sale on the festival website. I hope to place a few in *Chesapeake Bay Magazine* and the local newspapers."

Val sat at the counter, cradling the coffee mug. "You're branching out from wedding photography?"

"I'd like to." Monique took the seat next to her at the counter. "Tell me about your grandfather's weekend visitors."

"They came to plan a wedding here." Between sips of coffee, Val described each of the guests briefly. She put her mug down. "Now for the dramatic conclusion. I'm not supposed to give any details about this, but the bridesmaid died suddenly last night in our backyard."

Monique's eyes widened. "That's horrible."

"The police haven't said how she was killed, but they're treating it as a suspicious death. Don't tell anyone until the police make it public."

"I can't believe you're connected with another murder."

"Even worse than just connected to it, I might have been the intended victim." Val summarized her encounter with Chef Henri. "I'm afraid he might have mistaken the bridesmaid for me in the dark."

"Did she really look like you? Was her hair like yours?"

"No one's hair is like mine except Granddad's forty years ago. Fawn had light brown hair, flipped up at the ends, but her crab hat would have covered her head. The bride and I were about the same size as her. We all wore crab hats, so it's hard to say who the real target was."

"Don't you think a murderer would check that the person he's about to kill is the one he wants dead?" Monique didn't wait for an answer. "You sound paranoid. Understandable, after the murders the last few months."

Val welcomed her cousin's skepticism. "Okay. Let's test if a crab hat could have disguised Fawn's identity. If I can grab pictures of Granddad's guests from social media sites, can you use your photo editing software to put crab hats on them?"

"Sure. I'll need Fawn's photo, but why don't you just ask the rest of them to put on crab hats? Then take a picture of them."

"They'd want to know the reason. I'd rather not tell the bride she might have been the intended victim unless I know for certain that she resembled Fawn with the hat on. The maid of honor and the best man are my control group for this experiment.

In crab hats those two won't look as much like Fawn as Jennifer and I do."

"I think you're worrying for no reason. Do you really think a celebrity chef would murder you in cold blood?"

"I've met some vicious chefs. W. H. Auden said murder is more common among cooks than members of any other profession."

Monique laughed. "You have trivia for every occasion. Chef Henri can't get away with murder during the day at the festival. Too many witnesses. But in case your hunch is right, don't walk anywhere alone at night."

"I won't. What are you doing with Mike and Mandy while you take pictures at the festival?"

"Maverick's parents are driving here from Philadelphia today to babysit this weekend. They'll stay in the guestroom. That's why I put you in Mandy's room and the two kids together."

"Once the police are finished with my bedroom, I can move back in, but I'd be less nervous if I wait until the guests leave Monday."

"Stay as long as you like. The kids love the bunk bed in Mike's room. They take turns sleeping on the top bunk."

Val hopped down from the stool at the counter. "Thanks for the coffee. I'll see you at the festival."

"Aren't you going to stay for breakfast? I'm making something special. The kids always want cold cereal, but it's time they had more variety. I'm going to fix oatmeal with chicken broth and avocado and cheese. Doesn't that sound yummy?"

Cold cereal sounded yummier. Monique ruined

perfectly good comfort food like oatmeal with her elegant variations. At least Val had an excuse for not eating her cousin's concoction. "Busy morning. I'm making breakfast for Granddad's guests and going to the café to get the food ready for the booth."

"What are you fixing for breakfast?"

"Lemon ricotta pancakes with blueberry syrup." One of Val's favorite breakfasts, but maybe someone else would say she was ruining perfectly good pancakes. "Thanks for the coffee. Come by my booth and take some pictures."

"I will. See you later." Monique went back to looking at photos on her camera.

Early in the morning the road to Bayport was nearly empty. Val made it to her grandfather's house by seven. The guests expected breakfast by seven thirty. She parked in the driveway and went in the side door sandwiched between the sitting room and dining room. Not a creature stirred in the house.

She moved the twelve-cup coffee maker to the counter in the butler's pantry between the kitchen and the dining room. If any guests came down early, they could help themselves. She started the coffee brewing and set out mixing bowls, flour, and sugar on the island counter in the kitchen.

She was zesting a lemon when ferocious barking startled her into zesting the skin on her finger. RoboFido had detected motion. The noise stopped within seconds. It hadn't taken Granddad long to turn off the gizmo, but he might not have done it soon enough for Noah, whose room was above his.

Unless the best man was a deep sleeper, the barks would have woken him up. Better him than Sarina. She would storm down the stairs in protest at the noise.

Val washed the zester and rinsed the knuckle she'd scraped.

Granddad came into the kitchen. "I remembered to turn off Fido before I went to the bathroom in the middle of the night, but I forgot this morning. Did you hear the barking?"

"Loud and clear. How did you sleep?"

"Badly. Kept thinking about that nice girl lying there dead. You know, she reminded me a lot of you."

Not a welcome comparison.

"She really didn't look anything like me." Val took a carton of eggs from the refrigerator.

He sat down at the kitchen table. "I wouldn't say that. You're about the same size. She was cute like you, not hot like the bride. Her disposition reminded me of the way you used to be."

Val would much rather be hot than cute. "I was never, ever as bubbly as Fawn."

"Sure you were. Except for the occasional temper tantrum, you had a sunny outlook . . . at least when you were younger. People complain about teenagers being sullen. But the few years you all lived here with us, when your father was stationed in Annapolis, you always looked on the bright side. Nothing would get you down."

She cracked and separated the eggs, trying to conjure a memory of herself as a teenage version of the bridesmaid Fawn. Val couldn't. But compared to her brother, who'd gone through a surly stage during the three years they lived in Bayport, she must have come across as Little Miss Sunshine. "I loved living here with you and Grandma. We all did, but I don't have Fawn's cheerfulness."

"You don't have it anymore, that's for sure. You changed from upbeat to uptight after you went to New York. You were stressed out there. Moving here was the best decision you ever made."

She gave him a long, hard look. Had he somehow gotten wind of her job offer? "You've never said that before."

"Fawn brought back memories of what you used to be like." He took off his bifocals and wiped them on his plaid shirt.

He should clean the lenses he used for peering into the past. How could he possibly think he had a better memory of what she was like than she had? Well, different people made different memories from the same events. Chef Henri's version of what happened the night Val drove his vintage car bore no relationship to hers. To keep his pride intact, the chef had to point the finger at her. Her grandfather did his share of finger pointing too.

"I'm not the only one who's changed, Granddad." She whisked together the yolks, ricotta, and sugar. "Ever since I moved in with you, you've made me a scapegoat for anything that goes wrong."

He folded his arms. "I don't do that."

Whenever he had a cooking disaster, he faulted her recipe rather than his failure to follow it. But she didn't want to put him on the defensive. What he did from now on mattered, not what he'd previously done. "This weekend you can prove that you don't play the blame game. I suggested you rent your extra bedrooms to tourists. You agreed to it. That means we're in this together. From now on, let's both be more positive and less critical."

He gave her a thumbs-up. "It's a deal."

The first test of this resolution was coming. She brought him a cup of coffee, sat across from him at the small kitchen table, and told him about her encounter with Chef Henri.

Granddad sipped his coffee and set his cup on the saucer. "What's a hoity-toity chef doing in Bayport?"

"He's here to judge the cook-off. His restaurant failed because he spent more time being a celebrity than a chef. He didn't give his staff credit for their work and faulted them for his own mistakes. He did the same to me. If he finds out you're related to me, you have no chance of winning the cook-off." Granddad would at least have a valid excuse for losing.

His eyebrows lowered. "Just because you got on his bad side I'm gonna lose the cook-off?"

"That's coming close to blaming me for something I can't help. We can hope Henri won't find out we're related."

"Does he look like an aging Napoleon with a mustache?" She nodded, and Granddad continued. "He knows we're related. He came to the door looking for you yesterday when you were out."

A current of fear shot through Val. Henri had checked out where she lived. Maybe he'd come back here last night, intent on revenge, spotted a woman who resembled her, and strangled her. "What did he want?"

"He didn't say. I told him I was your grandfather and could give you a message. He didn't leave one or even tell me his name. With all the to-do about the guests arriving and Fawn's murder, it slipped my mind." Granddad peered at her over the rim of his cup. "You look pale. Are you okay?"

She didn't want to share her fears about Henri with him. "I'm fine. Our guests will be down for breakfast soon. I'd better get the pancakes ready." Cooking would calm her down. She returned to the counter. "How about cutting up the melon for a fruit salad?"

He stood up, went to the refrigerator, and took out a cantaloupe and a honeydew melon.

Val added flour to the bowl with the other ingredients and stirred vigorously when she should have done it gently. She forced herself to slow down her mixing and to rein in her fears about Henri. By showing up at her door, he'd reinforced her suspicion that he intended to hound her while he was in Bayport, but that didn't make him a murderer.

Her grandfather banged a drawer closed and opened another one. "What are you looking for, Granddad?"

"The good knife."

That's what he called her versatile five-inch knife. This wouldn't be the first time he'd misplaced it. Sometimes she'd gone for days without her favorite knife until it turned up in the unlikely spot he'd put it down—on a windowsill or the porch railing or most often, in one of his many junk drawers. "It's not in the knife drawer where it belongs?"

"I wouldn't be searching for it if it was. Maybe it's with the fondue forks and other stuff in the dish drainer." He checked the drainer. "Nope. Hey, there are only six fondue forks here. There should be seven."

"Did you wash seven yesterday?"

He scratched his head. "I dunno. The phone rang when I was in the middle of washing them. Ned called to say he was on his way to the pizza place. I was running late, so I finished washing the fondue stuff real quick. I didn't pay attention to how many forks were there."

He might have gone to answer the hall phone with a clean fork in his hand and left it somewhere between the kitchen and the hall. Another explanation for the missing fork occurred to Val. "Fawn might have taken a fork to the backyard last night, along with the strawberries and chocolate."

"I didn't see it in the yard when I went out there to check if she was really dead. And I looked around."

The missing fork didn't bother Val as much as the missing knife. "I'm sure the police did a more thorough search. The fondue fork is probably in an evidence bag."

The floorboards on the second floor creaked. Nothing unusual about that. You always knew when someone was walking upstairs. But after a murder in the backyard and a missing knife in the kitchen, familiar creaking noises sounded sinister. Probably Granddad had misplaced the sharpest knife in the house, but what if someone staying upstairs had taken it? A body in the yard was bad enough. One in a bed was far worse.

He looked up at the ceiling. "Better start cookin' the hotcakes. Those folks will be down soon."

Val reminded herself that she'd jumped to conclusions after each of the recent murders in Bayport. Now she was doing it again. Most of the time, a berserk chef is just a man acting out, not a murderer. Most of the time, a missing knife doesn't turn up as a weapon. Still, she couldn't help wondering how many people would come to breakfast.

Chapter 5

Granddad sliced a kiwi. "You know what else is missing besides the fondue fork and the knife? Fawn's cell phone. Last night after you left, the police called the number they got from the message she sent Noah. They were hoping the phone would ring somewhere in the house, but they only reached her voice mail."

Val monitored the pancakes. "Maybe the strangler called or texted her to arrange a meeting last night and then took the phone so the police wouldn't find out." Out of the corner of her eye, as Val flipped the pancakes, she saw Noah go into the butler's pantry, probably enticed there by the aroma of brewing coffee. How would he and the others deal with Fawn's death the morning after?

She hurried across to the kitchen to the butler's pantry. "Help yourself to the coffee. Breakfast will be ready shortly. I hope you slept well."

"I did, until a dog woke me up. It sounded really loud even though my window wasn't open."

"Yeah. I heard that barking too." Val scurried back to the kitchen.

She stacked the pancakes onto a platter as Sarina helped herself to coffee. At seven thirty Granddad took the platter to the table. Val brought in the fruit salad and moved the insulated coffee pot to the table.

Sarina and Noah were sitting across from each other in the same chairs they'd occupied yesterday for the fondue. They'd marked off their territory. No sign of Jennifer. A missing knife and a missing guest combined to make Val jittery.

She tried to sound nonchalant. "Where's the bride-to-be? Sleeping in?"

Noah eyed the pancakes. "She's on the phone with Payton. She told us to start without her."

Val relaxed.

Granddad gestured with an open palm toward the pancakes. "Dig in, folks. Another batch of hotcakes will be ready soon."

Noah pointed to the blueberry syrup. "That doesn't look like maple syrup. Do you have any of that?"

"Coming right up," Granddad said.

Val followed him back to the kitchen and poured batter onto the griddle for a second batch of pancakes. "The two of us can eat at the kitchen table instead of sitting with them in the dining room."

"They'll talk about Fawn's murder," he whispered. "We gotta listen and wait for someone to slip up. We figured out who the murderer was last time. We can do it again."

Last time they'd had a personal stake in identifying

the killer. Val held her thumb and forefinger a quarter inch apart. "You came this close to being arrested for the murder that time. We had a strong reason to identify the killer then. We don't have one now. Let the police handle it."

"We're involved because the murder happened here. Fawn was a nice girl, and I want to catch her killer." Granddad took the maple syrup from the refrigerator to the dining room table.

When he returned, he peered at the pancakes she'd flipped. "That's the way I like my hotcakes— a little brown. Don't overdo them."

"Cooking tips from the codger." She gave him a left-handed salute, while using the spatula to remove a pancake from the griddle.

"I've almost finished with my private eye course. Now I need practical experience. Identifying the murderer will give my new career a big boost."

So that was his real motive for wanting to solve the murder—self-promotion. None of his reasons to play detective persuaded Val to help him. She had a different reason to help. If they managed to prove that one of the guests was the murderer, she could stop worrying that Henri wanted to kill her.

She moved the last hotcake from the griddle to the serving platter. "Okay, let's sit with the guests and hope that stuffing pancakes into their mouths will force out incriminating words."

"I'll take the hotcakes to the table."

And, given the chance, he would take the credit for making them. She gave him the plate and followed him to the dining room.

As they took their seats, Sarina said, "Who found Fawn dead?"

"I did." Val put a pancake on her plate.

"Then you can tell us how she was killed."

Val didn't want to tell them the chief had warned her against talking about what she'd seen. She'd rather leave the impression of ignorance than of hiding what she knew. "I really can't. I was taking the trash outside when I glimpsed her. I saw only enough to know she was dead. Then I ran back inside. I was afraid that whoever killed her might still be out there."

Sarina's fork paused on its way to her mouth. "She was probably shot. With the fireworks going off, no one would have paid attention to a gunshot."

Jennifer came into the room, her eyes red-rimmed. She wore designer blue jeans and a crisp button-down shirt. "Good morning—no, it's not a good morning." She sat down in the same seat Fawn had occupied the day before, across from Val, with Granddad between them at the head of the table. He poured her a cup of coffee while the others passed her the pancakes and the two syrups.

Sarina peered across the table at her. "Are you coping?"

Jennifer nodded and put a pancake on her plate. "I called Payton to tell him about Fawn. He said I shouldn't stay in Bayport with a murderer on the loose. He wants me to go home today and not spend another night here."

Here, as in Granddad's home? Yesterday's dump had become today's death house.

Granddad leaned toward Jennifer, his face sympathetic. "Your fiancé is worried that you're in danger."

Noah stabbed a pancake with his fork. "Is Payton going back to Washington with you?"

Jennifer's eyes filled with tears. "He wanted to, but with a house full of guests, his parents can't spare him this weekend. They're throwing a big party tonight."

"The police chief asked us to stay in Bayport." Sarina swirled blueberry syrup around her plate with her fork. "You spent a lot of time setting up appointments to see party venues. If you leave, you have to cancel all of them."

"I'd do that even if I stayed. I'm too upset about Fawn to look at places for celebrations." Jennifer reached for her coffee cup. "I'll postpone the appointments to another weekend."

"If you wait, someone else might reserve the venues you want, and I won't be here to visit them with you. Saturdays and Sundays are the days I paint." Sarina cut a pancake into small pieces. "I set aside this weekend to help you make wedding plans, but I'm not coming back here again . . . until the wedding, of course."

Granddad frowned at Sarina. He probably thought the same thing as Val—that this bride needed a new maid of honor.

Jennifer wiped away a tear. "I don't know what to do. Should I listen to Payton or the police? If I stay, should I keep the appointments or not? What do you think, Noah?"

He laid down his fork and met her eye. "It's not *my* wedding, Jennifer."

More emotion went into that reply than into anything else Val had heard Noah say. Had he been jilted recently?

Granddad glared at him and then turned to Jennifer. "Do what *you* think is right."

She dipped a piece of pancake into the syrup on her plate. "I don't want to be by myself at home. At least here, I'm with other people and Payton's nearby."

Sarina flicked her wrist. "Payton's overreacting. One maniac killed a random woman in Bayport. In Washington the murder rate is much higher. How is going there safer than staying here?"

Noah's fork paused en route to his mouth. "Random murders by strangers get a lot of publicity, but most murder victims are killed by people they know. That's probably the case here. Fawn was divorcing a rotten man. She told me he'd gotten in trouble with the police. He could have followed her and killed her."

The statistics Val had seen on female victims supported Noah's view. A high percentage of murdered women were killed by their husbands or significant others, whether former or current. But why would Fawn's ex choose to kill her here and now? Val looked across the table at Jennifer. "How recently did Fawn break up with her husband?"

"I don't know exactly when they broke up, but at least six months ago." The bride-to-be turned sideways toward Noah. "I like your theory. If Fawn's husband killed her, he doesn't pose a danger to me or any of us. Will you convince Payton of that so he'll stop telling me I should pack up and leave?"

"I'll try." Noah checked his watch. "I want to get to the harbor early for the regatta. It starts at ten thirty. When do you expect Payton?"

"At eleven. I've got an idea. I'll suggest he meet us at the harbor instead of coming here so you can talk to him." Jennifer looked at Granddad. "When will the regatta be over?"

Granddad shrugged. "It'll take most of the morning. From the harbor, the boats will sail to the bay and go around the peninsula. They'll turn at buoys near the festival park and go back to the finish line at the harbor."

Sarina speared the last piece of pancake on her plate. "I'm going to take a camera to town and get some shots of the historic district and the harbor before they get too crowded. I might end up with a photo to use as the basis for a painting."

"Well, I don't want to be alone this morning," Jennifer said. "After breakfast the three of us can walk toward Main Street. You can take pictures, Noah can go look at boats, and I'll walk around town. We can all meet at the harbor at eleven."

Noah laid his fork and knife on his empty plate. "What else is happening at the festival today, Mr. Myer?"

"There's a boat docking competition this afternoon. You might like that. The harbor, the park dock, and nearby farms will all have special events. Val can tell you more about them. She was in on the planning."

"The Chesapeake Bay retriever demo is always

popular." Val didn't detect much interest among the bridal group in dogs playing fetch in the water. No point in telling them about the crustacean chalk circle. She couldn't imagine these city dwellers rooting for crabs scuttling to the edge of a chalk-drawn circle. "You can visit a corn maze on a farm about fifteen minutes from town. It has paths carved through a cornfield that goes on for acres."

"I've never heard of a corn maze," Sarina said.

"The maze has clues to help you navigate." Granddad pointed at Val with his thumb. "Ms. Trivia over there made up the questions. Answer correctly and you'll get on the right path."

"How does it work, Val?" Noah asked.

She pegged him as a fellow trivia buff. "You get a passport before you enter the maze and, once inside, you look for numbered signposts. When you see one, you answer the question in your passport that corresponds with the number. A correct answer tells you the next turn you have to make to get out of the maze."

"And an incorrect one leads you deeper into the corn jungle," Sarina said.

"You'll hit another sign before long. Every group gets a flag on a stick to take into the maze. You can use it to signal if you're lost." Val raised her arm and waved an imaginary flag. "The corn cops will find you and lead you back to the right path."

Granddad nodded. "At night the corn maze turns into an open-air haunted house. Scary scarecrows and sound effects." He pretended to be a monster about to pounce.

Jennifer smiled for the first time since she came

downstairs. "I've never been in a haunted maze, but I love haunted houses."

"You may want to go to the outdoor concert tonight at the festival park." Val certainly preferred a concert to a haunted maze.

The house phone rang. She jumped up to answer it in the front hall. The caller ID read Florida and a phone number Val recognized as her mother's. How would Mom react to the news about the murder?

Val decided to put off telling her. "Hi, Mom. I'm in a hurry. I have to leave for the festival."

"I won't keep you long. Your father's gone on a weekend fishing trip to the Keys. I decided to take a little trip myself. I'm sitting on a plane waiting for takeoff."

"Exciting. Where are you going?"

"To Baltimore-Washington Airport. Then I'll rent a car and drive to Bayport."

Oh, no. "Didn't Granddad tell you we have tourists staying in the upstairs bedrooms for the weekend?"

"He told me, but I thought one of them might not show up or would check out early. If not, there are plenty of hotels between Bayport and Baltimore."

"Everybody showed up." *And one checked out early.* If Mom was coming to town, she'd hear about the murder soon enough. Val had better prepare her for it. "A woman who came here for the weekend was murdered last night."

"*Another mur*—" Mom broke off, probably not

wanting nearby passengers to hear her. "Tell me more."

Val gave her a brief summary, leaving the worst for last. "It happened in our backyard." She heard nothing in response. Either the call had been dropped, or Mom was too stunned to speak.

"When I was growing up," Mom said at last, "we never had any crime in Bayport, and now this happens in the backyard. The flight attendant just said to shut off electronic devices."

"Have a good flight, and don't worry about the murder. The police will probably solve it by the time you arrive." Val didn't believe it, but maybe her mother would.

"The police department is in good hands with Earl Yardley. See you later." Mom hung up.

Val sighed. Twenty-four hours ago, the food for her booth had been her major concern and Granddad's guests a minor matter. Now, one of those guests was dead. A murderer was at large. Another guest, or even Val herself, might be the next victim. Her grandfather was playing sleuth. And to cap it off, her mother was coming. What else could go wrong?

Chapter 6

Val usually anticipated her mother's visits with mixed feelings. Nothing mixed about her feelings this time. Mom couldn't have picked a worse time to come.

Val returned to the dining room but didn't sit down. "Does anyone want anything else?"

Jennifer and Sarina shook their heads. Noah patted his stomach and said, "Not me. Great breakfast."

Val beckoned to her grandfather. They went outside to the front porch.

He joined her on the glider. "Who was on the phone?"

"Mom." Val recounted the phone conversation. "I broke the news about the murder."

Granddad groaned. "I'm always glad to see her, but any other weekend would have been better. Just don't tell her we're working on solving the murder, or she'll buy me a ticket to Florida and you one to New York."

Not the right time for Val to tell Granddad that she might buy her own ticket to the city and go back to her old job. "Mom says she'll stay at a hotel if—"

"I'd hate for her to do that. The police should be done poking around your room by the time she gets here. Your mother can take that room."

"You don't mind her staying here with a possible murderer in the house? Does she get RoboFido as a guard dog?"

"She gets better than that. I'll put a sturdy bolt on the door. Anyway, let's not jump to the conclusion that someone in the house killed that poor girl. The murderer could have come from the outside."

Val rocked the glider. "Who's your candidate? Sarina's homicidal maniac?"

Granddad cupped his hand around his mouth and leaned toward Val. "The groom. Yesterday, when Jennifer brought him into the dining room, you were on the phone. Fawn was outside smoking. He asked where she was. I wonder if something was going on between him and her."

"Just because he asked for her?"

"The man had dinner with his fiancée and then left her for the rest of the evening. Why? Where did he go?"

Good question, but not evidence of wrongdoing. "He didn't necessarily come here to lie in wait for Fawn and kill her. If his Washington law firm is anything like Tony's New York firm, Payton could have had to work on a case even on a Friday night."

"If Payton's anything like Tony, he could have

cheated on his fiancée when he was supposedly working late."

"Thanks for reminding me, Granddad." She stood up. "I have to go to the café to get the food ready for the booth today. Bethany's meeting me there to help."

"And who's gonna help me clean up after breakfast?"

She grinned at him. "Why don't you ask Sarina?"

"Because she'd bite my head off."

On the way to the café, Val picked up large bags of ice for the coolers she would take to the booth. It was almost nine by the time she pulled into the parking lot of the Bayport Racket and Fitness Club. Normally, the café opened at eight, but this weekend it was closed because of the festival.

She went inside the club and paused before entering the Cool Down Café. Small and utilitarian with its granite eating bar and handful of bistro tables, the café was the opposite of Granddad's Victorian house overstuffed with books, family photos, and soft furniture. But she felt at home in both places. One balanced the other. During her last few years in New York, she'd had Tony to come home to. If she went back there now, she might end up working constantly and losing the balance in her life.

From outside the café alcove, Val could see her weekend assistant and tennis teammate, Bethany, already at work. Val went into the café. Bethany had set out vegetables, fruits, and hummus on the food prep counter—ingredients for healthy alternatives to the burgers, hot dogs, and fries that other booths at the festival would offer. "Good morning."

"Hey, Val."

Val was used to seeing Bethany in primary colors that would appeal to the first-graders she taught. Today she'd gone for a younger look in pastels—a short lavender skirt with a lace trim at the hem and a pink top with puffy sleeves. The clothes would make a toddler look cute, but didn't flatter a sturdy ginger-haired woman in her twenties. "New outfit?"

"I bought it yesterday. Did you hear the news?"

Val could guess what news she meant, but hedged in case Bethany meant something else. "News, as in gossip?"

"No, I heard it on the radio as I was driving here. A woman was strangled last night. The police issued a bulletin asking for help. They described her and asked anyone who saw her at the festival to contact them. They also want to hear from people in your neighborhood who saw anything out of the ordinary last night between six and ten."

"The police better have operators standing by. They're going to hear from a lot of people. Bayport's never had a festival like this, so everything was out of the ordinary last night." At least the police hadn't announced exactly where the woman was killed, but in a small town everyone would know that before long. No reason to keep it from Bethany. "She was strangled in our backyard."

Bethany's eyes and mouth turned into O's. "Your poor grandfather. The radio said she was a tourist not a local. Was she one of the people staying at his house?"

"She was." While making the salads to sell at the booth, Val gave her assistant a rundown on Grand-dad's guests.

Bethany chopped celery for the Waldorf salad. "Those poor people. They come here to arrange a wedding and one of them is murdered. How are they dealing with that?"

"Better than you'd expect. The murdered woman wasn't a family member or very close friend. None of them knew her except the bride, who hadn't seen her for ten years."

"Don't most brides visit wedding locales with their mothers or sisters?"

"That's what my friends all did when they planned weddings." If Val hadn't broken off her engagement to Tony before they'd even set a date for the wedding, her mother would have gone with her to find a place for the reception. "I don't know if Jennifer's mother is dead, sick, or too busy to bother. The maid of honor is the mother substitute. The best man probably wouldn't have come except for the festival. He's more interested in boats than wedding plans."

Val's phone chimed. She pulled it out of her bag. Gunnar was calling.

"Glad I reached you, Val. I was worried when I heard a woman was strangled near your grand-father's house. The police said the poor woman didn't live around here, but first reports aren't always reliable."

"That one was accurate." She switched the phone

to her left ear so she could stir the cucumbers, olives, and tomatoes in the chopped Greek salad. "The woman was staying at our house. Keep that to yourself because I don't want any media attention." *Though Granddad, the publicity hound, probably felt differently.* If the police chief hadn't warned him to avoid the media, Granddad would be standing in front of a camera in his Codger Cook apron, cogitating aloud about the crime and brandishing a Sherlockian pipe.

"You're a magnet for murder, Val. I'll bet the New York homicide rate has gone down since you left."

"My magnetic power kicked in when I moved to Bayport." She gave the salad one last stir.

"I'm just grateful you'll be too busy at the festival to go sleuthing again."

"I can delegate what needs to be done at the booth, if necessary," she said, only half in jest.

"Delegate detecting to the police. The woman was a stranger, right? The police aren't accusing you or your grandfather, right? You have no skin in this game."

Unless the strangler had been after her skin. Val checked her watch. Time to load the coolers with the food. "When can I expect to see you at the festival?"

"We hope to finish the theater sets by noon. I'll stop by the booth after that."

If she gave him a mission, he'd be more likely to show up on schedule. "Would you bring some big bags of ice with you? We have enough for the food coolers, but I don't want to run out of ice for drinks."

"Okay. See you later."

Val tucked her phone in her jeans pocket and noticed a bulging plastic grocery bag next to the trash bin. The club's cleaning team came through every night to remove trash. So where had this bag come from? She picked it up, heard glass clinking, and checked the inside. It was full of baby food jars, all of them open and recapped. Some were half-filled with pinkish-grayish contents, others nearly empty except for orange or purple stuff clinging to the jars' insides.

Bethany zoomed over and took the bag from her. "Don't throw those away, Val. I'm going to take the jars home, wash them, and use them in my classroom for crayons and crafts."

Where had the jars come from? "Was anyone feeding babies in the café when you arrived? Sextuplets maybe? There are a dozen baby food jars here."

"Fourteen, actually."

"You counted them?"

"You bet I did. That was my breakfast. I have another fourteen jars for lunch. I'm on the baby food diet."

At least Val had heard of the diets Bethany had previous tried. Not this one. "Two months ago you were on the caveman diet. You've leapfrogged millennia since then. Now you're eating food that didn't exist until the twentieth century."

"The baby food is only for breakfast and lunch. Then I get to eat a light dinner of food I can chew."

Val took another look at her friend's outfit. Whether consciously or not, Bethany had picked out clothes that matched her diet. When eating like a cave man, she'd worn animal prints. Now on the baby food diet, she was wearing pastel frocks with smocking.

"After two meals of baby food, you'll be ravenously hungry and eat a heavy meal." Val wouldn't be surprised if the baby food diet resulted in weight gain. Bethany would look ten pounds slimmer in solid colors and simple styles, but Val wouldn't dare comment on anyone's wardrobe. Her own consisted mostly of black, white, beige, and the blue of jeans.

"Don't try to talk me out of this diet. I'm having a hard enough time with it. I now know why babies spit out their food. The meat is gross and the vegetables aren't a lot better. At least the strained fruit isn't bad, especially the applesauce."

This diet made even less sense than her previous one. Val would bet it wouldn't last any longer than the usual Bethany diet, five days tops. "Changing the subject to food for people with teeth, we need to load up this stuff for the festival."

The festival food booths were set up in the town parking lot, each one under a ten-foot-square canopy. The canopies lined a broad walking space for festival visitors. Val backed up her car to the booth. A popcorn vendor's machine two booths away permeated the air with a chemically enhanced butter fragrance that would entice some people and repel others.

With Bethany's help, Val set up the booth with a

long table at the front for serving customers, two folding chairs and a card table farther back, and coolers along the sides. An oilcloth table covering with a fall motif—yellow, orange, and red leaves on a green background—added a warm note to the stark booth. Val set out flyers for the festival events and discount coupons for the café at the club.

From ten until eleven, they had few customers, which gave them time to organize the booth for the influx of lunch eaters who lined up later. Whenever no one was lined up for lunch, Bethany took a break to eat baby food. She scraped every bit from twelve of her fourteen jars, but barely touched the spinach-apple-rutabaga combo and the macaroni and lentils with Bolognese sauce.

At one thirty Val took stock of the remaining food at her booth. The Waldorf salad with a vinaigrette dressing was almost gone. She still had plenty of the pasta-and-vegetable salad and of the chopped Greek salad. She also had enough bread to make more sandwiches though she doubted she'd use all of it, with the lunch rush over. The smoked turkey and cheese on rye and the hummus with roasted vegetables on whole wheat had sold equally well. The peanut butter and banana sandwiches had been a hit with youngsters.

"The iceman cometh." Gunnar adopted a voice of doom for his announcement. His dazzling smile undermined its effect. He was far from handsome, but that smile transformed his face. "I hope I'm not too late with the ice. Where do you want it?"

"In the two blue coolers." Val pointed to them. Judging by the whitish dust in his dark hair and on his sturdy workman's boots, he must have come straight from working on theater sets. "Are those new or old paint splatters on your jeans?"

"Old. We haven't started painting the sets yet. How are you doing, Bethany?"

"Fine. Good to see you again." She turned to Val. "I'd love to go home and make sure the neighbor's daughter took Muffin for a walk. Can you manage the booth alone for half an hour?"

Val nodded. "Sure. Gunnar can assist if things get busy, but I don't expect that."

Bethany picked up the plastic bag holding the remains of her lunch. "Thanks for covering for me, Gunnar. I'll be back soon." The baby food jars rattled in the bag as she left.

When Gunnar finished dumping the ice, Val asked, "Did you eat lunch yet? I can make you a sandwich. Or would you prefer a salad?"

"I stopped to eat at the burger booth at the end of this row."

"Ah. You'd rather not eat my lower-cal healthy food."

"I'll eat anything, but it's hard to pass up charcoal-broiled meat. I'll go get you a burger, if you like."

"No, thanks. I've been sampling the food here. Take a seat at the card table and I'll bring you cider and dessert." She poured ciders for both of them and brought over oatmeal cookies on a napkin. "This isn't just a food booth, it's an isolation booth. I've heard nothing about the strangling. Have you?"

"Rumors about a psychopathic tourist." He grabbed a cookie.

"Well, that's better than rumors about Granddad and his house of carnage." She sipped the cider.

"Fill me in on what happened."

Between interruptions to serve customers, Val described the wedding group. She was finishing her cider when she got to the part about finding Fawn in the yard.

Gunnar reached for her hand. "I'm sorry for calling you a murder magnet. I wouldn't have joked if I'd known you found her. Are you okay?"

"I'm good now." She could have used that hand enveloping hers last night.

"Did the murdered woman's friends cut short their weekend?" When Val shook her head, he tightened his grip on her hand. "You shouldn't sleep in the house with them. Why don't you stay at my place until they leave?"

"Thank you, but Granddad arranged for Monique to put me up at her house this weekend. You think it's dangerous to sleep in the house with the wedding group?" Or was Gunnar using the murder to nudge her toward moving in with him?

"Despite the rumors flying around, someone who knew the victim is a more likely killer than a psycho stranger. Do any of your grandfather's guests strike you as a possible murderer?"

"Hard to say who the murderer is without knowing who the victim was supposed to be." Judging by his raised eyebrows, she'd surprised him.

"I want to hear more about that, but right now,"

Gunnar pointed toward the front of the booth, "you have another customer."

She stood up and stifled a groan when she saw the sneering man with a mustache. She'd try to be civil to him. "Would you like to order something, Henri?"

"Certainly not. One of your former colleagues told me you planned to write a cookbook. I thought, *That can't be true.* You don't have a restaurant or a TV program. Now I see you do have a restaurant. Très elegant. Dining al fresco." He pulled a phone from his pocket. "I shall immediately send a photo to Monsieur Michelin. Perhaps he will come here and give you a star for this restaurant. Or maybe two stars."

"If you weren't too vain to put on your glasses, you'd know this isn't a restaurant." She gestured with an open palm toward the booth. "No stove, no refrigerator, no running water."

He squinted at the food listed on the whiteboard. "Ah, but you have a menu. Let us see what is on it. A peanut butter sandwich. How quaint. Fruit and cheese, but not French cheese, I'm sure. And hummus." He pronounced it *hyoo-mus* so it sounded like dirt.

"Hummus." Val corrected him through clenched teeth.

"Ooh-la-la! You make salads too. You are part of the raw food movement, perhaps. Now let us look up the meaning of the word *cook*." He punched buttons on his phone and held it up triumphantly. "Aha! To cook means to combine ingredients and heat them. So it is not a *cook*book you will write. You will write a *chop*book."

His tirade was attracting onlookers. She couldn't let him claim center stage unchallenged. She scuttled outside of the booth. She wanted to say, for the benefit of the crowd gathered around him, that her booth sold food she'd cooked not just chopped, but it took all her energy to control the steam rising inside her. An inner voice warned her against provoking a man who might want to kill her, and may have already tried.

"Your recipes will explain how to take something big and make little pieces of it." Henri mimicked chopping movements. "You think you know anything about cooking? Why? Because you promoted my cookbook? You didn't do a good job of it."

She erupted. "You can't cook without a brigade of helpers, the sous chef, the food prep team, the station cooks, and the pastry chef. You yell at them and chew them out. Is that what you call cooking? I call it the reason you don't have a restaurant anymore."

Henri raised his index finger and jabbed it toward her. "*You* destroyed my business."

Gunnar loomed behind him. "Scram, buddy." He had the kind of face that no one wants to see in a dark alley. With a crooked nose and a craggy complexion, Gunnar could answer a casting call for a hit man.

Chef Henri, however, wasn't cowed. He looked up at Gunnar the way most people look down on another person, as if he'd encountered a worm. "And whom are you?"

"*Who,* not whom," Val muttered.

"I'm her friend." Gunnar cocked his head toward Val, his voice quietly menacing. "Leave her alone, or you'll regret it."

For an amateur actor, he wasn't doing a bad imitation of a thug.

Henri's face turned puce. "You are threatening me?"

Gunnar stared down the chef. "I have not yet begun to threaten."

A man in the crowd applauded. "Great performance art. It wasn't even on the festival schedule."

"It isn't a performance," a tall gray-haired woman at the edge of the crowd said. "It's real. This man knows what he's talking about. He's the celebrity chef who'll judge the cook-off tomorrow."

Val might have known that Irene Pritchard, her former rival for the job of managing the Cool Down Café, would jump at the chance to criticize her and curry favor with the cook-off judge.

"Thank you, Madame." Henri bowed to Irene and extended both arms to the crowd. "I invite you all to watch my cooking demonstration tonight at eight at the Harbor Inn." He turned back to Gunnar and rose to his full height, which brought him up to Gunnar's chin. Eyes fixed on that chin, Henri said, "You do not scare me."

With that, he hightailed it away.

Bethany stepped forward. "What he said wasn't true. A lot of cooking went into the food Val's serving. She roasted the vegetables and baked the desserts. And it's all delicious. Her cooking is great, and her cookbook will be too."

"I'll second that," a man said, his voice coming from beyond the knot of people closest to the booth. "Val is a fantastic cook."

Val stiffened. Her insides knotted. She couldn't see the man because the crowd hid him from view, but she didn't need to see him. She'd spent enough time with him to recognize that gravelly voice and, if she'd forgotten what he sounded like, his recent voicemail message would have reminded her—Tony.

Chapter 7

Val stood rigid as her former fiancé sauntered toward her. The air around her seemed to buzz like a high-voltage wire. She'd suppressed her memory of how good-looking he was, his brown eyes framed by dark lashes, his high cheekbones. He had features that would have made the sculptors of ancient Greece swoon—a classic profile and a marble heart.

Val caught Bethany's eye. "Can you handle the booth by yourself for a minute or two?"

Bethany nodded and scurried under the canopy. Val reminded herself how she'd wasted five years thinking Tony was the love of her life. She moved closer to Gunnar.

Tony wore the crooked smile that women found so charming. "Good to see you again, Val. I've missed you."

Obvious that he'd lost weight. Missing her cooking? Starved for affection? "What are you doing in Bayport?" She kept her voice even, devoid of emotion, despite the turmoil inside her.

"Well, I didn't come for the Tricentennial."

"While you're here, enjoy the festival." *You won't get anything else out of this trip.* "Gunnar, this is Tony Nicolias. Tony, meet Gunnar Swensen."

Tony thrust out his hand.

Gunnar hesitated before shaking hands. "Tony. I've heard about you."

"Well, I haven't heard about you." Tony's eyes flicked from Gunnar to Val. "Can we talk . . . alone?"

She pointed to the booth behind her. "I'm working."

He glanced at the banner saying the booth would be open from ten to four. "I'll come by at four."

"I'll be busy then too. I'm sure you remember what it's like to work after hours." She instantly regretted her snide reference to the evenings he'd spent with his paralegal. She didn't want him to think his cheating still bothered her.

Val turned away from him and went back to the booth, with Gunnar following. The crowd around the booth was thinning out, but a knot of people clustered around the menu.

Bethany cocked her head toward them. "A bunch of people are talking about what to order."

"Great. A late-lunch crowd." Val smiled at Gunnar. "Business was slowing down before Henri came along. I hope he's nearby to see how his tirade made people notice my booth."

Gunnar folded his arms. "Why didn't you tell Tony you didn't want to talk to him?"

Val hesitated, surprised at the change of subject. "He already knew that. He left me several messages in the last month. I didn't respond to them." Voice mail, text message, e-mail. He'd tried them all and she'd deleted them all.

"What made him show up here?"

Val couldn't have been clearer about her negative feelings for Tony. Yet Gunnar was behaving as if she'd expected her ex-fiancé to come to Bayport. "You'll have to ask him, and I have to help Bethany wait on customers." She pointed to the line of people in front of the booth.

"I'll come back when you're less busy." He ducked out of the booth and walked stiffly away.

Val was glad he was taking a break. Given a little time, he might stop brooding about Tony.

For the next fifteen minutes, she was too busy waiting on customers to give any thought to him, Tony, Henri, or the Bayport strangler.

During a break between customers, Bethany said, "Would you do me a favor?"

"Of course." Val couldn't have run the booth without her this weekend and owed her a bunch of favors.

"I planned to go to the corn maze tonight with two of the other teachers. But one of them bowed out because her parents are visiting for the weekend, and the other caught the stomach virus that's going around. It's no fun to go through the maze alone, so will you go with me?"

Half an hour ago, Val would have nixed a visit to the maze, but now that she knew Henri would be busy with a cooking demo, she saw no reason not to go. A maze wouldn't appeal to criminals, whether purse snatchers or murderers. They couldn't depend on a fast getaway. "Okay. I'll go with you."

She spotted her cousin outside the booth. Monique moved around with her camera, apparently searching for a good angle. She took some shots of Val serving customers. When no more customers were waiting, she took more formal shots of Val and Bethany standing outside the booth, under the banner that read COOL DOWN CAFÉ ANNEX.

As Val smiled for the camera, she caught sight of Jennifer two booths away, clinging to a tall man. Had to be Payton. Long of leg and neck like a crane, he covered the same distance in a single stride as she did in three steps, wearing sandals with stacked heels. She'd changed out of the jeans she'd worn at breakfast into butter yellow capris, showing off her shapely calves. Noah in cargo shorts and Sarina in her usual tan gaucho pants walked a few paces behind the engaged couple, talking with their heads close together.

"The wedding group staying at Granddad's is coming this way," Val said in a voice just loud enough for Bethany and Monique to hear.

"Where?" Bethany glanced left and right.

"Two booths down. The woman hanging onto the preppy-looking guy is the bride-to-be." Val tilted her head in their direction. "They'll stop to talk if I'm right in their path. Why don't you go under the canopy, Bethany? It'll look more natural than if we're both lined up here."

Monique moved away. "I'll come back and take some photos of them."

While Bethany smoothed out the autumn table covering, Val stood outside the booth straightening the flyers on the table. She waved to the wedding foursome as they approached.

Jennifer pulled her companion toward the booth. "Hey, Val. This is my fiancé, Payton Grandsire. I don't think you got a chance to meet him yesterday."

Payton held his fiancée close with his hand roving on her hip and thigh. "Good to meet you. How is your grandfather after the tragedy last night? I hope it wasn't too much of a shock."

"Thank you. I hope so too."

"He seemed okay this morning," Jennifer said. "A little sad, but we all were."

Noah and Sarina joined the soon-to-be bride and groom. Val had just introduced Bethany to the four of them when Monique rushed over with her camera.

"Could I get some shots of this group? I'm Monique Mott, a festival photographer."

Val introduced everyone to Monique. "She's my cousin and the best wedding photographer in town."

"Could I have your business card, Monique?" Jennifer said. "Payton and I are planning our wedding. That's why we're all here this weekend."

"Fantastic. Photos of your planning weekend can be the first ones in your wedding album." With infectious enthusiasm, Monique arranged the group for the camera and coaxed natural smiles from them by prompting them to say *yes* instead of *cheese*. Even the formerly immovable Sarina was no match for Monique's irresistible force. Through a dozen shots, Payton never took his hands off Jennifer, though he did move them around to different parts of her anatomy.

"How about a few pictures with Val?" Monique said. "A souvenir photo of the weekend. Come and join them, Val."

Just what Val needed—a souvenir of a murder weekend. Like the others, though, she gave in to the energetic Monique.

Her cousin snapped three pictures of Val with the group and then pulled a pair of crab hats from her tote bag. "Now let's do a few pictures so you remember the festival that was going on while you were planning the big event. These are the official Tricentennial hats." She offered the bride-to-be a hat.

Jennifer took it. "We have our own hats, but not with us."

Val gave her cousin points for deviousness. Monique was saving herself the trouble of using software to put crab hats on people. When Sarina refused to wear a crab hat, Monique held it out to Val.

Val, who hadn't put on her own souvenir hat since finding Fawn dead, hesitated. Reluctantly, she donned the hat for the photo, though she couldn't quite manage a smile for the camera.

After a few clicks of the camera, Jennifer took off the hat and handed it to her fiancé. "Your turn, Payton!"

"Not unless Noah wears one too."

Val took off her hat, gave it to Noah, and moved out of the way of the camera lens. So many people had stopped to watch the photo shoot that they created a pedestrian tie-up near the booth. Val spotted her grandfather in the crowd and waved.

He returned her greeting, but the next time she looked, he'd disappeared. Maybe he'd gone to meet her mother, who should have arrived by now.

When Monique finished taking photos, she collected the hats and handed out her business cards. "You'll find the photos on the Tricentennial website with information about ordering them. Shoot me an email if you want to discuss photography for the wedding. I'm already taking bookings for June. Thanks much, folks." She hurried off.

Two women in designer slacks and chic sweaters approached from the other direction. Val recognized Penelope Grandsire, though until now she'd seen her only in tennis clothes. Payton sprang away from Jennifer. The resemblance between him and his mother was striking, both tall with a face shaped like an inverted triangle, broad in the forehead, narrowing to an elongated chin. The other woman, a willowy blonde with hair tied back at the nape of her neck, was about Payton's age.

"There you are, Payton." Penelope used the same tone as a mother would to a young boy who'd strayed away from her in a shopping mall. "Why don't you introduce your friends to Whitney?"

Payton did as he was told.

His mother nodded to Sarina when Payton introduced her, gave Jennifer a stiff hello, and exchanged a few words with Noah. She either didn't notice Val or didn't recognize her from their encounters on the tennis court.

Val shuffled the flyers on the table and kept her eyes and ears open to the drama taking place near the booth.

Noah glanced from the flustered Jennifer to the cool Whitney. "How do you and Payton know each other, Whitney?"

The blonde smiled fondly at Payton. "Fate put us together from the time we were born."

Payton didn't return the smile. "My parents and Whitney's have been friends a long time."

Penelope nodded. "Payton and Whitney played together as children and dated when they were older. Then Payton went off to law school and Whitney went to graduate school and to the Sorbonne. It's so nice to have her back home." She locked arms with the younger woman. "I've forgotten what type of work you do, Jennifer."

Jennifer perked up. "I'm an interior decorator. Residential. A lot of people move into and out of Washington after each election. It's very satisfying to help them find the look that will work for them."

"Such fun for you," Penelope said, "to go into the houses of the well-to-do and tell them what to do."

The little Val knew about the older woman suggested she also enjoyed telling other people what to do.

Penelope was still talking. "I'm sure interior decorating pays well too, for a job that doesn't require much education. Of course, you need a good eye."

"I have a B.F.A. degree." Jennifer's voice sounded half an octave higher than usual.

Penelope frowned. "I'm not sure what that is. Whitney is working on her second Ph.D."

Sarina glowered. "Bachelor of Fine Arts—that's what a B.F.A. is. And you need more than a good eye to earn one. You need talent and creativity."

"Are you an interior decorator too?" Whitney asked Sarina.

"No, I'm an artist. With a B.F.A. What are you getting a Ph.D. in?"

"Communication, Culture, and Media in their social, historical, and ideological contexts. It's an interdisciplinary program that fosters synergistic collaborative approaches to understand and solve problems."

Val watched the members of the wedding party go slack-jawed as Whitney continued in this vein, using terms like *ethnographic* and *sociopoetic*.

Sarina recovered first. "What sort of a job does that prepare you for?"

Her question echoed the one in Val's mind.

Whitney's pained expression made her look like a headache victim in an aspirin commercial. "Well, I've always believed the purpose of education is to enable you to live a full life, not prepare you for a specific job. That said, a leadership position in a foundation or nonprofit would be a possible outcome."

A possible outcome in the unlikely event she would need to earn a living.

Penelope touched her son's arm. "Your father's in a tizzy about getting the grills ready and the drinks set up for the barbecue. Don't dawdle here. We'll see you back at the house before long. So interesting talking to all of you." She and Whitney turned around and retraced their steps.

Looking at the two women from behind, Val would have taken them for sisters. The golden-haired Whitney and the platinum-haired Penelope weren't cut from exactly the same cloth, but they had a tailor who used the same pattern and scissors.

Sarina put an arm around Jennifer's shoulder and walked her in the other direction from Payton's mother. Noah and Payton followed.

Val went back inside the booth, grateful for the shade the canopy provided. She sat on a folding chair.

Bethany peered at her. "You look flushed. You okay?"

"I was standing in the sun too long."

"I'll get you a cold drink." Bethany gave her a paper cup of lemonade on ice and sat down across from her. "I feel sorry for Jennifer. Did you notice how Penelope looked at her?"

"You mean, like she was going to drill a tennis ball right at her?" Val guzzled the lemonade.

"I still have a circular black-and-blue mark on my shoulder, where she hit me a week ago. If you'd found Jennifer dead instead of Fawn, I'd know who did it."

And if Penelope had failed the first time, she'd certainly try again. Val could think of no way to find out where Payton's mother had been last night, but maybe she could talk the chief into checking on Penelope's alibi. "Imagine having her as a mother-in-law. Love is all well and good, but when you marry someone, you also marry his family."

Bethany focused over Val's shoulder, her eyes widening. "Hi, Gunnar."

He had slipped into the back of the booth without Val noticing him.

"Who's marrying whose family?" he asked.

Val saw the tension in his close-mouthed smile though he'd sounded nonchalant. Maybe he was still obsessing about Tony. "We were talking about the bride-to-be who's staying at my grandfather's house and her potential in-law problems."

Bethany's head swiveled from Gunnar to Val. "You could use a break, Val. Why don't you go for a walk with Gunnar? I can manage on my own."

"Okay. If it gets busy again, call me. We'll go to the park." Close enough that she could return within two minutes if Bethany needed help and far enough from the booths to breathe air that didn't reek of buttered popcorn.

Bethany pointed to her straw hat with a four-inch brim. "Take my hat, Val. The sun's brutal."

Val put it on. *Much cooler than a crab hat.* She and Gunnar went behind the canopies to the parking lot perimeter. They weren't the only ones avoiding the crowds visiting booths. Val stopped walking when she saw Jennifer and Payton ten yards away.

She pointed them out to Gunnar. "His mother was less than cordial to his fiancée a few minutes ago. I wish I could hear what Jennifer and Payton are saying. Well, maybe I can. No harm in trying." She pulled down the brim of the sun hat so her face was less visible.

Gunnar bent down and peered under the brim. "Nosy, aren't we?"

"You can hang back if you have qualms. I'm going to park myself closer to them."

"You'll be less obvious if I'm with you." He grabbed her hand. "Now look at me as if I'm your secret lover and we're wrapped up in each other.

When you're close enough to hear them, stop walking and take my other hand. We'll gaze into each other's eyes and listen to what they're saying."

Gunnar's plan worked well. They halted near enough to hear the engaged couple talking.

"When you said your parents had invited friends, I assumed they were old people," Jennifer said. "Now I find out you have an ex-girlfriend staying at the house."

"I didn't know my mother was going to invite her. I swear I didn't, Jennifer. I haven't seen Whitney in years."

"It's pretty clear why your mother invited her. She wants to break up our engagement."

Safe conclusion, Jennifer. Val stole a glance at the couple.

Payton held Jennifer by the shoulders. "My mother doesn't control who I marry."

"She's controlling your time. That means she's controlling you."

"She invited a whole bunch of friends to a barbecue. She needs me there to help with the drinks and the food."

Val was fairly sure the Grandsires could afford to cater a barbeque.

Jennifer put her arms around Payton's neck. "I could help at the barbecue."

He pulled her closer. "You don't want to take drink orders and stand over a hot grill. Go out and have a nice dinner with Sarina and Noah. Or get picnic food and eat it during the outdoor concert. I'll join you as soon as I can get away."

"*If* you can get away." She wriggled free of his

grasp. "We're not going to any concert. We're going to the corn maze tonight."

"Jennifer, please don't do that. You've got to be careful after what happened to Fawn. I wish you would listen to me and leave Bayport."

"Of course you wish that. Then you could spend the whole weekend with Whitney Oglethorpe."

Jennifer stalked off, leaving Payton standing alone. He didn't try to go after her.

"The curtain goes down," Gunnar said softly. "I missed the opening scenes, but I followed the plot anyway. Two young lovers kept apart by interfering elders, class differences, or previous romances. Where have I heard that story before?" He tapped his forehead. "Oh, yeah. Hollywood. Shakespeare. Jennifer should take heart. It turns out well in the end."

"Except when it doesn't. Remember Romeo and Juliet? And Jennifer has all three obstacles working against her—elders, class, *and* former flings."

"But no feuding families, so she's good." Gunnar steered Val across the street to the park. "Let's find a place to sit. Something you said has been bothering me, and I haven't had a chance to ask you about it."

Well, he'd had several chances to ask about Tony and seized them all. Maybe this time he had a question about something else.

Chapter 8

Children and their parents waited at the park dock for boat rides along the creek and clustered at the face-painters' tables. A banjo-mandolin-fiddle trio played bluegrass on the bandstand. Val spotted a patch of green grass in the dappled shade of a small tree and hurried to it. She sat on the ground with her legs curled under her.

Gunnar stretched out, leaning on one elbow, and faced her. "Before the chef showed up at your booth, you said you didn't know who the strangler intended to kill. What did you mean by that?"

Oh, good. He wasn't asking about her ex-fiancé this time. She much preferred talking about murder than about Tony. "Have you seen the crab hats?"

"How could I miss them?"

"Fawn wore one last night, and so did Jennifer, who's about Fawn's size. In the dark it would have been hard to tell the difference between them. I'm worried that the killer mistook Fawn for Jennifer and will try to correct that mistake. Do you think I should tell Jennifer?"

"You might be frightening her for no reason. Tell the police instead. They can warn her if your idea makes sense to them."

"I'll talk to Chief Yardley about it." Maybe the bride-to-be would listen to the police even though she'd ignored her fiancé's warning. "It's also possible I was the intended victim."

Gunnar jerked upright. "*What?* Why do you think that?" Worry lines added to the roughness of his face.

"I'm about the same size as Fawn and Jennifer, and I wore a crab hat last night too. Chef Henri saw me in the hat, followed me last night, and went ballistic, screaming that I ruined his life. He's always blamed me for the injuries he got in the car accident. He knows where I live, and he'd like to wring my neck." Val massaged her throat.

"Yelling at you isn't the same as strangling you. Did you ever see him attack anyone physically?"

"No, but I've seen him verbally violent with his underlings and me. Verbal abuse often leads to physical abuse."

"But he just made his hostility toward you obvious to a lot of people near your booth. Would he do that if he tried to kill you last night and planned to try again? He'd have to be insane."

"He has an anger-management problem, temporary insanity. Last night he was like that. This afternoon he was crazy like a fox. He was feeding his ego and drumming up an audience for his cooking demo. I was just the instrument he used."

"Stay out of his way and tell Chief Yardley. If he's concerned, he can get his officers and the festival security force to keep an eye on Henri." Gunnar ran a finger under the collar of his plaid work shirt. "I'm sorry, but I have to back out of dinner tonight. I'll make it up to you when the festival's over."

Again? "Tonight was a makeup for last night. And now the makeup for tonight can't happen until after the festival? Are you still constructing sets for the play?"

He shook his head. "One of the guys in the theater group arranged a gig for tonight and to-morrow night. He came down with a stomach bug and asked me to take his place."

Val sighed. Gunnar wouldn't refuse a request for help. That's who he was, and she liked him that way, so she couldn't complain. "What kind of gig?"

"I'm going to be a zombie scarecrow at the corn maze."

She laughed. "That, I've got to see. When you take up your duty station, text me where you are in the maze, and I'll find you."

He winced. "I don't want you going into the maze alone after last night's murder."

"I won't be alone. Bethany asked me to go with her. She's giving up her weekend to help me at the booth, so I couldn't turn her down. Anyway, if someone wants to get away with murder, the maze isn't the place to do it. One way out, hard to find, no easy getaway."

"I still wish you wouldn't go there. But if you insist, call me when you go in. How do I explain where I am in a maze?" Gunnar traced curlicues with his finger in the grass as if designing an ant maze.

"You can give me the number of the last signpost you passed and tell me which way you turned after that. I should be able to find you. I've been all over that maze to check where the signposts for the trivia questions are." She stood up and brushed off her jeans. "I'd better get back to the booth. I don't want to work Bethany too hard or she may not come back tomorrow."

As they crossed the street to return to the booths, Gunnar said, "There's Chief Yardley. I'll give Bethany a hand in the booth if you want to talk to him now. Oh, wait. A woman just came up to him, and they're hugging.

"Where?"

Gunnar pointed. "Over where Jennifer and Payton were standing earlier. Does the chief have a sweetheart?"

"It wouldn't surprise me. He's been divorced for a while." Val craned her neck, but the chief blocked her view of the woman. "This doesn't look like the right time to talk to him. Maybe we'd better walk a little further before we cut over to the festival tents. It's not the quickest way back to my booth, but I don't want to interrupt him."

"They're clenched so tightly that I doubt the chief would notice if you brushed against him."

The chief released the woman from his embrace, giving Val a clear view of . . . her mother?

Maybe the woman just resembled her mother.

Val took off her sunglasses and squinted at the couple.

Definitely her mother with the chief, the two of them so intent on each other that they might as well have been in a cocoon.

Val felt as if her lungs had compressed, leaving no room for oxygen. Did Mom use Dad's fishing trip as an excuse to spend time with Earl Yardley? Her mother and the chief, both close to sixty, had known each other when they were growing up. After leaving town to go to college, Mom didn't return to live in Bayport until Val was a teenager, and then only for a couple of years. By then, Earl Yardley had left Bayport to work elsewhere. He'd moved back here in the spring, and this was Mom's first visit since then. The two of them probably hadn't seen each other for many years.

Satisfied that she'd worked it out, Val put on her sunglasses again. "That's not the chief's sweetheart, Gunnar. I think he's just greeting an old friend with a hug."

"I doubt it. You hug an old friend with your arms. The chief and that woman were hugging with their bodies, and it lasted a lot longer than a greeting-your-old-friend hug."

Val put her hands on her hips. "That's my mother."

"Oh, sh—" Gunnar covered his mouth. "Your mother? Where's your father?"

"In Florida with his fishing buddies."

Gunnar gave her arm a brief squeeze. "I must

have been wrong about that hug. Why didn't you tell me your mother was in town?"

"I only found out this morning that she was coming here. This is the first I've seen of her. I was hoping you'd have a chance to meet her, but this isn't the right time."

"Definitely not. I don't want to meet your mother dressed like this." He gestured toward his faded jeans and stained shirt. "How long will she be here?"

Val shrugged. "I'll let you know when I find out. Now let's just give her and the chief a wide berth."

Back at the booth, Val told Bethany and Gunnar that she could manage alone until closing time at four. Her mother stopped by the booth shortly after they left.

"Welcome to Bayport, Mom." Enveloped in a hug, Val momentarily forgot the embrace she'd witnessed earlier.

Her mother let go of her. "You look so much better than last February. No dark circles under your eyes."

Her mother's short, brown hair had more streaks of gray than Val remembered, but otherwise she looked the same. Not like a woman contemplating a huge change in her life. "How's Dad?"

"Happy to be on a boat." Mom pressed her lips together, looking stern. "When you told me about the murder, you left out that you tripped over the body. Your grandfather gave me all the details."

A pair of teenage girls approached the booth and ordered lemonade and cookies. Her mother sat down at the card table while Val served the girls.

Once they left, Val joined her mother at the table. "I saw Granddad walking by earlier, but he didn't stop. Is he still here?" And had he seen Mom and the chief together? Maybe he could explain that overly friendly greeting.

"He's home, turning your bedroom into a fortress so I'll be safe sleeping there. I reserved two rooms in a motel this side of Annapolis, one for me and one for him, but he refuses to leave his house. I won't let him stay there alone, so I cancelled the reservation."

"Why? Are you staying at the house to protect him from his guests?"

"In a way. I doubt they'll kill us in our beds, but they might make too many demands on him. While I was at the house, they came back so the bride-to-be could change into more comfortable shoes. She was nuts to walk around in high heels for hours." Sitting at an angle to the card table, Mom crossed her legs and showed off stylish beige flats that went well with her ankle-length pants. "They're all going out for crabs tonight, so we'll have the house to ourselves for dinner."

Val envisioned the shelves of the refrigerator at home. Not enough of anything there to feed three. "What would you like for dinner? I'll have to stop by the store."

"I brought Florida shrimp with me. Frozen solid and in an insulated bag. There's enough for four. Do you want to invite Gunnar? I'd like to meet him."

"He can't make it tonight. How long are you staying?"

"My plane back leaves Monday evening."

Val noticed her cousin approaching the booth. "Here comes Monique."

"I haven't seen her in a long time." Mom intercepted Monique outside the booth and gave her a quick, though awkward, hug. "I'm so glad to see you. We usually meet only at funerals. Val has told me how good a friend you've been to her since she moved here. Thank you for that, and also for putting her up this weekend."

"She's been a good friend to me too." Monique raised her eyebrows at Val as if asking how much she should reveal.

Val shook her head, signaling her cousin to say nothing about the dangers Val had faced while trying to prove Monique innocent of murder.

Mom fiddled with the festival flyers on the table, looking ill at ease. "My father hasn't been a friend to anyone on your side of the family for a long time, Monique. I'm glad he's finally mellowing about that. Come sit under the booth canopy. I want to hear about your children. I hope I get a chance to see them this weekend."

"They're with my in-laws today. We're getting together at the park at four." Monique checked her watch. "Fifteen minutes from now. You're welcome to come along and meet the little guys."

"Mom would love to do that." Possibly not true, but Val wanted to give her mother no choice. "When I close the booth at four, I have to drive to the café to refrigerate the leftovers and get a head start on the food for tomorrow."

She planned a quick escape from the booth to avoid Tony. He might show up, though she'd warned him she would be busy even after the booth closed.

By four o'clock she had already loaded the coolers in her car. She was about to climb into it when she noticed something colorful under her windshield wiper—a frizzy-haired miniature Raggedy Ann doll, with VAL printed in marker on its pinafore. The five-inch high doll had another personalized feature.

Val's stomach clenched. Someone had stuck a dozen straight pins into the doll, one between the eyes. A Raggedy Val voodoo doll.

Val was so shaken that her hand trembled as she reached for it. She stopped before she touched it, took out her phone, and snapped photos of it. Now she had proof that someone hated her, but no evidence of who. If Chef Henri had put Raggedy Val on her windshield, as she suspected, he would have made sure no one had seen him do it. Val removed the doll, holding it by a few strands of its yarn hair, wrapped a tissue around it, and put it her trunk so she wouldn't have to look at.

As soon as she maneuvered through the traffic in town, she pulled into a strip mall and phoned the chief. When he answered, she told him about the doll and her encounters with Chef Henri La Farge, describing him as a man with a grudge against her. "I think he left that thing on my windshield."

"Nasty, but not dangerous, unless the voodoo works," the chief said.

She took a deep breath. "True, but I wonder if

Henri could have strangled Fawn, mistaking her for me."

"Hmm. First, he tries to kill you and, when he fails, he resorts to voodoo? The other way around makes more sense."

"Henri's unstable. He doesn't always make sense." But the chief had a point. As long as she had him on the phone, she'd give him a chance to shoot down another theory. "It's also possible that Jennifer was the intended victim. She and I are about the same size as Fawn. All three of us wore crab hats."

Chief Yardley took a moment to respond. "I'm not ruling out anything, but for now the investigation is focused on the victim we have. We also want to make sure there isn't another victim. I told your granddaddy's guests not to go anywhere alone until this case is solved."

"I hope they take your advice." As long as the three of them stuck together, there was less chance of another murder, either *by* or *of* one of them.

"The same goes for you, Val. Safety in numbers. Safety in daylight. Don't walk around alone in the dark."

"I won't." Though she'd have to drive alone to Monique's house tonight.

At the café Val made dough for the cookies and brownies she would bake in the morning to sell at the booth.

She arrived home at six o'clock and found Grand-dad in his easy chair, drinking a beer, and Mom on the sofa with a glass of white wine. Val plopped down next to her.

"How did everything go at the booth today?" Granddad asked.

"Fine, except for when Chef Henri came by. He's the man who came to the house yesterday asking for me." Val told them the story, imitating the chef's voice and making them laugh. She said nothing about the voodoo figure because she didn't want them to worry about her. "Gunnar no sooner ran him off than another Ghost from New York Past showed up at the booth—Tony."

Granddad frowned. "Your rotten ex-fiancé? What's he doing here?"

"Good question." Granddad's reaction, a mixture of surprise and annoyance, didn't surprise Val. Her mother's lack of reaction did. Mom got up off the sofa, crossed the room to the shelves by the fireplace, took out a book, and shifted it to a new location on the same shelf. Val watched her rearrange books, a suspicion forming. "What do you know about Tony's visit, Mom?"

Her mother wheeled around. "He called me a few days ago to ask my advice because you wouldn't respond to his messages. I told him that you were busy getting ready for the festival and that he might like to visit Bayport during the festival."

"*What?*" Val jumped up. "It was your idea for him to come here and ambush me?"

Her mother ran a hand through her curly hair. "Ambush isn't the right word. He has something to say, and you won't give him the chance. He just wants to talk to you."

Granddad waggled his index finger at Mom. "How can you take his side, Diane, after what he did?"

"You're turning on me too, Pop? I only wanted to do what's best for Val."

Val hugged herself, holding in the anger bubbling inside of her like lava. The image of Penelope Grandsire superimposed itself on her mother's face. Her mother had meddled, just as Payton's mother had, both fanning old flames, possibly with the same goal—to ward off a new romance. She gave her mother a defiant stare. "What makes you think you know what's best for me?"

Mom returned Val's steady look. "If you can't bring yourself to even talk to Tony, you haven't put that relationship behind you. Unfinished business can haunt you for years."

"It's finished as far as I'm concerned, Mom."

Shaking with anger, Val marched out of the room toward the kitchen. *Running away?* Yes, but with a good reason. A full-blown argument with her mother would ruin the weekend, not only for the two of them, but also for Granddad.

A loaf of crusty French bread rested on the kitchen counter. Her mother must have picked it up at the bakery on Main Street. Val hacked off the narrow end, crunched down on it, and chewed vigorously. Then she sliced off another piece and slathered it with butter. She felt calmer, partly because bread-and-butter was the ultimate comfort food and partly because of the tranquil aura her grandmother had left behind in the room where she'd spent so much time.

Val opened the refrigerator door and spotted the

plastic bag of shrimp her mother had brought from Florida. The shrimp were still slightly frozen. She took the bag from the fridge.

Granddad came into the kitchen and set his empty beer bottle on the counter with a bang. He still looked tense, but not as angry as before. "You got plans for those shrimp?"

"I have an easy recipe you can use for your column, a simplified version of a Greek dish with shrimp, tomatoes, and feta cheese."

"Good. What do you want me to do?"

Val took his rare offer to help with the cooking as a sign of support for her in her quarrel with Mom. "Shell and devein the shrimp. I'll run water on them first so they don't freeze your fingers." She put the shrimp in a colander and took them over to the sink. "Where's Mom?"

"Gone upstairs to grade papers. She says she's not ready to retire from teaching. But, as usual, she retires from the kitchen pretty quick whenever it's close to mealtime. Cooking never interested her. Your grandmother was tickled when you took an interest."

Val fetched olive oil, garlic, and a can of diced tomatoes from the pantry. "I was tickled to learn from her." Even when she could barely see over the kitchen counter, she'd insisted on helping Grandma cook.

Granddad leaned on the counter, his face grave. "Just as well your mother left us alone so I can tell you how my investigation is going. I found out what the strangler did before killing Fawn and how the murder went down."

Really? He often touted his cooking expertise, though he had none. Boasts about his investigative skills wouldn't surprise Val. On the other hand, he might have learned something important. Either way, she'd rather her mother not know anything about his so-called investigation.

Val glanced toward the staircase that ended in the kitchen. If Mom came down the back stairs, she might overhear Granddad talking at the counter.

He motioned for Val to follow him to the breakfast table on the other side of the room. "Let's go over there. If we keep our voices low, your mother won't catch anything we say."

Joining him at the table, Val adjusted the position of her chair so that she could see if Mom came to the kitchen from either the back staircase or the butler's pantry. "What did you find out?"

Chapter 9

Granddad moved his chair closer to Val's at the small kitchen table. "I walked through the neighborhood, talking to folks and looking real hard for clues. Halfway between here and the historic district, there's a house with flowers in pots hanging from the porch roof. Lots of pots, nice flowers."

Val conjured an image of a bungalow no one would notice except for the hanging garden on the porch. Pink petunias and blue vinca cascaded from planters held up by long rope hangers. "I know where you mean."

"Each pot hangs from sixteen strands of jute rope, four in each of four places around the pot. One of the pots was on the ground. It had two missing strands. It looked like someone sliced them off below the top knot and at the lower end." He demonstrated a cutting motion and clicked his tongue. "Those strands are like the rope used to strangle Fawn."

Val's heart sped up, but just a little. He might

be mistaken about the rope. "Did you notify the police?"

"I did some investigating on my own first so I wouldn't raise a false alarm. I knocked on the door of the house with the flowers. Nobody was home. Then I talked to a neighbor. The folks with the hanging plants have been on vacation for a week and aren't due back until next weekend. The neighbor said all the pots were okay yesterday afternoon when she watered the flowers. The rope was cut sometime between then and this morning."

Was he trying to solve this murder on his own? "When are you going to tell the police?"

"I told them and stood guard over the pot until they arrived. First a young officer came by, then a sheriff's deputy, and then the crime scene unit."

"The crime scene unit. I'm impressed, Granddad. You may have discovered where the strangler got the rope." Obviously, the police were taking his discovery seriously.

"I sure hope they give me credit for that when the story comes out. The police are sitting on a lot of information they haven't released. But I found out a few things."

"From the chief?" Granddad had served as a father figure after the chief lost his own dad, and the chief always treated him well.

"Nope. He wasn't there. It's a good thing you talked me into getting a hearing aid. When the police first got to the house with the hanging plants, I kept cupping my ear and asking them to repeat what they said. Pretty soon they were talking like I wasn't there. I turned up the volume." He touched the back of his ear to demonstrate. "Then I could hear real good."

She should know by now how wily he was, but he always surprised her with his ploys. "What did you hear?"

"Fawn was strangled from behind. Her killer slipped a looped rope over her head."

Val's stomach turned. She'd learned in a self-defense class how to break the hold of someone trying to choke her from the front. With a rope tightened from behind, Fawn wouldn't have had much chance to fend off the attack. "She might not have even seen her attacker."

"And the strangler didn't necessarily see her face either. What if that rope was supposed to go around someone else's neck?" He leaned toward her. "When Monique was taking pictures of the wedding bunch near your booth, I saw how much like Fawn you looked in a crab hat. You gotta watch your back, Val."

She tensed, not just because the voodoo doll had reinforced her anxiety about Chef Henri. She also feared Granddad would go on the offensive. A few months ago, when he'd believed her in danger, he'd taken down his shotgun. That time the police had let him get away with threatening someone at gunpoint, but would they be so generous if he did it again? Even worse, this time he might shoot someone, or the person he was threatening might grab the shotgun and use it on him.

To keep him from overreacting, she decided to

downplay the threat to herself. "Jennifer also looks like Fawn in a crab hat."

He tilted his head to one side and then the other, as if weighing her idea. "Could be, but she'll have to get someone else to protect her. I don't know who *her* enemies are, but I know of two people who'd want to go after you."

"Two?" Bad enough she had to look over one shoulder to make sure Chef Henri wasn't following her, now Granddad wanted her to look over the other shoulder too. "You seriously think two people would want to strangle me? Who?"

"That chef and Tony."

"*Tony?*" She laughed.

"Shh." Granddad pointed to the ceiling. "Lower your voice. Your mother will hear you."

She whispered, "Tony is too wrapped up in himself to go to the bother of murdering anyone. Trust me on this."

"Why would I trust you when it comes to Tony? You missed what he was doing right under your nose when you were engaged to him."

"Then ask Mom about him. She's his confidant."

"Don't be so hard on her. She means well. And don't ruin tonight's dinner by talking about the murder."

Or about Mom's clench with the police chief. Val stood up, went to the sink, and ran water over the shrimp. "What topics are acceptable?"

"One topic. Family. She's gone to California to see your brother and his brood twice since the last time she came here. She'll have plenty to tell us about the grandkids. And you can talk about the café and the cookbook you're working on." He joined her at the counter and peered at her index card with the shrimp recipe on it. "Let's see what you've got here. Hmm. This looks easy enough."

So easy that he could have cooked it himself, but he just watched Val do it. Her mother stayed upstairs until dinner was on the table. When she took her first bite and raved about the shrimp dish, Granddad thanked her as if he'd made the dish himself. Then he fed her questions about his great-grandchildren, keeping the conversation on one track through most of the meal. Val did her part with some follow-up questions.

When dinner was almost over, Mom said, "So much for the California branch of the Deniston family. Now let's hear about the Bayport branch. I spent some time this afternoon with your grandniece, Dad. I like Monique. Don't you?"

Val glanced at her grandfather. This probably wasn't the family conversation he wanted to have.

He broke off a piece of French bread and sopped up the sauce on his plate. "She's okay. Can't say I think much of her husband." He popped the bread in his mouth.

Val watched her mother push what was left of her dinner around the plate, possibly trying to decide how to deal with Granddad's brief, grudging response.

Her mother put down her fork. "Don't hold her husband against her . . . or her father. You haven't given Monique a fair chance because of what her father did. It's time to put that to rest. Men who fled to Canada during the Vietnam War have been welcomed back in this country for decades. He didn't come back, but he probably would have if he hadn't died so young. You can't blame her for something that happened almost fifty years ago."

"I don't blame her. Heck, I don't even blame him anymore. Maybe he really had moral qualms about that war."

"So why keep his daughter at arm's length?" Mom held both hands out with her palms up. "Monique moved to Bayport eight years ago, and I saw her once—at Mom's funeral. She came, even though none of us went to her mother's funeral the year before. We've been here every Christmas since then, and you never asked her to join us."

Granddad's eyes blazed. "You don't know the whole story. Sure, I was outspoken when my nephew dodged the draft. My sister never forgave me for saying that her son was shirking his duty as an American. She told people I sent him hate mail, calling him a traitor. Somebody may have done that, but I didn't."

Mom touched his arm. "Your sister died almost twenty years ago, Pop. Let it go."

He returned her steady gaze. "I can't do that, Diane, because she took her anger out on your mother."

Val had never heard this part of the story and never even met Granddad's sister. "What did she do to Grandma?"

"She told lies. She spread rumors at church and at the woman's club about your grandmother's loose behavior when she was young. It took a long time, even after my sister moved away from Bayport, for your grandmother to get the respect she deserved in this town."

Val was incensed that anyone, least of all a family member, could treat her kind, gentle grandmother so badly. "That's terrible." She understood now why Granddad found it hard to reconcile with his sister's branch of the family.

Mom frowned. "Why didn't I know about this?"

"You were on your way to college when we found out what she was saying. Your mother didn't want you bothered by it." He took off his bifocals and wiped his eyes. "She's been gone six years. I think about her every day, and it still makes me mad when I remember what my sister did to her."

Val's eyes stung with tears. Maybe his anger at his sister's family made it easier to cope with his grief over Grandma's death.

Mom reached for his hand. "You have every reason to be angry with your sister, Dad, but don't transfer your anger to Monique. It's no better than your sister transferring her anger at you to someone else."

He downed his remaining beer.

Poor Granddad. What made him think family would be a safe subject?

Val stood up. "Bethany's coming by for me in twenty minutes. We're going, uh, out for a while, and before I leave, I want to make a breakfast casserole for tomorrow."

Fortunately, Mom and Granddad were too engrossed in talking about the past to ask her about her plans. If they knew she was going to the maze in the dark, the night after a murder, they would have worried about her. Knowing that Henri would be giving a cooking demonstration tonight eased her own fears. The maze, bound to be a popular attraction, would offer safety in numbers.

It took Bethany and Val fifteen minutes to drive to the cornfield maze off a rural road outside town. Val called Gunnar as they waited to buy tickets.

Just inside the entrance, a maze monster gave a flashlight to each group coming in. Val and Bethany started down a dark path, sandwiched between a group of six teenagers and a family of five. The family included twins Bethany had taught the year before. After ten minutes of tramping between eight-foot high cornstalks on paths lit only by tiny flashlights, the twins were bawling.

Val didn't blame them. "This place is creepy for little kids."

Bethany glanced behind her. "The family's turning around. You've gone through the maze already, haven't you?"

"Yes. Under different circumstances."

Val had enjoyed finding her way through the cornfield with a blue sky above. But on a moonless night, she found it disorienting. In the dark, the maze resembled a tunnel with walls that rustled in the breeze and reached out to brush against her. Her mild claustrophobia kicked in. She'd never experienced it until she tried spelunking in college.

Now she avoided caves, but who would expect to be claustrophobic in a cornfield?

Don't panic, she told herself. One step after another, flashlight and eyes on the path ahead, not on the living walls closing in on her.

A screech came from within the corn wall. Val jumped away from it. Wailing followed.

Bethany laughed. "I remember that from last year. They have motion detectors with speakers hidden among the corn."

The banshee version of Robo-Fido.

Bethany stopped short as screams came from the group of teenagers twenty feet in front of them.

Val tensed and then immediately relaxed. "They're adolescents fooling around. Come on, or they'll get way ahead of us and we'll be all alone on the path."

Bethany hurried up. "Shouldn't we see another signpost? It's been a while since the last one."

"Yes, it has. We're looking for signpost five. Gunnar texted me to turn left there and go straight ahead until we see a path to the right. That's where he's hiding out."

A skeleton jumped out in front of them. Bethany shrieked and clutched Val's arm.

Cackling, the skeleton disappeared down a side path.

Bethany laughed nervously. "That's why the teenagers screamed."

Val couldn't believe how her heart was racing. The skeleton had rattled her. She wouldn't fall for that again. "We have to be prepared to see scary scarecrows. Gunnar the Zombie isn't the only one lurking in the maze."

After a few steps, Bethany stopped again. "Are you sure we're going the right way?"

She was balking every other minute, and Val was losing her patience. "You're the one who wanted to do this. While you were on the caveman diet, you took all sorts of risks. Now you go on the baby food diet, and you're totally timid."

"Don't blame my diet. When I was here last year, there was a moon out. Now it's pitch black and easy to get lost. Also, there's the murderer to worry about."

Val tamped down her annoyance. Bethany was young, only twenty-five, and entitled to an occasional rash decision. She needed reassurance. "We're not alone here. Up ahead you can see the teenagers' flashlights. If we think we've lost our way, you wave that flag on a stick while I shine the flashlight on it. The corn cops will come and rescue us. Besides that, we have our phones."

"But will we have the time to wave a flag or call 911 if the Bayport strangler comes after us?"

"Well, *one* of us will have the time." Val poked Bethany with her elbow to show she was joking.

"You're not helping, Val." Bethany moved forward, but even more cautiously than before.

They must have walked beyond the reach of electrical wires because no more noise came from banshee motion detectors. Now the only sounds were screams from nearby paths where skeletons, zombies, and other scary creatures were doubtless jumping out at people.

Whoops and howls came from behind them. Val turned around and made out movement in the darkness. A band of preteen boys wearing crab hats stampeded past. One boy jostled the flashlight out of Val's hand, and the light went out. *How annoying.* She stooped and patted the ground. It couldn't have fallen far.

"Where are you, Val? I can't see you." Bethany sounded panicky.

Val fought her own case of nerves. "The flashlight fell. I'm trying to find it. Oh, wait. My phone has a flashlight too." She pulled the phone from the back pocket of her jeans, turned on its light, and trained it on the ground.

"I don't have my flag, Val. The boys grabbed it."

Val spotted the tiny flashlight at the edge of the cornstalk wall. She picked it up and turned it on. "The light works. Don't worry about the flag. We're not going to get lost." She tucked her phone away.

They started walking again, but could no longer see beams from other flashlights in front of them. Maybe the path ahead curved and, once they rounded the bend, they'd see the lights again. Odd, though, that no one behind them had caught up with them after the time she'd spent searching for the flashlight. A lot of people must have opted for the concert instead of the maze tonight.

Val saw a post in the beam of her flashlight. "Here comes a signpost. Now we're good. Gunnar's just around the corner. Hold the flashlight while I get my question list. I want to double check that we should turn left." She definitely didn't want to take a chance on turning the wrong way. She gave Bethany the light and fished a small booklet, the maze "passport," from her pocket.

Bethany held the flashlight toward the post. "Didn't you say this is supposed to be signpost number five?"

"Yup." Val opened the booklet. "Shine the flashlight on this, would you?"

"Okay, but it's useless to look at question five because this is signpost number six. We must have missed one. We'll have to go back."

"Huh?" Val had concentrated on finding the posts. How could she have missed one? Maybe she hadn't. Bethany needed glasses, as her bad line calls in tennis games suggested. She could have mistaken a five for a six. "Shine that light on the post again."

With the number illuminated, Val clearly saw a six. She also saw something odd about it. The number looked larger than the ones she'd previously seen on the posts. She touched the surface and felt a raised edge of a rectangle around the number. *Mystery solved.* She used a fingernail to get under the corner edge of the rectangle.

"What are you doing, Val?"

"This is signpost five. Somebody, probably one of the kids who ran by us, slapped a stick-on number on top of the five. I'm peeling the number off."

"Kids like that are why I teach first grade, not middle school."

"They may have done the same thing on a previous signpost after we passed it. If they did, everyone behind us answered the wrong question and took a different path. That would explain why we're alone." Had Jennifer, Sarina, and Noah been among the latecomers diverted onto the wrong path? Or had they entered the maze earlier, before the pranksters?

"What's the trivia question for signpost five?"
Bethany asked.

Val put the paper under the beam of the flashlight.
"What time is it on a Saturday night in Billy Joel's
song *The Piano Man*?"

"What time? I thought the answer to all these
questions is left or right. Oh, I get it. The answer's
nine o'clock, isn't it? We turn left like you said."
Bethany checked her watch. "That's eerie. It's just
about nine o'clock on a Saturday night."

Val laughed. "I don't know if that's a good omen
or a bad one."

"Only one way to find out—turn left."

Bethany sounded more cheerful now that she
was sure they weren't lost. They turned onto a path
that looked like the last one, but even narrower.
Not a soul on this one. The only sounds were
muted howls from remote paths. They tramped for
fifty feet before the flashlight illuminated a break in
the corn wall.

"Gunnar should be near that clearing up ahead.
Here Zombie, Zombie," Val called out as they
neared the cross path. "Show yourself, Zombie. We
know you're there."

A zombie scarecrow shambled into the path. His
face, lit from below by a flashlight, was dead white
and his eyes had black rings around them. Maroon
streaks suggested dried blood dripping down his
forehead and from a gash on his cheek.

"Yow!" Bethany backed up.

"Sorry I scared you. Not really. My job is to scare
you." Gunnar brushed aside strands from his twisted
cotton mop wig. "You took so long to get here I

was getting worried. A lot of people came past here earlier, but no one's shown up lately."

Val told him her suspicion that kids had covered the numbers painted on the signposts with stick-on numbers. "That happened at signpost five. If the kids tampered with the numbers below that, the people who entered the maze after us may have gone off the main path."

"The maze owner will have to send out rescue teams. And I'm doomed to spend the next hour alone with no one to scare."

A scream came through the cornstalks from a path on the left. "Help me," a woman yelled. "Help!"

Val froze, torn between rushing to help the woman and fleeing in the opposite direction.

Gunnar trained his flashlight on the path opposite the one where he'd hidden. "Stay here!" He headed toward the cries for help.

"Let's go with him." Bethany took off behind Gunnar.

Val sure as heck wasn't staying by herself. She followed, using her flashlight to illuminate the path ahead. "Hurry, Bethany. We don't want to lose him."

They lost him in less than a minute at a point where they had to choose between turning left or right. No sign of Gunnar's flashlight between the tall stalks lining both paths.

While they talked about which way to go, Val glimpsed a light on the path to the left, a flashlight belonging to a couple who came toward them. "Did you guys pass a zombie?" she asked.

"Yes, just a moment ago," the woman said.

"Let's go." Val led the way along the path to the left. When it curved, she aimed her flashlight ahead and saw the back of a man, his white mop wig swinging as he ran.

Someone in front of the zombie screamed.

"Wait up, Gunnar," Val called out.

The monster turned, tall and hulking. *Not Gunnar!* Bethany shrieked and ran back. Val tore after her.

Chapter 10

Val's heart pounded as she ran away from the zombie. If the man in the zombie getup had been hired, like Gunnar, to stay at his post and frighten people, why would he chase after her and Bethany? She glanced behind her without slowing down. No flashlight, no movement. Unless the zombie was wearing night-vision goggles, he wasn't following them.

Ahead of her, Bethany turned onto a path to the right.

"Stop, Bethany! We've been that way. Go the other way."

The two of them nearly collided at the intersection.

"I want to go back to the last signpost." Bethany panted. "Then we can get trace our way back out of the maze."

Val was all for getting out, but not going back. They were more than halfway through the maze.

"It's faster to keep going. Gunnar can't be far ahead of us."

"What if the strangler jumped him?" Bethany's voice verged on a whimper.

"It would take a gang of stranglers to get the better of him." Val sounded more certain than she felt. "Let's try this other path. If we don't find him in a couple minutes, we'll turn around and back-track."

Bethany followed her. "Don't run. I'm out of breath."

A minute of fast walking brought them to a path on the right. Val heard a murmur of voices coming from that direction. "Let's wait for these people. Maybe they've seen Gunnar."

"Jennifer, where are you?" a woman on the path shouted.

Val's pulse sped up. "That's Sarina." Was Jennifer playing hide-and-seek in the maze or was she lost . . . or worse?

"*Jennifer?*" a man bellowed.

Val trained her flashlight toward the voices. "Noah? Sarina? It's Val."

Noah sprinted toward her. "Have you seen Jennifer?"

"No. Why isn't she with you?" Val said.

Sarina joined them, breathless from trying to keep up with Noah. "I tried calling her cell phone. No answer."

A woman yelled for help. Val ran in the direction of the voice, farther along the path she was already on. She led the way with her flashlight, the others running behind her. Why hadn't Gunnar found

Jennifer? Maybe he had, and that was the problem. The zombie disguise might have frightened her. "Gunnar? Wait up. We're coming."

"Who's this Gunnar?" Noah roared. Without waiting for an answer, he elbowed his way in front of Val.

Val couldn't believe how fast Noah, who'd struck her as a desk potato, was moving. She had trouble keeping up with him. "Gunnar!"

"I'm here," Gunnar called out from somewhere off to the left. "I saw a woman running on this path."

Noah turned onto a path to the left. Val and Bethany followed a second later. Sarina brought up the rear, calling out Jennifer's name.

Gunnar stood aside for them, his back up against the cornstalks.

Jennifer emerged from the dark path ahead and ran to them. "Someone was chasing me. I was so scared after what happened to Fawn." She cried on Noah's shoulder and then on Sarina's.

When her sobs died down, Val asked her how she became separated from her friends.

Jennifer sniffed. "A brawny kid in a crab hat tried to take my flag. I wouldn't let go, so he pushed me down into the cornstalks. When I got up, there was a crowd of people standing around in the dark. Then a woman with a flashlight yelled that some bigger kids were on the rampage, coming toward us. When she said *Let's get out of their way*, I followed her and the guy with her. I thought Sarina and Noah were behind me."

"We were searching for our flashlight," Noah said. "The kids knocked it out of Sarina's hand. Why didn't you stay with the couple you followed?"

"I nearly tripped on my shoelace and stopped to tie it. By the time I got up, they had disappeared. Then I heard someone coming up behind me in the dark. I got scared and ran. I yelled for help a few times, but no one came. Whenever I slowed down, I could hear the person behind me getting closer. I kept running until I came to a dead end."

Val shivered, imagining herself in Jennifer's shoes. "Then what did you do?"

"I ran deep into the corn and kept quiet. I turned off my phone in case it rang." Jennifer took a tissue from the pocket of her jeans and blew her nose.

"Why didn't you use your phone to call for help?" Bethany asked.

"I thought the glow from the display would give away where I was hiding. After I didn't hear anything for a while, I crept back to the path. Then I saw the zombie with a flashlight coming. I yelled and hid again."

Val pointed to Gunnar, who was talking on his cell phone. "There's your zombie with the flashlight. He was with Bethany and me when we heard you cry for help."

Gunnar announced to the group that the GPS on his phone was guiding the maze manager and a sheriff's deputy to this spot. They would conduct everyone to the exit.

Jennifer dabbed her eyes. "Thank you, thank you."

She looked so grateful that Val expected her to kiss the zombie.

For the next two minutes, they had to flatten themselves against the corn plants as other maze visitors filed by them.

When the maze manager arrived with a young sheriff's deputy, he gave Gunnar directions to the nearest signpost. "Stay at that location and call me if those damned kids come by. We're trying to round them up and get them out."

Gunnar went to his post, while the manager and the deputy escorted Val, Bethany, and the wedding group out of the maze. A brisk five-minute walk brought them to the ticket shack. They exited the maze on one side of the shack, while visitors entered it on the other.

The deputy pointed out a picnic table near the maze entrance. "Let's go over there. You can tell me what happened and I'll file a report about it, if necessary."

Jennifer sat on a bench, flanked by her two friends. Val perched across the table from her, between Bethany and the deputy. He took notes as Jennifer repeated what she'd told the others earlier, this time without tears. Now that they were all safely out of the maze in an oasis of light near the ticket shack, the cornfield chase sounded less frightening. Val would have chalked it up to Jennifer's nerves getting the better of her, if it weren't for Fawn's murder.

"Can you describe the person who ran after you?" the deputy asked Jennifer. "Male or female? In costume or not?"

She massaged her temples as if trying to coax a memory to the surface. "I'm sorry. I couldn't see anything in the dark, but it was probably a man. I run a couple of times a week, and I'm fast for a woman. Whoever was behind me was keeping up with me. If that was a woman, she either runs regularly or has long legs."

"What did you two do," the deputy said, pointing his pen first at Sarina and then at Noah, "while your friend was lost?"

Noah spoke up. "We shouted and searched for her on the paths closest to where we'd lost sight of her. We were still searching when we ran into Val and Bethany. We all took the only path none of us had tried and heard Jennifer shout. Then we found her. She'd run away from a man in a zombie costume. Val knows him. Maybe she can tell you why he was chasing Jennifer."

Val didn't pick up immediately on Noah's cue. Her attention was on a group of preteen boys the maze manager was escorting to the exit, most wearing crab hats, none of them burly enough to be the one who'd shoved Jennifer.

"The zombie's name is Gunnar Swensen," Bethany said. "I can tell you why he was running after Jennifer."

She explained at length how Gunnar responded to a woman's cries for help and what she and Val did as they followed him.

Val kept watching people filing out of the maze. A security guard herded a dozen or so boisterous teenagers out of the maze, possibly the ones who'd gone on the rampage when Jennifer was separated

from her friends. A tall woman in a crab hat exited the
maze next and mingled with a group of middle-
aged visitors walking toward the parking lot. The
woman in the hat had the same body type as Payton's
ex-girlfriend, the long-legged Whitney Oglethorpe,
but the hat made it hard to see her face.

Sarina spoke up when Bethany finished talking.
"Noah left something out when he told you how we
looked for Jennifer. He and I split up for a while
to check two different paths."

Val jerked to attention. The deputy's head
swiveled from Sarina at one end of the table toward
Noah at the other end.

Noah smacked his forehead with his palm.
"Right. I forgot."

"Lawyer, liar, pants on fire," Bethany whispered
in Val's ear.

Val coughed to cover a laugh. Noah might not
have lied, but he'd certainly had a convenient
memory lapse. By leaving out part of what had
happened, he'd given himself and Sarina an alibi
for the whole time Jennifer was alone. Once Sarina
drew attention to the gap in his story, his *I forgot*
made a good excuse. No one could prove what
someone else remembered or forgot.

The deputy turned to Sarina. "How long were
the two of you apart?"

"Six minutes. I took the path behind us, where
we'd just been, in case Jennifer had retreated that
way. Noah took the path to the left. He used the
light on his phone, and I had the flashlight. We
agreed to go as far as we could for three minutes

and then turn around. If we located Jennifer or came to a dead end, we would return sooner."

Val decided to go through the maze tomorrow in the daylight and try to work out which paths they'd all taken.

The deputy thanked them for their help, stood up, and hailed the maze manager.

Sarina put an arm around Jennifer's shoulder. "You could probably use a stiff drink."

Jennifer managed a feeble smile. "You're right. Let's go to the Bugeye Tavern. Payton and I ate there last night. I'll call and tell him what happened. Maybe he'll join us there."

In the car Val asked Bethany if she'd noticed a tall woman in a crab hat leaving the maze. She hadn't. Bethany wasn't her usual talkative self while driving back to Bayport. A week of first graders, a day at the festival, and a night at the maze must have tired her out. And, of course, it was way past the bedtime of anyone eating baby food.

While Bethany concentrated on driving, Val pondered whether the maze chase had anything to do with the murder, aside from making everyone jumpy about something they would otherwise have laughed off. The same person might be responsible for both strangling Fawn and chasing Jennifer. Maybe the murderer had meant to kill Jennifer last night and pursued her tonight, hoping for another shot. In that scenario, Payton's ex-girlfriend made a good suspect. If Val pointed that out to her grandfather, he might give up the idea that she was the strangler's intended victim and leave his shotgun locked up.

Bethany dropped her off at Granddad's house, and Val walked up the path to the house. As she climbed the steps to the front porch, she heard a motor start up. She turned around and saw a flame flicker inside a car across the street. *A cigarette lighter?* She heard a deafening bang and hit the porch floor, her heart racing. Another bang. She rolled toward the front door. Tires screeched and an engine roared. Val waited until she heard the engine noise fade and then scrambled up.

Her mother opened the door. "Who's setting off firecrackers out there?"

Firecrackers, not gunshots. Of course.

Before last night, Val would have identified the bangs as firecrackers, especially after seeing the lighter in the car across the way. Tonight she'd mistaken the sounds for gunshots because the murder, the voodoo doll, and the claustrophobic maze had given her the jitters.

Though she preferred firecrackers to bullets, the person who'd tossed them from the car had obviously intended to scare her. Henri, of course. She hadn't heard a car engine that loud since she drove his 1960s Pontiac. If he'd replaced it after the accident with another vintage car, it would make more noise than newer passenger cars.

She went into the sitting room with Mom. Granddad was reclining in his chair, his eyes closed and a newspaper on his lap.

Val collapsed into the armchair near the sofa. "What have you been doing tonight, Mom?"

"Not getting those graded." Mom pointed to a stack of student papers on the coffee table. "The phone's been ringing nonstop. Someone posted a video online called *Strangler's Rope*. It showed the police examining a rope plant hanger while your grandfather stood watching."

Oops. "So reporters were calling to talk to him?"

"Yes, and I got rid of them with a *no comment*. The neighbors called too. Someone saw the emergency responders arrive last night. Now everyone knows where the strangling happened. They warned me that murders would decrease the value of the house and make it hard to sell."

Granddad opened his eyes. "Who's selling the house? Not me."

"You'll want to sell it someday, Pop. I didn't mean now."

Nice job of backpedaling. Eight months ago Mom had tasked Val with nudging Granddad toward selling the house, the sooner the better. Val had put that task at the bottom of her to-do list at first and erased it entirely since then. Mom would have to deal with Granddad's resistance.

"Where did you and Bethany go tonight?" Mom asked, wisely changing the subject.

"To the corn maze."

Granddad scowled. "You shouldn't have gone there with a murderer on the loose."

"Bethany had her heart set on going to the maze, and I didn't think she should go alone." Granddad and Mom would probably hear what had happened there tomorrow at breakfast. Val might as well tell them now. "Jennifer got lost and frightened in the maze. When Gunnar, Bethany, and I found her, she was a wreck because someone had run after her. She got away by hiding among the cornstalks."

"Where were her friends?" Mom asked.

"Jennifer got separated from them. They split up to search for her at first, before they joined Bethany and me to look for her."

Granddad's eyes lit up. "Sarina and Noah both had the opportunity to chase after her when they split up."

Mom straightened the stack of student papers on the coffee table. "They're Jennifer's friends. Why would they want to run after her?"

Val thought of an answer that might convince Granddad she wasn't the strangler's target. "Maybe Sarina or Noah wanted to do more than scare Jennifer. Neither of them has an alibi for Fawn's murder. Whoever killed Fawn might kill a second time out of fear of exposure, or just for the heck of it."

"Just for the heck of it. Hmm." Granddad glanced at his video collection across the room. "I see a connection between what happened tonight and the strangling, but that doesn't mean the same person killed Fawn and ran after Jennifer."

Mom frowned. "You're speaking in riddles, Pop. Explain what you mean."

"There's a pattern. It may not solve the mystery of what happened yesterday, but it could give us a clue to what will happen tomorrow."

Val agreed with her mother about Granddad's riddle-speak. He'd gone from Codger Cook to Delphic Oracle. "Give *us* a clue what you're talking about. What pattern?"

"Use your noodle." He pointed to the ceiling. "Go upstairs and walk down the hall. You can't miss it."

The hall? Oh, the posters! Val thunked herself on the forehead. "I get it. Someone strangled with a rope. Someone pursued through a cornfield. Welcome to Hitchcock."

Chapter 11

Val licked her thumb and held it up toward Granddad as if giving him a gold star. He'd hit on the common thread in the strangling of Fawn and the pursuit of Jennifer. "*Rope* and *North by Northwest*. And the murder in *Rope* is committed just for the heck of it." Was that true also of Fawn's murder?

From the sofa her mother waved her arm like an A-student with all the answers. "Hello? In *North by Northwest* Cary Grant ran from a crop duster not a person."

Val could raise objections to her grandfather's theory, but that wasn't one of them. "For an English teacher, you're awfully literal, Mom. Let's assume, for the sake of argument, that there's a connection to the posters. Does that help us figure out who the culprit is, Granddad?"

"It narrows down who chased Jennifer to the people staying in this house. No one else knew about the posters."

Val shook her head. "Jennifer or the others could have told Payton."

Mom raised her index finger. "Who's Payton?"

"Jennifer's fiancé. He's staying with his parents at their house on the bay. His mother arranged for his ex-girlfriend, Whitney Oglethorpe, to spend the weekend at the house." Val gave her mother a long look. Would Mom see a mirror of herself in Payton's interfering mother? "I glimpsed a woman who re-sembled Whitney leaving the maze. Whitney looks athletic and could have chased Jennifer."

Granddad's eyebrows shot up. "If Payton knew about the posters, he could have told Whitney about them. Why would she have run after Jennifer?"

"To scare her into leaving Bayport. Then Whit-ney would have Payton all to herself this weekend."

"You've both been watching too much Hitch-cock." Mom pointed to the video collection on the shelves near the fireplace. "Jennifer was pursued in a cornfield because that's where the maze was. Why assume the person running after her targeted her specifically? Didn't the maze owner hire people to dress in costumes and scare the visitors?"

Her mother had a theory that would let her sleep tonight. Val decided to support it rather than argue against it. "That's true, Mom. And Jennifer wasn't the only person frightened tonight at the maze. Gangs of teenagers were running around scaring people and making them scatter. That's how Jennifer got separated from Noah and Sarina."

Mom gathered her students' papers and stood up. "One of those kids probably peeled off from the gang and ran after her. You're dreaming up complicated explanations when simpler ones are more likely. Someone who doesn't know Jennifer chased her in the maze as an ugly prank. Or she panicked when she found herself alone and imagined someone was following her."

Granddad stroked his chin. "Possible, but not the only explanation."

Mom gave him and Val a quick hug. "You two can stay up all night spinning fantasies, but I'm going to bed."

"Promise me you'll bolt your door," Granddad said.

Mom held up her right hand as if taking an oath. "I promise, though I won't lose sleep worrying that one of your guests will attack me." She went into the hall and up the staircase.

Granddad motioned to Val. "Sit closer to me, Val. Then we can both keep an eye on the door and make sure the wedding group doesn't sneak up on us. We need to talk more about this Hitchcock business."

Val changed seats, moving to the sofa near her grandfather's chair. "Mom's probably right about the Hitchcock connection. It's far-fetched."

"I'd be more willing to believe there isn't a Hitchcock connection if a knife hadn't disappeared."

"We've had knives go missing before. They always show up." *Would the fondue fork show up too?* "There isn't a Hitchcock movie with a fondue fork as a weapon, is there?"

"No, but there are knifings. In *Rear Window* Jimmy Stewart suspects the man across the way of using a knife to kill his wife and a saw to dismember her."

"Ouch." Val had forgotten the plot of *Rear Window*. "That covers three of the four posters upstairs. We don't need to worry about the remaining one. I doubt our Hitchcock killer, if we have one, can make birds swoop down and peck us to death. Noah said he was a Hitchcock fan. Does Sarina know anything about those movies?"

"Enough. When I took them upstairs to show them the rooms, I told them whoever stayed in the *Birds* and *North by Northwest* rooms would have to share the hall bath. Sarina said that was okay with her, as long there wasn't a *Psycho* poster outside it. No worries, I said. The bathroom has a tub, not a shower stall. She and Noah laughed, and Jennifer said she didn't get the joke."

Val had watched *Psycho* once, but with her eyes shut during the gruesome knifing in the shower. She crossed the room to the shelves with Grand-dad's videos, removed *Psycho*, and slipped it behind the other movies in the collection. "Out of sight, out of mind. I hope you're wrong about a Hitchcock-inspired killer."

"Right or wrong, we know one thing for sure— someone strangled a woman who might have been mistaken for Jennifer or for you. Don't let down your guard, and don't go to the maze tomorrow night."

"No more haunted mazes for me. I promise." Val kissed him on the cheek. "Goodnight, Granddad. Please don't worry about me."

He levered himself out of his chair with effort. "I should have stretched my legs sooner." He took car keys from his pocket.

"Are you going somewhere this late?"

"I'm driving behind you to Monique's house, making sure no one else does."

"Don't do that. You can't see well driving at night."

He walked toward the hall. "I know the peninsula road like the back of my hand. I'll be right behind you and watch you until you're inside her house."

Useless to argue with him, once he'd made up his mind. "Okay, Granddad, but please phone me when you get home, or else *I'm* going to worry about *you*."

"I'll call you with my cell phone. The hall phone isn't private with folks staying here."

Twenty minutes later, Val waved to her grandfather as the door to Monique's house opened.

A plump, gray-haired woman let her in and extended her hand. "Hello, I'm Deedee Mott, and you must be Val. Monique told me she was expecting you."

Val shook hands with Monique's mother-in-law. The aroma of baked cookies permeated the house. Val sniffed butter, sugar, and chocolate. A faint pungent smell mixed with it. "Something smells great."

"I made chocolate chip cookies." The woman lowered her voice. "Monique made a large batch of her—uh—creative cookies to enter in the dessert cook-off tomorrow. I didn't think the children would care for them, so I whipped up a batch of the good old-fashioned kind. Come into the kitchen and try them."

"Thank you. I love chocolate chip cookies." She followed Mrs. Mott into the kitchen-family room. "What did kind of cookies did Monique bake?"

"Something with weird spices." Mrs. Mott pointed to a plate stacked with chocolate chip cookies. "Help yourself to *my* cookies."

Val took a bite of one. Crispy outside. Chewy inside. Lots of chips. Amazing how a chocolate chip cookie could almost make up for a bad day.

Monique bustled into the room. "Hi, Val. I brought up the photos I took at your booth on my computer. Oh, you're having Granny's cookies. You should try one of mine. They came out great."

Val held up her hand. "No, save your cookies for the dessert contest. You'll have to give out lots of samples. The chocolate chip cookies are fantastic, Mrs. Mott."

"Thank you. I'll say goodnight now. Good to meet you, Val, and I hope—" She gave a startled cry and pointed to the sliding glass door to the backyard. "I just saw someone out there. In the backyard."

Monique rushed to the door. "I don't see anyone."

Val followed her cousin and peered out. "Neither do I." The exterior fixtures lit up the perimeter of the house, but beyond a distance of four yards away, total darkness prevailed. Dozens of people could lurk there without being seen from the house.

Monique closed the vertical blinds, making it impossible for anyone to peek inside. "What did the person look like?" She sounded more curious than concerned.

Her mother-in-law hugged herself. "A man, I think. I saw him for a second near the patio and then he disappeared. I'm going to wake up Maverick and tell him."

Monique rolled her eyes as her mother-in-law scurried down the hall to the bedroom wing. "Where she lives, the neighbors are close enough that she can gossip across the driveway. She says she feels isolated here. She's been jumpy ever since she heard about the murder."

Mrs. Mott returned to the kitchen with her son in tow.

Maverick wore a T-shirt and running shorts. He raised a hand in greeting to Val, his eyes half open and his hair tousled. He crossed the room toward the sliding door. "I'll check outside, Ma."

She followed him and grabbed his arm. "No! The strangler might be out there. Just call the police." She wrung her hands.

"Okay." He put his arm around his mother and looked over her head at his wife, who shook her head. "It'll take half an hour for a deputy to get here. And whoever you saw is probably gone by now. How about we station ourselves at the windows for the next five minutes? If any of us sees something moving, I'll call 911. You go to the window in the living room, Ma. We have motion-sensing lights on the front of the house. If anyone's out there, the lights will flip on."

"Suppose whoever is there sees me at the window?"

"We'll turn off the living room lights so no one can see you, and you can stand to the side of the window."

Val flipped off the kitchen lights and peered between the slats of the sliding door's blinds.

Monique and Maverick stood sentry at the windows in the bedroom wing. Five minutes later, after no one had seen anything move outside, Maverick called them off guard duty, coaxed his mother to go to bed, and announced he was going back to sleep.

Monique set her laptop on the kitchen counter and brought up the photos she'd taken at Val's booth. "You and Jennifer don't look all that similar in crab hats in the daylight. Let's see what happens when I apply a night effect to this photo." She clicked around the screen of her photo-editing software.

Val watched as day turned to night in the photo. "Yes, I look more like Jennifer under the dim light, but the question is whether either of us looks like Fawn in a crab hat. I didn't have time to search online for a photo of her."

"I found one on her Facebook page. She hadn't posted anything for a long time, but the page had a headshot of her. I'm working on layering a crab hat onto the photo."

Val's phone chimed. Granddad's cell phone number popped up on the display. She thanked him for remembering to call her. He asked to talk to Monique. Surprised, Val passed the phone to her cousin.

"Hello." Monique listened for twenty seconds and then said, "I can do that. . . . They'll be ready for Val to take to you in the morning. . . . You're welcome." She handed Val the phone.

"What was that about?"

"He saw me taking pictures of the wedding group near your booth. He wants headshots of each of them, with and without crab hats. I'll give him one of Fawn too. I'll crop the photos and print them tonight. He didn't say why he wanted them."

"I don't know what he's going to do with them." And Val was too tired to care. She yawned.

"You look worn out. Why don't you go to bed? You have another two days of working in the booth."

"Okay. Goodnight." Val left the kitchen, not expecting a good night. She'd probably dream about a zombie chef in a crop duster chasing her through a cornfield.

She put her head on the pillow and woke up when her phone's alarm tune played. Nightmares hadn't disturbed her sleep after all.

Unlike the day before, Val didn't smell coffee brewing. She went into the kitchen. Monique wasn't there. Maybe she was sleeping in.

Val was trying to figure out how to get plain coffee from the espresso-latte-cappuccino machine on the counter when the sliding door opened and Monique came in. It was starting to get light outside, though the sun wouldn't rise for another hour.

Monique slid the door closed with a bang. "My mother-in-law was right. There *was* someone out there last night."

Chapter 12

Val felt a chill as if she'd been doused with ice water. A prowler outside a house where two pre-schoolers lived scared her far more than a maze stalker. She clutched her cousin's kitchen counter to steady herself. Maybe Monique had jumped to a conclusion with no proof. "What did you see out there?"

Her cousin stomped from the sliding door to the counter. With her face flushed and her eyes narrow, she gave off vibes of anger. "Food wrappers and a drink can. Someone was out there long enough to need a snack, staking out the house."

Possibly the strangler, looking for his next victim. Val's stomach knotted up. The maze incident had almost convinced her that if the murderer had mistaken Fawn for someone else, Jennifer was probably the intended victim. But with a prowler here, Val's fear that the rope had been meant for her own neck returned. Granddad had driven behind her last night to make certain no one else did, but did he look in his rearview mirror to check if someone had followed him? An obvious precaution, but maybe he hadn't taken it because, with his eyesight, he needed to concentrate on the road when he drove in the dark.

The good news was that the prowler had left something behind. "I hope you didn't get rid of the trash, Monique."

"I didn't want to touch it with my bare hands."

Val would stop mocking her cousin's germ phobia. Sometimes it was useful. If there were fingerprints on the can, they would be intact. Val pointed to the phone on counter. "You'd better report this right away."

Monique eyed the phone. "I'll do it later, when my kids and my in-laws leave the house. I don't want them frightened by seeing police in the backyard."

The delay bothered Val. "You're giving the prowler time to come back and pick up the trash."

"It's unlikely he'd return in the daylight."

Unlikely, but possible. By the time the children left with their grandparents, it might be too late to collect evidence. Next best thing—get the evidence now. "Go back outside and take photos of the trash. I assume you have latex gloves." Anyone obsessed with germs would.

"Of course. What for?"

"I'm going to take that soda can to Chief Yardley. The prowler might have left fingerprints on it." *Or even DNA.* "I'll need a paper bag to put it in."

Monique gave her the gloves and bag. They went outside. Except for the patio adjacent to the house and the clearing along the creek near the dock, the deep lot was dense with trees and bushes. The trash lay behind thick shrubbery, which would have provided complete cover at night and made it hard to see the prowler in the dawn or twilight. Val stood back from the trash and glanced around. She couldn't see anything else the prowler had left behind.

Her cousin took photos of the collection of the trash from different angles. "I'll ask my in-laws to take the children home with them to Philadelphia."

"Maybe you should go to Philadelphia with them."

"Maverick and I can't leave. He's doing a program at the boatyard, and I'm committed to taking pictures the whole weekend." She stopped aiming her camera. "I doubt even a crime-scene technician would take more pictures of this pile of trash than I just did."

Val moved closer to the trash and peered at it. The person who'd left it had consumed a canned espresso, a packet of macadamia nuts, and a bar of imported chocolate. Pricey snacks for your average vagrant, but not for Chef Henri. She could imagine him eating the nuts and the chocolate. He preferred freshly brewed coffee, but he couldn't expect that in the woods around Monique's house. Val picked up the drink can with a gloved hand, put it in a paper bag, and went back to the kitchen with her cousin.

Monique approached the coffee maker with her finger poised to press its buttons. "You want a latte or a cappuccino?"

"I don't have time for either." Val was running

late after the backyard excursion. "Do you have the photos Granddad wanted?"

"In the envelope on the hall table. I included one of Fawn with a crab hat courtesy of my photo-editing software."

"Thanks. See you tonight." Val left with the drink can and the photos.

Fifteen minutes later, she pulled into Granddad's driveway behind her mother's rental car. In the rearview mirror, she saw a slate-gray Jaguar slow down in front of the house. The Jag's driver made a U-turn and parked across the street. As she walked to the front porch, Payton unfolded his legs and climbed from the sports car.

He hailed her and joined her at the front door. "I'm glad to see you. I was afraid if I rang the bell, I'd wake up the whole house. I wanted to get here early and talk to Jennifer in private."

Val unlocked the door and let him in. The house was so quiet, she decided to whisper. "It doesn't sound like anyone's awake. Is Jennifer expecting you?"

"No, but I'll just knock quietly on her door." He bounded up the stairs.

Did he know where to knock? Val crept up the steps behind him and peered around the wall where the stairway turned. He rapped on the first door to the right in the hall. Jennifer must have told him which room was hers. He might have even visited that room between Friday night and this morning.

Val tiptoed back down the stairs. On the way to the kitchen, she stopped in the butler's pantry to start the coffee maker. She preheated the oven for the casserole she'd assembled before going to the maze last night. At least this breakfast didn't require her to make batter and stand over the stove as she'd done yesterday for the pancakes. While the oven preheated, she took the translucent envelope with the photos from her tote bag.

Monique had made five-by-seven prints of the wedding group, one with no one wearing a hat, one with Jennifer and Val in crab hats, and one with the two men in the hats. She'd also printed three-by-five close-ups of each guest, with and without hats, in full light and with the night effect. The crab hat Monique had superimposed on Fawn's head fit her badly, but it was better than nothing.

The creaking floorboards above the kitchen alerted Val that her mother was awake. Granddad probably didn't want to tell Mom why he'd requested these photos. Val hastily stuffed them back in the envelope. The photos weren't safe from her mother's prying eyes anywhere in the kitchen. She headed to the hall so she could slip the envelope under her grandfather's bedroom door or give it to him if he was awake. As she reached the hall, Payton was standing at the foot of the staircase. Val was so startled that she dropped the envelope. It fell with a photo showing through the translucent envelope, a close-up of Fawn in a crab hat.

"I'll pick that up for you," Payton said.

Val stepped on the envelope to cover Fawn's picture, possibly too late. He might have already glimpsed the photo. "That's okay. I'll get it." She crouched to hide the envelope, slipped it from under her foot, and clapped it against her thigh. If it weren't for the photos of Fawn, Val could just hand the envelope to Payton, saying her cousin had made prints for the wedding group.

She stood up, holding the envelope firmly against her thigh. "Was Jennifer awake?"

"Barely. She just got out of bed and didn't want to talk until she had a shower and got dressed." His eyes traveled from Val's face to her thigh.

Val glanced down and stiffened. She'd put Fawn's photo against her body and assumed that the visible side of the envelope would show the blank back of another photo. But no, one of the group photos was face out. Her hand wasn't large enough to cover the whole picture. The envelope was too big to slip into her pants pocket. She slid it toward the rear of her thigh. "So you'll be back in a little while to talk to her?"

"No, I'll wait. She should be down soon." He looked wistfully at the sitting room. "That coffee smells wonderful."

Val regretted brewing the coffee. Without its aroma, he might have waited in his car or on the porch, not in the house he'd called a *dump*. She gestured toward the sofa. "Take a seat. I'll bring you some coffee."

"You don't have to wait on me. I'll serve myself. Just show me where the coffee is." He gave her a toothy smile worthy of a successful politician.

What should she do? Scurrying down the hall and shoving the envelope of photos under her grand-father's door would just draw attention to it. What if the envelope was too thick to fit under the door?

No, she'd better hold onto it until she could tuck it away somewhere when Payton wasn't looking.

"Follow me." She couldn't have pressed her hand more tightly against her side if she were stanching the blood from a wound. When they reached the butler's pantry, she said, "The coffee's here. Help yourself."

"Thank you." He reached for a mug near the coffee maker. "Do you have any milk or cream?"

"Of course." She went to the refrigerator.

Instead of waiting for her to bring him the cream, he tagged after her. She held the photos tightly with one hand. With the other, she opened the fridge door, took out a carton of half-and-half, and put it on the kitchen island.

He doctored his coffee, took a sip, and set his mug on the island. "If I'd gone to the maze last night, I wouldn't have let Jennifer out of my sight. I feel guilty about helping my parents with their party instead of being there with her."

Did he expect Val to absolve him of blame, or did he have another reason for confessing to guilt feelings? "You were at your folks' party all night?"

"Until Jennifer called to tell me what happened. I drove to town and met her in the tavern." Payton clutched his mug and stared into it, frowning as if it contained tea leaves he was having trouble reading. "Sarina and Noah were with her. They said you helped them find her at the maze. Do you think she panicked, or was someone really chasing her?"

Val shrugged. "I don't know. I found the maze disorienting and was glad to have someone else with me. If I'd been alone, I might have freaked out." Instead of allaying his guilt, she'd just rubbed it in—not on purpose, but she'd told the truth.

"Jennifer should leave Bayport for her own safety. She won't listen to me. She might listen to the police. One of the guests at my parents' party said you and your grandfather are friends with the police chief and even helped solve a murder recently. Could you use your influence and get the police to urge her to leave?"

Ah. That's why Val couldn't shake him off this morning. He wanted something from her. Why should she tell Payton she had no influence? He might be more forthcoming if he owed her something. "Okay, I'll talk to the police. Have you and Jennifer known each other long?"

He tilted his head from side to side. "Yes . . . and no. We met briefly when I was finishing law school, and then we met again in May. I'd thought about her during those ten years, but never imagined we'd see each other again."

A ping from the stove told Val the oven had preheated. With one of her hands occupied holding the envelope of photos against her thigh, getting the casserole from refrigerator to oven would require several steps. Behaving like a one-armed woman might draw Payton's attention to the arm she didn't lift. She'd better distract him with questions.

She opened the refrigerator door. "How did you get together with Jennifer after so many years?"

"It was a blind date." He raised the mug to his lips and slowly sipped the coffee. "A double date with Noah, actually."

His hesitation gave her time to take out the

casserole, put it on the counter near the oven, and close the fridge. "You both had blind dates? Or was Noah going out with someone who knew Jennifer?" Val opened the oven door.

"No. He was going out with Jennifer. He asked if I'd go on a blind date with one of her friends . . . Sarina, actually." Payton ran a finger under the collar of his polo shirt. "When we all met for dinner, Jennifer and I were amazed to see each other. And, well, we hit it off."

Val was so surprised she nearly lost her grip on the casserole as she put it in the oven. Strange that Payton would tell her he'd horned in on his friend. Whatever the reason for his frankness, she could now fathom why Noah or Sarina might play a nasty prank on the bride-to-be. Noah might resent Jennifer because she'd thrown him over in favor of Payton. Sarina might resent her because Jennifer had set her up with a rich, handsome man and then claimed him for herself. With the two losers roped into helping the two winners plan their marriage, an occasional note of irritation was bound to crop up. Val remembered Noah saying, *It's not my wedding,* when Jennifer asked him about looking at venues. Sarina hadn't shown any negativity, though, except in her treatment of Fawn.

Fawn. With Payton in a talkative mood, this might be Val's chance to find out if he had a connection to the dead bridesmaid, as Granddad had suggested. "You first met Jennifer ten years ago. She must have been quite young."

"She was about to start college."

"That's when she was friends with Fawn. Did you know her too?"

"I met them both in passing."

Val eyed the shoulder bag she'd left on the kitchen table. If Payton stayed where he was at the counter, she could tuck the envelope into her bag and he wouldn't get a glimpse of the photos. She walked toward the table as nonchalantly as she could with one arm glued to her leg. "Jennifer came back into your life after ten years. When did you reconnect with Fawn?"

"After Jennifer invited her to be part of the wedding. Jennifer had a get-together for her attendants. I stopped by for a few minutes." Payton crossed the room toward the table and set his mug on it. "Fawn was her one link to the past and the place where she grew up. Jennifer's really broken up about what happened."

Val felt Payton's hovering presence. So much for the idea of putting the photos in her bag. Her right arm ached. She longed to move it and flex her fingers, but she was afraid the envelope would slip to the floor. "Jennifer has no family or other friends where she grew up?"

"No siblings, and her parents are dead. They didn't give her much while they were alive. She put herself through college. Everything she's accomplished, she's done on her own without any help from family. I admire her for that."

Val detected defiance in his statement as if he expected her to argue against it. Maybe his mother had belittled Jennifer's achievements. Payton's upbringing had certainly differed from his fiancée's.

"At least Jennifer studied what she wanted." Unlike Gunnar whose father pressured him into an accounting career. "Family help sometimes comes with strings attached."

"Tell me about it." He banged his mug down on the table, like a judge using his gavel to cut off discussion.

"Good morning!" Mom had come down the back staircase into the kitchen.

Val introduced Payton to her mother. As Mom made small talk with him, Val excused herself and hurried to the front hall. Her grandfather emerged from his room as she was about to knock on his door.

She heard the floor above creaking. "Here are the photos Monique made for you. Put them out of sight, unless you want to tell our guests why you asked for them."

Granddad took the envelope into his room.

Jennifer came down the stairs and gave Val a strained smile. "Good morning."

"Same to you. I hope you slept okay. Payton's waiting for you in the kitchen."

"Thanks." Jennifer reached into a back pocket of her yellow capris and held out a credit card. "Could I ask you for a refund on Fawn's room?"

"No problem." Val took the credit card as Jennifer went into the kitchen.

Granddad came out of his room and grumbled about the refund. Val pointed out that, with Mom occupying the bedroom, he couldn't insist a guest pay for it.

By the time they went into the dining room,

Mom had set the table. Val invited Payton to stay for breakfast. In quick succession, the other guests came downstairs. Granddad put the casserole on the table as they all sat down.

Val was so engrossed in her own thoughts about Monique's prowler and Payton's revelations that she tuned in only intermittently to the table conversation. When the chase in the corn maze came up, Payton urged Jennifer to leave town. Noah did too, offering to stay with her if she was afraid to be alone in her apartment in Washington. Sarina cautioned against overreacting, saying that a teenager had probably run after Jennifer for kicks. After much discussion, Jennifer decided not to leave.

The group then discussed plans for the day, which included the knot-tying contest. At first, only Noah was going to enter the contest, but Jennifer proposed that they all do it. Granddad suggested the group go to the dessert cook-off that afternoon and cast their votes for his fondue.

Val ate quickly, excused herself from the table, and went into the study for a map of the maze. The maze manager had provided a detailed map with the signposts marked on it so she could work out the trivia questions for each spot. In the daylight, she might be able to trace the route Jennifer had taken when pursued and figure out if either Noah or Sarina could have chased her. She stuffed the map into her shoulder bag and went out to her car.

As she turned the Saturn's ignition key, her mother dashed out the front door toward the driveway.

She climbed into the passenger seat. "I'm going with you to the club."

"Why?" Surely not to make salads and bake sweets for the festival booth.

"I've never been to the Cool Down Café. I'd like to see where you work. Also, I haven't had much chance to talk with you alone."

Visiting the café was Mom's excuse for the jaunt. Her real reason was to talk *to*, not *with*, her daughter. As a teacher, she liked lecturing to a captive audience, and that's what she'd do for the fifteen minutes it took to drive to the club. But Val had a captive audience too. Maybe this was her chance to ask Mom about the chief, assuming she could interrupt the lecture.

Chapter 13

Val backed the Saturn out of her grandfather's driveway. "What do you want to talk about?" She could guess what Mom would say.

"Your grandfather. Losing your grandmother and two old friends hit him hard. You've lifted his spirits since you've been here. I can't thank you enough for that."

Val was too surprised to say anything for a moment. She'd expected the Tony-talk. "Granddad gets in the dumps less, but he hasn't given up the grumps."

"Before you came here, he ate badly and did nothing but watch old movies. Now he's eating better and writing a newspaper column, of all things. It gives him status in town. He takes more interest in life now."

And in murder. "He's always willing to tackle something different."

"Take a leaf from his book." Mom crossed her legs and adjusted her sandal strap. "Now that you're sure he's in a good place, it's time to get on with *your* life. He'll do fine without you."

"You really think so?" How he would do without her had been on Val's mind ever since her former boss had phoned with the job offer. "Granddad likes having someone around to spar with."

"He'd find another sparring partner if he moved to Florida near us or even to the senior community here."

But he didn't want to move, even though his good buddy, Ned, lived at the senior village. "You figure he'll sell the house sooner if I'm not here?"

Her mother shrugged. "That's not the reason I brought this up. Don't narrow your choices because of him. He's on a roll with that newspaper column. Just keep feeding him simple recipes. He'll give them hokey names and throw in some homespun advice. He can do that without you being here."

For the first time since Friday, Val could think about returning to her job without feeling guilty about leaving her grandfather. On the other hand, she no longer had him as an excuse for turning down the offer. Now she had only one criterion for accepting the job—whether it was right for her. *Was the job a step forward or a step back?* "Thanks for saying that, Mom. I wasn't sure how he'd react if I told him I was moving out."

"He'll react badly, but he'll get over it. Now that you've given him a taste for good food, he'll learn to cook for himself. It's time to take off the training wheels."

Val hit the accelerator as she left the town limits

behind. "Even with the training wheels on, he crashes in the kitchen. Batter on the walls, cookies baking on the oven door, and a thick haze of smoke all over the house."

"I've had similar results in the kitchen. Your culinary genes didn't come from either of us." Her mother fidgeted and uncrossed her legs. "Cooking isn't the only thing I mess up. I hope you forgive me for springing Tony on you this weekend. I could have handled that better, but I still think you need to talk to him. You shouldn't rush into another relationship without having closure on one that lasted for five years."

Her mother had given her the spoon full of sugar. Val should have known that the foul-tasting tonic would follow. "Tony doesn't have closure, or he wouldn't be here. But I have closure. He gave it to me. And who said I was rushing into a relationship?"

"Within a few months of breaking your engagement, you start seeing a man who—"

"Am I supposed to have a longer period of mourning?"

Mom pursed her lips at the interruption. "Almost immediately, you started seeing a man who sounds like Tony's opposite."

"That's what I like about him." Whatever her mother knew about him had come from her grandfather. "Did Granddad tell you Gunnar looks like a troll?"

Mom laughed. "No, like a hit man."

"Gunnar can't compete with Tony on looks. Luckily, I'm not shallow enough to care about that."

"I don't care about looks either. Tony is a hard worker. He's on track to be a partner in his firm. He has a bright future."

"And Granddad told you Gunnar walked away from a secure government job to pursue an acting career." No wonder Mom was suddenly so enthusiastic about Tony.

"A lot of people want to be actors. They work at it for a while, get it out of their systems, and settle down with a steady job before they're thirty."

"Gunnar did it in reverse. He's always wanted to study acting, but he had family issues that prevented him. He spent a dozen years at a steady job and then inherited some money. Now he can do what he really wanted to do all along."

"A downturn in the economy can wipe out an inheritance fast."

Pointless to tell her mother that Gunnar could expect an income from his accounting practice once it took off. Mom wouldn't consider a small start-up business a sufficiently reliable source of money.

"I get it, Mom. You're afraid Gunnar can't provide for me with my lavish tastes. I'm used to luxury after living in a tiny city apartment and a ramshackle house here." Val turned onto the road leading to the club. "Well, don't worry about it. Gunnar and I are far from making a commitment."

"Things move fast when you're on the rebound. You risk exchanging one set of problems for another unless you take the time to put the past in perspective. Figure out what was good about your relationship with Tony, not just what was bad. Then you'll have a better idea what you want for the future."

Her mother gave meaty lectures. "I don't disagree with you, Mom. You could have said all that without bringing Tony here."

"Tony the Cheater is the image you have of him because that's what he was the last time you saw him. But you should see him again so that you get past that one-dimensional view."

"And give him another chance?"

"Talk to him for your own benefit . . . and Gunnar's. A rebound relationship isn't fair to him either."

Her mother didn't know that Gunnar too was on the rebound. She'd probably say that two rebounds are like two wrongs—they don't make a relationship right. They double the pitfalls.

Val pulled into the club's parking lot. Every morning when she did this, she looked forward to working at the Cool Down Café. Did she enjoy managing the café only because it was a rebound job? Here she didn't have to deal with people like Chef Henri La Farge. Just as Tony's cheating overlaid everything else in their relationship, Chef Henri's nastiness kept her from putting her old job in perspective.

Her mother gave her a long, hard look. "What are you thinking?"

"I'm thinking that while Bayport is celebrating its past this weekend, my own past is assaulting me." *On two fronts.* She had to make peace with it. "Okay. I'll listen to what Tony has to say."

But she'd have to put off her talk with Mom

about the chief. The private time with her mother was over.

While Val mixed the batter for pecan mini muffins, Mom helped Bethany chop the vegetables and fruit for today's salads. With an extra set of hands, they finished preparing the food earlier than they had the day before and loaded the coolers into Val's car quickly. Her mother hitched a ride back to town with a high school classmate who'd been exercising at the club.

As Val and Bethany unloaded the coolers, a teenage girl who'd worked at the Cool Down Café in the summer showed up.

"Hey, you two." Tanisha radiated energy.

Val hugged her. "Welcome back."

"My turn." Bethany enveloped Tanisha in a bear hug. "How's Swarthmore?"

"I have a lot of reading and papers, but I'm keeping up. I'm really glad fall break is at the same time as the festival. You need any help in the booth this weekend?"

Val nodded vigorously. "I can use some time off." To talk to the police chief, visit the maze, and make sure her grandfather was set up for the cook-off. "How many hours can you spare?"

"Whatever you need."

Val huddled with Tanisha and Bethany to work out when they'd each cover the booth. Then she got on the phone to schedule an appointment with Chief Yardley. He could see her right away.

She drove to the Bayport Police Department

headquarters at the edge of town. The chief met her in the reception area of the converted farm-house and led her to his Spartan office.

She took a seat in a straight-backed metal chair facing his desk. The chair was as hard and the room as cold as she remembered it. At least the chief's smile was warm as he lowered himself into his cushioned desk chair.

He pointed at the grocery sack she held. " Is that for me? The last time you came here, you brought some sweet bribes. What have you got this time?"

"Pecan mini muffins." She passed a plastic bag with three muffins across the desk to him. Then she pulled a small paper bag from the grocery sack. "This contains an empty can of espresso. I brought it from my cousin's house."

"Why?"

She told him about the trash Monique had found and the prowler her mother-in-law had seen in the backyard. "I brought the drink can with me in case you want to test it for fingerprints."

"Your cousin lives outside the town limits, the county sheriff's territory, not mine. Up to her whether she wants to pursue this, but I'd blame the litter on festival visitors." The chief took a muffin from the plastic bag. "A tourist staying at the B&B on the peninsula could have walked along the creek to your cousin's house, stopped to enjoy the view, and munched on some snacks." He ate half the muffin in one bite.

"The can and the wrappers weren't visible from the house. It's certainly possible someone dropped them during the day yesterday." Yet Val couldn't shed her fear that Chef Henri had followed her to her cousin's house. "No matter who left the litter, my cousin's nervous about a prowler, especially after a murder."

"She should have called 911 right away. If her mother-in-law can describe the man—"

"She can't."

The chief finished the muffin. "Not much to be done now. Whose fingerprints do you expect to find on the can—the celebrity chef's or your former fiancé's? Your granddaddy believes one of them tried to kill you."

"He might be right about Chef Henri, but my cousin's afraid her children might be the next victims of a serial murderer."

"A lot of folks are calling in worried that the strangler will strike again." He tapped his pen on a blank page of a notebook. "I want to hear tips about the victim we already have. Instead, I get theories about who's next on the list."

"I'm sure a lot of those theories are far-fetched. Have you heard what happened to Jennifer Brown in the maze last night?" At his nod, she continued. "You can't blame her for thinking she could be the murderer's next victim. Her fiancé would like you to pressure her to leave Bayport because it's too dangerous for her here."

"Why should she leave? Because we have a serial killer confined to the town limits? That's the only situation that would make it more dangerous for her here than elsewhere."

Val should have picked up on that herself. "I get it. A murderer who planned to kill Jennifer specifically could do it anywhere, so there's no reason for her to leave town. Maybe she figured that out, and that's why she's reluctant to leave. Here, at least, she's staying in a house full of people."

The chief took another muffin from the plastic bag. "Even before that incident in the maze, you said Jennifer might have been the murderer's target. Got any ideas on who'd want to kill her?"

"A few. Jennifer dumped Noah in favor of Payton. She also snatched Payton from Sarina." While the chief ate his muffin, Val told him about the blind date that resulted in a shuffling of couples.

He brushed crumbs from his hands. "Which of them told you about the blind date?"

"Payton. He's a lawyer, trained to choose his words carefully, and yet he volunteered information that put him and Jennifer in a bad light. Maybe he did that to suggest that Sarina and Noah have a reason to resent Jennifer." Val leaned forward in the hard chair. "Someone staying at the Grandsires' house also has a reason to resent her."

The chief laced a rubber band through his fingers. "Who?"

"Whitney Oglethorpe, Payton's ex-girlfriend. Mrs. Grandsire invited her instead of Jennifer for the weekend. I wonder if Whitney has an alibi for Friday night when Fawn was killed and last night when Jennifer was in the maze." Val decided against mentioning her possible sighting of Whitney at the maze. The chief liked definites, not possibles.

"History repeats itself. You find someone murdered and bring me a list of suspects. You want me to check their alibis because you've thought of motives for them. At least the last time, those motives had to do with the actual victim, not a supposed victim."

"And potential next victim, Chief. That's my main concern."

"And mine is capturing Fawn Finchley's killer. She was divorcing a man with a criminal record and a warrant against him. He's been on the run for months. We now have police looking for him in a lot of states. We will find him." The chief sipped coffee from a foam cup, made a face, and put the cup back down on his desk. "You know, a third of all female murder victims are killed by current or former husbands, lovers, or boyfriends."

And two-thirds were killed by other people, harder to identify than the usual suspects. Val swallowed the comment because she had something more important to say. "Let's hope history doesn't repeat itself in another way. The police focus their investigation on the obvious suspect. Then someone else is murdered. Oops. Maybe you can prevent a second murder by casting a wider net for suspects in the first murder."

The chief's face puckered as if he had a lemon wedge in his mouth. "You want me to question the Grandsires and their guests because one of them has a motive for a murder that hasn't taken place? How many lawyers do you suppose are staying in that house?"

If Val had a white flag, she'd have held it up. "Okay. They'd probably alibi Whitney anyway. Keep her on your radar if anything happens to Jennifer."

Val held up the paper bag with the soda can. "So I should just toss this out?"

"No, leave it with me. If the fingerprints belong to Fawn's husband, we'll know he's in the vicinity. Someone reported seeing her talking to a man just as the fireworks were starting."

Val waited for more details about the man, but the chief didn't supply any. "Does Fawn have any other family?"

The chief grunted. "The hardest part of my job is talking to the victim's family. I spoke with her parents. The mother's coming here today. I told her I couldn't release her daughter's body because we're still waiting for the autopsy results from Baltimore."

"Is an autopsy necessary?"

"Suspicious deaths always trigger autopsies, though there isn't much doubt what killed Fawn. The rope around the neck did the trick."

"Did she have any other injuries, like bruises or wounds?"

"Only those consistent with struggling to save herself and clawing at the ligature." The chief leaned back in his chair. "According to the medical examiner, Fawn was eating strawberries and chocolate when she was killed."

A final act that any chocoholic would appreciate. "Granddad served fondue in the afternoon. Fawn helped herself to seconds Friday night. Did you find a fondue fork in the yard? One of ours is missing."

"No, and we looked for a fork. We figured she must have used one because she didn't have strawberry juice and chocolate on her fingers, only around her mouth."

"We also have a missing knife. Maybe the killer took the fork and the knife." Both might still be in the house. "Can you search the bedrooms at the house for evidence? Granddad would give you permission."

The chief smiled. "Your mother asked me the same question. Didn't she tell you what I said about that?"

Val couldn't resist walking through the door the chief had opened. "Mom doesn't talk to me about her conversations with you." No sign of discomfort or embarrassment from Chief Yardley, but of course he'd had years of practicing the poker face while interviewing suspects.

"Then I'll tell you what I told her. Except for the victim's room, we can't even go into the other bedrooms unless the people who paid to stay there let us. We can turn those rooms upside-down if we have a search warrant, but we need probable cause to get one." The chief checked his watch. "Anything else you want to talk about?"

Yes. What's going on with you and my mother? Val bit back the question. That was no more her business than her relationship with Tony was Mom's business. "Nothing else. Thanks for your time."

The chief escorted her to the door. "By the way, Fawn's mother said she wanted to see where her daughter died. I'm sure your granddaddy won't mind. I'll phone him when I know what time she'll be there, probably this evening."

Once outside police headquarters, Val called Gunnar and was surprised that she'd woken him. Being a zombie must have been tiring if he was still asleep at ten thirty. He agreed to meet her at the booth at eleven so they could go to the maze.

The missing fondue fork occupied Val's mind on the short drive back to the festival. Fawn's killer might have taken it to make sure the police didn't test it for incriminating evidence. Maybe Fawn had shared her fondue and fork with the person who then strangled her. She'd only do that with some-one she knew and didn't fear. Hard to imagine she'd share her chocolate with the husband she was divorcing and whose debts she had to pay.

When Val arrived back at the booth, she heard business had been slow.

"A lot of people are probably at church," Tanisha said. "A really gorgeous guy came looking for you half an hour ago. Dark hair, nice smile."

A description of Gunnar, except for the gorgeous part. "That would be Tony, my former fiancé."

"*Former* fiancé? I told him you'd be back soon. He said he'd stop by again at eleven. I hope that's okay."

"That's fine."

Or was it? Val looked at her watch. Gunnar was picking her up for their trip to the maze just about the time Tony planned to return. She could call Gunnar and suggest they go to the maze later, but heck, why should she adjust her schedule for Tony? He rarely showed up when he said he would anyway.

He broke with tradition this time, arriving two minutes early.

She grabbed her shoulder bag and met him out-side the booth. "I can't talk to you now, Tony. I have—" She was about to say an appointment. With Gunnar approaching, she changed her mind. "I have a date."

Tony's face sagged. "I've checked out of my hotel. I don't want to stay here another night, but I also don't want to leave without talking to you."

"I'll make time, but not now."

"Call me when you're free, okay? Or I'll call you."

It sounded like an ultimatum. He would bug her until she heard him out. She stepped toward Gunnar, smiling.

No answering smile from him. "My car's this way." He pivoted and took big strides walking back the way he'd come. "I thought you weren't going to have anything to do with Tony. Now he's going to call you or you're going to call him?"

Her shoulders tensed. She felt like a rope in a tug-of-war, her mother yanking her one way, Gunnar pulling the other way. "I had no idea you had such a jealous streak."

"This isn't about me. It's about you and Tony."

She had trouble keeping up with Gunnar because he was walking so fast. "I told you Tony meant nothing to me. That doesn't mean I won't talk to him. I don't *owe* him a hearing, but after he's come all this way, I'll give him one."

Tony's arrival had touched off something in Gunnar she'd never seen before. If he couldn't handle her talking to another man, they had no future with each other. They walked in silence for a minute.

He stopped and faced her. "I'm sorry. I'm not

usually like this. Something about Tony just rubs me the wrong way."

Val's shoulders uncramped. "You're a good judge of his character." But not of hers. "Let's not talk about him."

As Gunnar drove to the maze, they stuck to a safe subject—the murder. She told him what she'd learned from Payton and the chief.

Once inside the maze, he stopped at each intersection where they turned and took photos, like digital breadcrumbs. Without eerie noises and scary scarecrows, strolling on corn-lined paths was pleasant. The cornstalks rustled in a wind stronger than last night's, but seeing the stalks swaying in the breeze made the sound less ominous. Along the way, they encountered families with children and groups of less rowdy teenagers than those who'd visited the maze last night.

Val marked their progress on the maze map. "The last time I went through the maze in daylight, I took the most efficient route and didn't pay any attention to the other paths. According to the map, if you make a wrong turn at a signpost, either you'll come to a dead end and have to go back, or you'll circle around to the same spot. You can't get lost. You'll just take longer to go through the maze."

They arrived at signpost five in half the time it took Val and Bethany to reach it last night. From there they turned onto the path to the left.

Gunnar slowed down after a while. "This looks like a familiar bunch of cornstalks."

Val studied the corn plants on either side of the path. They looked the same as all the corn in the maze. "Seriously? Growing up in the Midwest means you can distinguish one group of corn plants from another?"

He laughed. "Just joking. When I took up my post yesterday, I counted the number of paces from the last turn to my hiding spot."

"Now for the challenge. Which paths did you take when we heard Jennifer call for help? Bethany went running after you, and I followed her, but I wasn't paying attention to how long we stayed on one path before we turned on another."

Fortunately, Gunnar had an unerring sense of direction and a feel for how long it would take them to walk as far as he had run the night before. They soon reached the place where they'd come upon Jennifer the previous night.

He walked a little further along the path and pointed to flattened cornstalks. "There's where she hid among the corn."

"Now let's go back to the intersection where Bethany and I met Sarina and Noah. From there, we might be able to figure out where those two started their search for Jennifer."

They reversed direction on the path. Something on the ground under the cornstalks caught Val's attention. A really long worm? She stopped short and bent down for a better view.

No, not a worm. A rope with loops, like the one she'd seen around Fawn's neck. Val felt a sudden chill.

Chapter 14

Val crouched for a better look at the cord on the ground. She pointed to it. "Look, Gunnar."

He squatted next to her and took off his sunglasses. "A length of rope perfect for a strangler. You have a loop at each end for your hands. You cross your wrists." He stood up and crossed his wrists, pretending to have a rope in his fists. "You slip the rope over the victim's head and tighten it by yanking sideways on the ends."

Val recoiled at the sudden outward jerk of his arms and nearly fell over. "Where did you learn how to strangle someone?"

"From a buddy who went through combat training. You approach from behind so the victim can't see you coming and fight you off. Is the rope the same type the strangler used?"

"I don't know. I didn't study it." She stood up. "That looks like a complicated knot. Who would know how to tie it?"

"It's actually a simple knot—a bowline. Boy Scouts

learn it. Boaters use it. It's easy to tie or untie if the rope is slack, tight and reliable if the rope is taut." Gunnar stepped to the side of the path to allow a family with two preteens to go by.

Val said nothing until she was sure the family couldn't hear her. "I was ready to chalk up what happened in the maze last night to Jennifer's panic, but the rope suggests that Fawn's strangler was here or that someone wants to give that impression."

"Don't rule out a sick joke. The strangling is big news. Imagine a teenager telling his friend, *Don't mess with me, or I'll make you my next victim. I've got my rope right here.* He pulls it out of his pocket." Gunnar reached into his jeans pocket and pulled out a phantom rope. "Then the kids horse around, drop the rope, and can't find it in the dark."

"I'd be more willing to believe that if this rope were lying somewhere else, not on the path where Jennifer ended up." Val rummaged in her shoulder bag for her cell phone. "Chief Yardley has been working on the theory that Fawn was murdered by her ex-husband. The second rope may convince him that Fawn wasn't the target. Jennifer was, and she's still in danger."

While she called Chief Yardley, Gunnar studied the maze map. The chief told her to stay where she was and make sure no one touched the rope. He would relay her news to the sheriff's office, and someone would call her with further instructions.

"Should I alert Jennifer about it?" she asked.

"If I think she needs to know, I'll tell her. Don't say anything to anybody about this. Too much information is leaking, making folks nervous." The chief clicked off.

Gunnar pointed to where they were on the map. "This is an alternate path to the maze exit. Plenty of people could have walked along here and dropped the rope, either before or after Jennifer was here."

"Sure, other people *could* have come this way. Sarina and Noah definitely did. Either of them could have brought the rope with them, Sarina in her tapestry shoulder bag and Noah in a pocket of his cargo pants. And they both have a reason to resent Jennifer."

"Why would they ditch the weapon among the corn?"

Val paced on the narrow path between the cornstalks. "We were all standing in this spot when you announced that the maze manager was coming to fetch us with a sheriff's deputy. The person with the rope might throw it away in case the deputy searched people for weapons as they left the maze. In the dark the rest of us wouldn't have noticed someone dropping a rope."

Val's phone chimed. She answered it. Deputy Holtzman from the sheriff's department was at the maze entrance and asked if she could guide him to her location. She suppressed a groan. She and the deputy had clashed during a previous murder investigation. He would be an obnoxious addition to the weekend's already foul stew. She'd love to direct him to paths that would get him hopelessly lost, but that would just delay her return to town. She used the map and Gunnar's photos to put the deputy on the most efficient route.

When the deputy had one more turn to make, Val muted the phone and said to Gunnar, "The last time this deputy investigated a murder, he accused me of playing Nancy Drew. I don't want to listen to that again. Don't tell him we're trying to reconstruct what happened last night." She tucked the map in her shoulder bag.

The grim-faced Deputy Holtzman wore a Stetson-like hat that shaded his protruding eyes and most of his doughy face from the sun. The deputy accompanying him was the young one who'd asked questions last night after Jennifer was chased. Val pointed out the rope under the cornstalks.

After peering at it, Holtzman asked Gunnar to provide his colleague with contact information. As they moved a few yards away, Holtzman turned his raptor eyes on Val. "No need to give us your contact information, Ms. Deniston. We have it in our files. Why did you call the police about this find of yours?"

"It resembles the rope I saw in the backyard the night Fawn Finchley was strangled."

"You realize, Ms. Deniston, that you and your grandfather are the only people outside law enforcement who know what the rope used in the murder looked like."

As usual, Val's blood pressure rose in his presence. When he was investigating a murder three months ago, he'd treated her like a suspect and implied she was withholding evidence. *Here we go again.* "Are you suggesting I planted that rope?" Or possibly even committed the murder?

"I'm curious how you happened to find it. It's

well camouflaged." His bulging eyes narrowed with suspicion. "Is this where last night's chase occurred?"

"The place where Jennifer hid from her pursuer is farther along this path." Val swiveled and pointed toward the place where the cornstalks had been pushed aside.

"Why did you come back to this path today?"

He made it sound as if she'd returned to the scene of her crime. She'd lost her temper with him in the past, and now he was needling her, daring her to do it again. She wouldn't give him the satisfaction of rising to his bait. Taking deep breaths and counting to ten, she quelled her anger. "To enjoy a daytime visit after my night visit was cut short."

He waved her away as the young deputy and Gunnar joined them. "You can leave now. Keep quiet about this rope. If word gets out, I'll know who to blame."

Val marched away, seething, and grabbed Gunnar's arm. "Let's go." She tugged him away.

They quickly reached the intersection where she and Bethany had met Noah and Sarina while searching for Jennifer last night. Val unfolded the maze map.

Using the map and Gunnar's estimates of the time between Jennifer's first and last cries for help, they found the spot where the wedding group had split up.

On the map Val traced the paths that Jennifer, Noah, and Sarina had taken, based on what the three had said the night before. "See how the path on the left, which Noah took, eventually converges with the path Jennifer took. So he could have chased her."

Gunnar looked over Val's shoulder at the map. "You said Sarina was supposed to take the path back in the direction they'd come. She wouldn't have met up with Jennifer that way."

"But what if Sarina switched paths, once Noah was out of sight? If she went to the right, instead of back, she could have caught up with Jennifer and chased her part of the way."

"I'll buy that either of them could have chased her, but not to put a rope around her neck. They would be the obvious suspects if she were found strangled."

True, but Val had another idea. "What if they didn't want to kill her, only scare her? Drop a rope on the path, pretend to find it, and convince Jennifer that a strangler was after her."

A middle-aged couple approached them. The man looked at the sky, and the woman asked, "You have a map? Could we see it, please?"

After the couple returned the map, Val said, "I think we're done here, Gunnar. Let's head out. Do you want the map?"

"It's imprinted on my brain. Let's go." He led the way. "You sound convinced that Noah or Sarina brought a rope to the maze and chased Jennifer to frighten her. I don't buy it. If Sarina resented her because the blind date didn't turn out as planned, she'd have dropped her as a friend. She wouldn't take part in the wedding or wait months to take a lame-brained form of revenge."

Val couldn't argue with him. "True, and hardly anyone expects blind dates to work out. But Noah has more reason to resent Jennifer."

"Why? She's probably the only pretty woman who ever looked twice at him. And he introduced her to his rich, handsome friend. What an idiot. He's kicking himself, not blaming her, and he's hanging around, hoping the dude dumps her. Then she'll cry on Noah's shoulder and, if he's lucky, decide she really loved him all along."

When Val first met Gunnar, he'd shown more regret than resentment over the fiancée who'd broken up with him. She had to admit that Noah's behavior and demeanor were consistent with what Gunnar had said. "There's another person who might have brought a rope to the maze—Payton's ex-girlfriend, Whitney. Last night I saw a woman here who resembled her. I couldn't see much of her face because she was wearing a crab hat."

"Why would she bring a rope?"

"Either to strangle Jennifer or to convince her that Bayport has a serial strangler and she'd be better off cutting her weekend short. But after Jennifer freaked out and law enforcement showed up, Whitney couldn't risk being caught with the rope. So she threw it away."

Gunnar steered her by her elbow onto a path to the right. "That's a long shot. You don't even know for sure that she was here. But you skipped over someone who was definitely here and had the best chance to pull off a hoax last night."

"You mean Jennifer." He nodded. Val tried to remember if Jennifer had anywhere to stash a rope.

"She had a narrow, quilted bag about ten inches long hanging from her wrist. The rope would have fit in there. She could have faked the chase too."

"Is she the kind of person who likes to be the center of attention?"

"She'd like more attention from her fiancé. She expected to spend the weekend with him. Instead, he's been busy at his parents' house, to which she was not invited. If she faked the chase to get his sympathy, she succeeded. When she told him what happened, he left his folks' house and drove to town to comfort her."

Gunnar reached for Val's hand. "It's also possible that pranksters brought the rope and chased her."

"Yes, but I can't rule out that someone really was trying to kill Jennifer. Even if the strangler couldn't count on finding her alone last night, no harm in trying. I came up with lots of possibilities here, but no conclusions." Wandering in the maze hadn't brought Val any closer to knowing who had killed Fawn and what the killer's next move might be. "Still, this trip wasn't wasted. I've enjoyed strolling amid the corn with you." She squeezed Gunnar's hand.

"We could find a secluded path and stay a while." He wiggled his eyebrows.

She laughed. "No path is secluded enough for what you have in mind. Can you come to Granddad's for dinner tonight? You can get to know Mom and, after dinner, you and I can go someplace together."

He grimaced. "I'm sorry. Tonight I'm stuck being a zombie again."

Darn. Compared to all the other bad things that had happened this weekend, though, this one was minor. "Well, Mom will be here most of the day tomorrow. I'll find a time when we can all get together before then, though we may be rushed."

They walked in silence to the maze exit and the car.

Val climbed into the Miata's passenger seat and took out her phone.

Gunnar pulled out of the parking space. "Are you calling the chief to give him your conclusions?"

"I haven't reached any conclusions yet. I don't want to tell him what we talked about, especially the idea that Jennifer might have faked being chased. This morning I spent a lot of time trying to convince him that she was in danger of being the murderer's next victim. That's still true, even if she pulled the stunt in the maze."

"You're afraid that the police will brand her as the bride who cried wolf and that they won't go to her aid when the real wolf comes after her. You underestimate them." Gunnar steered onto the country road heading for the main drag to Bayport.

No one would lose money underestimating Deputy Holtzman. "Jennifer doesn't need the sheriff's deputy badgering her, after everything else that's gone wrong for her this weekend."

Gunnar turned onto the main road to Bayport. "Where to? Straight back to the booth?"

"I'm not sure until I talk to Granddad." She speed-dialed the landline at his house. After six rings, he answered. "Hey, Granddad, do you need me to pick up anything for the fondue?" *Or stir the chocolate to keep it from burning?* "I can come by the house and give you a hand with it."

"No! Don't come near here. I don't want people like Irene Pritchard saying I didn't make this dish myself."

"Well, she's used that line before." At least this time, he could honestly say he'd done it on his own. That wouldn't necessarily stop Irene from making her usual accusation. "My alibi is solid. I have a witness who'll swear I was elsewhere while you were making the fondue."

Gunnar nodded, pointing to himself.

"Funny you should talk about a witness. I found one this morning who will change how the police are thinking about the murder."

"Who?"

"Your mother's coming in the door. I gotta put her to work cutting up fruit for the fondue. I'll call you back." He hung up.

Val clicked her phone off, her curiosity roused about the witness Granddad had found. If he didn't call her in fifteen minutes, she'd phone him again. "I can go straight to the festival. My grandfather says he doesn't need my help with his chocolate fondue."

"I have fond memories of fondue. My grand-mother used to make it. Is it having a comeback?"

"The comeback was about twenty years ago. Now it's out of style again." The word *comeback* reminded Val that she had yet to mention her job offer to Gunnar. "Between the murder and the maze, I forgot to tell you about *my* shot at a comeback. My former boss offered me my old job back. With a nice raise."

Gunnar's eyebrows rose. "You asked to go back?"

"No. He called me out of the blue. I told him I'd give him my decision on Tuesday."

Gunnar braked harder than he needed to for a stop sign. "I thought you were settled here. I didn't know you were thinking of going back to New York."

"I wasn't, until I got the phone call."

He glanced at her, frowning. "Why would you go back there after the way he treated you? He fired you for no good reason."

She turned away and looked out the side window. "He shuttled me off to a position I didn't want, and I quit. It's not the same as being fired."

Gunnar pulled past the stop sign. "Right. If you're fired, you usually get severance pay. Your boss figured out how to get rid of you cheaply."

She winced. "The accountant's viewpoint. The money didn't matter to me. I quit because my pride was hurt."

"Your pride should keep you from going back." Gunnar drummed the heel of his hand on the steering wheel. "The traffic's picking up and getting on my nerves. I don't mean to badger you. It's your decision."

"Of course, it's my decision." But if he said what she'd hoped to hear, that he wanted her to stay, she'd have one more reason not to go back.

He slowed down and looked intently at her. "Does Tony have anything to do with your sudden interest in going back to New York?"

"Certainly not." So that's what was bothering Gunnar—not the idea of her leaving, but of Tony influencing her decision.

Her phone chimed. Granddad was calling her back at the perfect moment. Without the interruption, she and Gunnar might have said something they'd later regret. "That's my grandfather. I have to take his call. He says he's found a witness."

Chapter 15

She answered the phone as Gunnar hit the accelerator. "Hey, Granddad. Tell me about this witness you found."

"This morning I knocked on all the doors from here to the festival. I showed folks those photos Monique gave me." His voice came through the phone, full of energy. "I wanted to know if the neighbors saw any of our guests Friday night."

"The police must have already canvassed the neighborhood."

"Not with photos of our visitors in crab hats. A lot of the neighbors saw people in crab hats Friday night, but no one paid attention to what they looked like, except for Bill James. He's the fella who just bought the ugly yellow house on the next street. He saw Jennifer in her crab hat walking toward Main Street a few minutes before the fireworks started. She came from the direction of our house."

"How could he be sure it was her with that hat on?"

Granddad laughed. "Her legs attracted his attention. He checked *them* out first and then her face. He figured she was a neighbor he hadn't met yet. He sure wanted to meet her. She had a lot of leg showing between her skirt and—what did he call them?—her cross trainers. Another name for sneakers, I suppose. Didn't she leave the house earlier wearing high heels?"

"You took a good look at those legs too, Granddad." Val caught Gunnar's amused look and took it as a sign that he wasn't dwelling on Tony. "I focused more on Jennifer's shoes. She wore sandals with stacked high heels. Walking on brick sidewalks with those heels had to be a challenge. She probably went back to the house to put on more comfortable shoes."

"The chief asked her what she did after dinner with her fiancé. She didn't say she came back here. She made it sound like she was at the festival the whole time. Why did she lie about it?"

Val imagined herself in Jennifer's shoes, the metaphorical ones, not the high heels. There was another explanation besides deliberate deceit, for Jennifer's failure to mention being at the house. "If I'd just found out an old friend was dead, changing shoes earlier in the evening would have slipped my mind too."

"Hmph. Now that she's over the shock, she should correct what she said. When you lie, you look guilty."

Val would have reminded him that his newspaper column was based on a lie if Gunnar hadn't been listening. Like most people who didn't know

Granddad well, Gunnar had fallen for the ruse that the Codger Cook knew all about cooking. Her grandfather would be ticked off if she outed him to anyone.

"What does Jennifer look guilty of, Granddad? Not murder. She was at the house before the fireworks started. Fawn was still at the festival then."

"Who said so?"

Val must have inherited her skeptical streak from her grandfather. "The chief told me someone reported seeing her talking to a man when the fireworks first started."

"How could that witness identify her if she was wearing a crab hat?"

"Excellent question." Exactly the one she'd asked Granddad a minute ago. He often turned the tables on her. "Maybe Fawn wasn't wearing it when the witness saw her."

"Jennifer's on top of my suspect list because she lied. She'll stay there until I know for sure that Fawn was still alive when Jennifer left the house. I gotta get back to the fondue."

"See you at the cook-off." Val put her phone in her bag.

The police hadn't released information about when Fawn died, possibly waiting for the autopsy results. The local medical examiner must have estimated the time of death. Maybe Val could coax the information from the chief.

She gave Gunnar the gist of the conversation. By the time she finished, the car was crawling toward the Bayport historic district.

"Look at this." Gunnar pointed at the windshield.

"It's like being back in Washington with cars bumper to bumper. Day-trippers."

Val smiled. He'd been a day-tripper himself a few months ago. "They're coming for the food. Between the restaurant chefs' cook-off and the amateurs' dessert cook-off, I'll be lucky to have anyone buy food at my booth this afternoon." And at this pace, she'd be lucky to get to the booth by closing time. "Can you let me out? I'll move faster on foot. Maybe we can meet for an early happy hour before you change into your zombie clothes."

"Happy hour with a zombie doesn't appeal to you?" A ghost of a smile crossed his lips. He pulled over to let her out. "I'm going to turn around and run some errands in Treadwell. Then I can stop by the booth, unless the traffic gets even worse."

"See you later." She stepped out of the car.

After she'd walked a block on the narrow sidewalk, a man came up behind her—Roy Chesterfeld, deputy sheriff from a nearby county. He'd responded when she reported finding a murder victim in that county a few months ago. Blond and broad-shouldered, he looked just as handsome in casual clothes as in the uniform she associated with him, but younger. He couldn't be much over thirty. His gray T-shirt clung to his toned body.

"Hey, Val. You're looking good. Going to the festival?"

She nodded. "To work at my booth, the Cool Down Café Annex at the festival."

Roy fell into step next to her. "I'll walk over with you, okay?"

"Sure." She looked for Gunnar's Miata among

the cars inching along the street, but he must have already turned off. *Whew.* If Gunnar saw her now, with his jealousy stoked by Tony's presence, he might assume she'd left the car to meet up with the hunk walking next to her.

"I hear you found another dead body."

"The police haven't made it public who found the body. You must have inside information about the case."

"I have access to the reports. We're on standby, in case the Bayport Police Department and the deputies from this county need assistance."

"I found Fawn dead around ten o'clock. Do you happen to know what time she died?" The last time she'd found a body, he'd been less closed-mouthed than other deputies.

"I'll check what the medical examiner said and let you know."

He caught her eye. "I kept your phone number. Are you still seeing someone?"

"I am." *But for how much longer?*

"That's too bad. How's your grandfather doing after another murder on his property?"

Val turned the corner onto a side street with fewer people on it and picked up her pace. "He's upset but making the best of it." *By throwing himself into detecting.* "He's competing in the dessert cook-off this afternoon. If he sees you, he'll twist your arm to try his dessert and vote for his entry."

"I'll skip the cook-off. I'm not big on desserts."

She glanced at his tight abs. Not dessert territory. As far as she knew, he subsisted on protein bars, which he carried in his pockets. The only protein bar she'd ever tried had tasted like pressed sawdust mixed with ground gravel. She'd rather eat baby food. To be fair, she'd never dined with Roy. Just as well. To him a square meal might mean an actual square of pulverized protein. Gunnar couldn't compete with the deputy in looks, but at least his taste buds were compatible with hers.

"What's going on today besides the cook-offs?" Roy said.

She gave a rundown of the activities she remembered from the schedule. As they crossed the street toward the festival booths, Tanisha was crossing the opposite way.

"Hey, Val." She darted a look at Roy. "I'm taking a break from the booth. I'll be back in half an hour."

"Okay." Val would have introduced her to Roy, but Tanisha zoomed off. "See you later."

Val and the deputy joined the crowd strolling between the rows of booths. "My booth's smack in the middle of this row. You're welcome to a cool drink, on the house. We have sandwiches and salads if you haven't eaten lunch yet." She was looking forward to lunch herself.

"I'll take you up on some ice water."

To wash down his protein bar? Val spotted Jennifer, Noah, and Sarina near her booth. "Are you off duty, Deputy Chesterfeld, or working undercover in plain clothes?"

"Would I tell you if I was working undercover?"

"I just want to know how to introduce you to some murder suspects."

"Go with my name, not my job."

They arrived at the booth as Bethany gave a

cranberry spritzer to Jennifer, a lemonade to Noah, and an iced tea to Sarina.

Noah slapped a ten-dollar bill on the table. "Keep the change."

"Thank you. Hey, Val. I was just telling Jennifer that you went to the maze to look for clues to who chased her." She leaned across the serving table toward the wedding group. "Val has solved murders that stumped the police."

Val cringed inwardly. "That's not true."

"It is too." Bethany said, sounding like one of her first graders. "Val's really modest. She dug up most of the evidence."

Val glanced at Roy, who covered his mouth, probably to stifle a laugh.

"I hope you found some evidence in the maze." Jennifer sipped her spritzer. "No one should get away with terrifying people."

"I didn't find anything that would identify the person who chased you." Val watched Jennifer and her friends. None of them looked relieved that she'd failed to find evidence. She caught Bethany's pointed look at Roy. "Everyone, this is my friend, Roy Chesterfield. Roy, meet Bethany O'Shay. She helps me at the café when she isn't teaching first grade."

"Hi, Bethany." Roy leaned toward her, shook her hand, and gave her a warm smile.

When he let go of her hand, she kept it outstretched, apparently too mesmerized to let her arm drop.

Now for the suspects. "Roy, these are the guests

staying at my grandfather's house." She introduced Jennifer, Sarina, and Noah. He shook hands with them, giving them the same smile he'd bestowed on Bethany. "They took part in the knot-tying contest today. How did it go?"

"I came in first," Noah said.

"Congratulations." Val shook the winner's hand, which surely knew how to tie a bowline.

Roy and Bethany also congratulated Noah.

Jennifer beamed. "He won a fantastic prize. A gift certificate for dinner tonight at the Inn on the Bay. I wanted to check out the restaurant there this weekend, but I couldn't get a reservation. Lucky for us they set aside a table for the contest winner. We're all going. Payton too. He's meeting us there."

Val moved out of the way of a middle-aged couple checking the menu at the booth. "How did Payton do in the contest?"

"He had something else on his agenda," Sarina said. "I managed to tie all the knots correctly except one. Jennifer was hopeless."

The bride-to-be shrugged. "I didn't learn to tie my shoes until I was in third grade. Well, nice talking to you all. We're going to the cook-off. Will you be there to cheer on your grandfather, Val?"

"I'm planning on it."

The wedding group left. The middle-aged couple continued to study the menu.

Bethany looked up at Roy with the same brown-eyed adoration that her dog Muffin gave her. "Would you like something to eat? We have lots of choices."

Val knew what was coming next. She'd had no chance to warn Bethany.

Roy removed a wrapped protein bar from his trouser pocket. "In my job I'm never sure when I'll get a chance to eat. I carry my own food. Would you like to try one?"

Bethany nodded, her ginger curls bouncing. "I'd love one."

No, you wouldn't.

Bethany took the bar Roy gave her and tore into the wrapper as if it were a longed-for birthday gift. She bit off a chunk and chewed. An expression of bliss came over her face. "Oh," she moaned.

Roy must have heard an *oh* like that from other women, but only after he'd given them something besides a protein bar.

"Oh," Bethany moaned again. "This has *so much . . . texture.* And *flavor.*"

Compared to baby food, yes.

"I'm glad you like it." Roy's delight looked genuine.

Maybe he'd found his soul mate, at least for the time being. Once Bethany gave up her baby food diet, she wouldn't take so much joy in protein bars. She and Roy might as well enjoy the honeymoon.

Val owed Bethany some time off. "Why don't you give Roy a tour of the festival and check out what's happening on Main Street."

"Can you handle the booth on your own for a while?"

"I can handle it." Val appreciated Bethany's dependability. No matter how much she longed to do something, she wouldn't renege on a commitment. "Tanisha will be back soon. Have fun, you two."

Tanisha returned just as the lunch crowd increased.

When the number of customers dwindled, she said, "Could I ask you something, Val? Bethany said the guy you left with this morning was like your boyfriend, and he was an actor, and really nice."

"Gunnar. Yes, he's nice."

"The dark-haired guy who was here before him and the blond guy I saw with you half an hour ago look like they belong in the movies. I wonder if maybe Bethany mixed up who's the actor and who's your boyfriend or something."

Val laughed. Her love life was probably not the subject of whatever question Tanisha hadn't quite managed to ask. "Bethany got it right. Are you asking why I prefer the man who isn't handsome to the two who are?"

"Well, yeah. I guess you're going to say that looks aren't everything."

"And that's hard to believe when you're eighteen. I can give you a simple example of why Gunnar appeals to me more then the other two guys. Did you notice Tony's smile when he was here this morning? It's lopsided. A lazy half-smile. He only gives so much of himself and holds the rest back." *A cheapskate with his emotions.*

"Well, the blond guy was smiling big at you."

"Roy has a huge smile, but it's the same for everybody." *Or at least every female body.* "When Gunnar looks at me, his smile transforms his face, and that smile is for me and no one else."

Tanisha nodded solemnly. "I get it. He makes you feel special."

"Right. When you go back to Swarthmore and two guys make a play for you, don't choose the one your friends think is hot. Pick the one who's right for you."

Tanisha stepped back "How did you know about the two—?"

"Lucky guess." Val checked her watch. Three o'clock. Bethany didn't usually take such a long break. She'd probably lost track of time with Roy next to her. "I figured Bethany would be back by now. My grandfather's in the dessert cook-off. I hate to miss the judging."

"Go ahead. Business has slowed down. I can manage the booth alone."

"Thanks."

Val weaved around the people visiting booths and jogged across the street to the park, working up a sweat in the afternoon heat. People milled around the party tents where the contestants were serving desserts. She couldn't find her grandfather because of the crowd, but she could see Henri. He stood on a raised platform at the far end of the park, sharing a microphone with the cook-off chairperson, the mayor's wife.

She spoke into the microphone. "Now that the chef has given us his opinion of several of the dessert entries, we come to the moment we've all been awaiting. Chef Henri La Farge, tell us your choice for the best dessert in the Bayport Festival cook-off."

Henri took over the microphone. "This was not a hard decision. I knew the moment I took my first bite that this was an extraordinary taste experience. By far the best dessert is the Quinoa Carrot Coconut Cardamom Cayenne Cookie." His voice rose to a crescendo that cried out for applause.

Incredible. Monique's cookie had won. Val clapped enthusiastically for her cousin's winning entry, but only a few other people joined in, possibly those who, like Val, hadn't tasted it. No hope now that Val would get away without sampling the winning cookie. Maybe it would surprise her and taste great. . . . *Nah.*

Henri continued. "This delicacy came from the kitchen of Madame Monique Mott. Monique, such a wonderful French name. Her dessert is sweet and hot, with the spicy complexity of cardamom and ginger, and a kiss"—he kissed his fingers—"a kiss of coconut nectar and a hint of almond. It has a certain je ne sais quoi that sets it apart from all the other cookies."

"Hot pepper!" someone yelled.

Laughter erupted. This crowd probably had less enthusiasm than Chef Henri for complex flavors in cookies. Sweet would have sufficed without hot and spicy.

The mayor's wife leaned toward the microphone. "Is Monique Mott here? Please come up and receive your prize."

Monique climbed the steps to the platform and

accepted an envelope from the mayor's wife, who thrust the microphone toward her.

"Thank you, thank you, Chef Henri. I'm overwhelmed by the honor of winning. I've tried every single dessert here. They're all wonderful and just as deserving of the prize as mine."

Thundering applause came from the crowd.

Monique then thanked as many people as the average Academy Award recipient, including the members of her family, the owners of the spice shop in town, and the organizers of the food cooperative where she bought grains. Camera crews from a Salisbury TV station shot video. Photographers from the *Treadwell Gazette* and other Eastern Shore newspapers took pictures of Monique with Chef Henri.

"Congratulations, Monique," the mayor's wife said into the microphone. "And a huge thank you to Chef Henri La Farge for acting as the judge. Those of you in the audience who haven't yet submitted your ballots for the people's choice dessert, you have another fifteen minutes to vote. We've counted the ballots we've received thus far. It's a close race. Mark your ballot for your favorite dessert. Every vote counts. Now let's welcome the high school choral group who will sing favorite American classics."

While the mayor's wife talked, the professional photographers and media interviewers with microphones turned away from the platform. They hurried en masse toward one of the party tents.

Val pushed her way through the crowd to congratulate her cousin. "Fantastic win!" She hugged

Monique and turned to Maverick. "Finished giving boatyard tours for today?"

"I have one more session at five. Then Monique and I are going to celebrate her win and a night without the kids." He reached for his wife's hand.

The corners of Monique's mouth turned down. "I wish the kids could have seen me take the prize. I'm sorry your mother wasn't here too, Maverick. She was pretty snarky about my cookies."

Val congratulated her cousin again and excused herself to search for her grandfather. She checked the closest party tent. Her mother and Granddad's buddy, Ned, presided over the table offering fondue. People were lining up for the chance to skewer a chunk of fruit and dip it into a bowl of melted chocolate. Two bowls rested on stands with tea candles under them.

Val found her grandfather outside a party tent, wearing an immaculate Codger Cook apron and facing a video camera.

A reporter with a microphone stood next to him. "What's your reaction, sir, to the cook-off judge's comments on your dessert? He said it should be disqualified because the other contestants baked something and you did nothing but chop and melt." The reporter, a perky young woman who reminded Val of Fawn, tilted her mike toward Granddad.

"Someone should have told that fella that this isn't a bake-off. It's a cook-off. Maybe he doesn't understand the meaning of the word *cook*. It means to combine ingredients and heat them. That's what I did to make the fondue."

Val liked how Granddad parroted what Henri had said yesterday at her booth. She looked for the chef among the people standing nearby. Too bad he wasn't there to hear his definition of *cook* thrown back in his face.

The reporter angled the microphone toward herself. "The chef also said it takes less time and effort to make fondue compared with the other entries. What does the Codger Cook say to that?"

Granddad leaned toward the mike. "When I went to school, you earned grades for results, not effort. I know that's changed in schools, but in the real world, results matter. Who should come out on top? The cook who spent the most time in the kitchen or the one who made a dessert you really want to eat?"

Applause erupted from the festival visitors close enough to hear the interview.

"Words of wisdom from the *Treadwell Gazette*'s own Codger Cook."

Val heard murmurs from the group.

"That chef is a jerk."

"The Codger Cook is the real deal."

"I'm going to try his fondue."

Henri's attempt to put down Granddad was backfiring. Val searched the crowd for the chef. Telling him that he'd chosen her cousin as the cook-off winner would give her great pleasure. She would also suggest he watch the coverage of the cook-off on the local evening news so he could see Granddad's interview.

Val didn't see Henri in the crowd, but she noticed Jennifer striding past the party tents and heading behind them. She was alone, without her friends or her fiancé to protect her. Nothing bad was likely to happen to her in broad daylight, but if it did, Val would feel awful about turning her back on Jennifer. She hurried after the bride-to-be.

Chapter 16

Val followed Jennifer to the area behind one of the tents and watched her join the festival goers waiting to use the portable lavatories. For the first time in her life, Val was happy to see a line outside the facilities.

She rushed to take the spot behind the woman she'd tailed. "Hi, Jennifer."

"Hey, Val. Aren't those painted panels on the stall doors fantastic?" Jennifer pointed to the row of johns with landscapes painted on them. Instead of being eyesores, the stalls blended into the surrounding trees and shrubs. "After I saw those yesterday, I went online and found you can rent panels that look like white trellises covered with pink flowers. Perfect for a big outdoor wedding."

All roads led to her wedding, including the one near the portable johns. "If only they could be as pretty inside as outside," Val said.

"They weren't bad yesterday morning, but I'm guessing they've gone downhill since then. The cook-off was great fun. Your grandfather's fondue was outstanding. Sarina and Noah said it was better than the one he served when they arrived."

"I haven't had a chance to try it yet. Too many people were waiting for a taste." And not enough were waiting here. The line was moving faster than Val liked. No time for small talk. "I've been meaning to ask you something. One of our neighbors said he saw you leaving our house just before the fireworks started Friday night. That surprised me. You didn't mention going to the house when the police chief asked what you did after dinner."

Jennifer blinked rapidly. "I thought he wanted to know when we all got back to the house after the fireworks."

No way she could have interpreted the chief's question so narrowly. She'd told him what she'd done right after dinner and then skipped over everything else until the fireworks ended. *Why leave out the middle?* She wouldn't want the police to know she'd gone to the house if, while there, she'd murdered her friend in the backyard. But in that case Jennifer would deny being at the house at all and challenge the witness who said he saw her. So what else would she want to hide?

"You should call the police to revise your statement before the witness reports seeing you at the house." Val hoped that scare tactics would prompt Jennifer to tell the truth. "If you don't, the police will take you for a liar. You'll be answering a lot of questions in the interrogation room, especially if Fawn was murdered around the time you were at the house."

"If she was there then, I can't help the police. I didn't see or hear anything. I was uh . . . busy." Jennifer wiped sweat from her brow and leaned toward Val. "After we finished dinner, Payton and I drove to your grandfather's house for a quickie," she whispered.

Ah. That explained how Payton knew where her bedroom was. "So Payton can give you an alibi for at least part of the evening when the murder took place. Why didn't you mention that to the police?"

"I didn't think I needed an alibi." Jennifer shuffled forward as the line for the johns shortened. "And it was embarrassing to talk about it in front of a room full of people."

She must have had a strict upbringing. Admitting to a tryst with her fiancé wouldn't embarrass any woman Val knew. "The police will respect your privacy if you tell them."

"I have the chief's card. I'll call him. Thanks for the advice."

"You're welcome." Val estimated she had less than a minute to coax information from Jennifer about the others in the wedding group. "This morning while Payton was waiting for you, he mentioned the double date he and Noah had with you and Sarina. Obviously things have worked out for you and Payton. What about Sarina and Noah?"

Jennifer held up crossed fingers. "I've been hoping they'd get together. It would be perfect for her. Her family wants her to settle down and have kids. Noah has a good income. If she married him, she could quit her job and devote herself to painting.

I pushed for Noah to come here this weekend so they could spend time with each other."

"On Friday, before you arrived at the house, Fawn was flirting with Noah." *To Sarina's obvious annoyance.*

Jennifer advanced to the front of the line. "Fawn was in such dire financial straits, she'd have thrown herself at anyone with a steady income. I should have told her that Sarina had first claim to Noah. See you later, Val." Jennifer marched to a just-vacated portable lavatory.

By the time Val returned to the front of the tents, the mayor's wife was calling for attention from the platform.

She spoke into her microphone. "Ladies and gentleman, I'd like to thank all of you—cooks, tasters, and voters—for making the cook-off a success. We're ready to announce the people's choice dessert." She paused. "The winner is the chocolate fondue made by Don Myer, the Codger Cook."

Val whooped and jumped up and down. She gave Granddad a high-five when he passed her on his way to the platform. The camera crew shot footage as he accepted the prize, thanked the organizers, and praised the desserts made by his competitors. Much as Val wanted to stay around and celebrate with him, she felt guilty about leaving Tanisha on her own in the booth any longer.

As Val crossed the street, she saw Tony at the edge of the parking lot where the booths were located. He was punching the screen of his smart phone.

He looked up, waved to her, and met her as she walked toward him. "Can we finally talk?"

She glanced at her watch. "Briefly. I need to relieve my assistant at the booth in a few minutes." She hadn't promised Mom she'd be cordial.

He tucked his phone into his jeans pocket. "I'll go straight to the point. I want to apologize for my fling. I let you down, and I let myself down. I can't tell you how sorry I am."

A large number of *I*'s in four short sentences. He hadn't apologized eight months ago. What had changed? Maybe his paramour had dumped him. "You did me a favor by cheating right after we got engaged instead of waiting until we were married. Thank you for that."

His head reared back as if she'd slapped him. "I deserve that. I only hope you'll forgive me."

"You didn't ask me to forgive you when it happened. Why do you care now?"

"I feel guilty about it."

So what bothered him was guilt found not love lost. Val crossed her arms. "Good to know you have a conscience. Maybe you won't cheat on your next fiancée."

"I promise I'll never do anything like that again." He ducked his head and looked at her like a little boy sent for a time-out, afraid his mother would stop loving him. "If you can't forgive me, there's no hope you'll come back."

"Everybody makes mistakes." Hers was falling for

him. "I've made a lot of them myself, but I don't make the same one twice. We're done."

"Okay, the break-up was one hundred percent my fault, but after all the time we spent together, you're heartless not to give me another chance. You're taking revenge."

Here was the Tony she remembered. He would admit to a lapse and follow it with a *but*, shifting the focus to her faults. "You really don't know me, Tony, if you think I'd take pleasure in revenge."

"We were together a long time. Can we at least part as friends? No hard feelings."

She'd do whatever she had to do to get rid of him, except say that she had no hard feelings. She extended her hand. "Have a good trip back to New York."

He looked at her hand, but didn't shake it. Instead, he enveloped her in a hug.

Her heart beat faster. Her body responded to his as it always had. He was like a glass of champagne, sparkling and tangy at first, but ultimately flat. She broke away from him. "Good-bye, Tony."

She turned and saw Gunnar in front of her, watching from the same spot where he'd spied her mother and the chief together. Wishing he hadn't seen her with Tony, she walked toward him.

"What was that about?" he said.

His question put her teeth on edge. "I'm not sure what you mean by *that*. If you're talking about Tony hugging me, that was a final farewell after he ambushed me."

"I can't believe he would show up here without any

encouragement from you. You don't need to spare my feelings by acting as if he took you by surprise."

"Acting?" She felt steam rising inside her, under pressure from the murder, Henri, Tony, and now Gunnar. She couldn't control her temper any longer. "Only one of us is an actor. I never pretended to be someone I'm not. You can't say the same. You were following a script when we first met, so where do you get off accusing *me* of acting?"

She stomped toward the booth, but slowed down to calm herself. Taking deep breaths, she replayed her brief exchange with Gunnar and saw it in a different light. He wasn't blaming her so much as protecting himself from disappointment, wanting to know where he stood. Instead of listening to the subtext of his words, she'd transferred her anger at Tony to him. She might not be ready for another relationship yet, as Mom had said. Too soon for a commitment.

She went into the booth. Tanisha and Bethany, their heads close together, sprang apart when they saw her.

"What's going on?" Val asked.

Tanisha shrugged. "Nothing. Business has been slow, but steady. Is it okay if I leave now?"

"Sure. You've been here a long time."

The girl scurried away.

Bethany straightened the stack of flyers on the table though they looked neat enough already. "Tanisha warned me against getting serious about Roy, based on what you said about his smile."

Uh-oh. Val should have known better than to tell an eighteen-year-old anything that she didn't want repeated. "Tanisha took what I said out of context. That wasn't meant as advice for you."

"I like Roy. He's a lot of fun and, at my age, that's all I want. Nothing serious. I don't have to worry about my biological clock yet." Bethany's hand flew to her mouth. "I didn't mean that you need to worry about yours."

Val stifled a laugh. "I probably should, but my worry basket is filled to capacity this weekend. No room for a biological clock in it. And I'm glad you had a good time with Roy."

Twenty minutes after closing the booth, Val was hauling the last cooler from her car into the café. She glanced toward the club's fitness machines arrayed in the open area beyond the reception desk. Only a few people were using the equipment.

A golden-haired woman on a recumbent bike caught her attention. Whitney Oglethorpe, Payton's ex-girlfriend, was reading a book while her legs pedaled. No one was on the bikes to either side of her. Adjacent exercise bikers resembled airline passengers seated next to each other. Strangers would talk to each other in both situations, though getting away from an inquisitive person was easier in a gym.

Like it or not, Whitney, you're about to have company.

Val shoved the cooler behind the counter at the café and hurried to the locker room to change into the shorts and T-shirt she kept there in case a chance to play tennis came up. By the time she returned to the exercise area, she still hadn't thought of a way to get Whitney talking. Val would have to play it by ear.

She climbed on the bike next to Whitney's and put her feet in the rubber stirrups on the pedals. Wearing beige shorts with pockets for tennis balls, she must look like a newbie biker to Whitney, who was cycling in form-fitting biking shorts. Asking for help was always a good icebreaker.

Val leaned forward on the bike contraption to peer at the console with its LED display, myriad buttons, and a number pad. "Excuse me, can you tell me how to work this thing?"

Whitney looked up from her book. "If you don't know what program you want, you can just pedal and press the Quick Start button." She went back to reading.

"Thank you." Val started pedaling, pressed the big green button, and gave Whitney a long look. "Didn't I see you yesterday at the festival with Penelope Grandsire? I play tennis with her here at the club."

The name-dropping worked.

Whitney bent the corner of her page and closed her book. "She's very into tennis. I'm staying at the Grandsires' house this weekend. I'm Whitney."

"I'm Val. Nice to meet you." Val glanced at the title of book Payton's ex-girlfriend had closed— *La Cousine Bette* by Balzac. Val had read it in English translation during the summer when she focused on long novels. She remembered little about the plot except that it took Bette five hundred pages to exact an exquisite revenge. Did Whitney have any vengeful urges toward the woman who replaced her in Payton's affection? "Speaking of the Grandsires, I just met Penelope's son, Payton, this weekend."

Whitney pedaled more slowly. "Oh? How did you meet him?"

"I live with my grandfather. He got roped into renting his extra bedrooms to festival visitors. Payton has friends staying at the house, so he came by this morning. I'm sure you've heard that one of them was strangled Friday night."

"Not one of Payton's friends. He hardly knew her. She was a friend of his fiancée, Jennifer. She must be staying at your grandfather's house, too." When Val nodded, Whitney continued, "Do you know Jennifer? I mean, is she a friend of yours?"

Val suppressed a laugh. Two women pumping on bikes were pumping each other for information. "I never met any of the people staying with my grandfather until they checked in two days ago." *Sorry, Whitney, I can't tell you anything about Payton's fiancée, but feel free to rant about her.*

"How strange that she stayed on here after her friend's murder. Nothing, not even death, will interfere with her weekend plans." Whitney attacked the cycle with new vigor. "Penelope doesn't think Jennifer's right for Payton. He has a future in politics, but not if he's married to her. The press will jump on him for having a wife who was involved in a murder."

Val couldn't let this unfair comment go without a protest. "No one can hold her responsible for her friend being murdered." *Not even the press.*

"You're known by the company you keep. And most murders involve drugs."

Implying that Jennifer was involved in both drugs and murder? Therefore, she would be a bad wife for a politician, whereas Whitney would feel at home in the political arena, able to use innuendo like a weapon.

Were words the only weapons she'd used against Jennifer? Val would love to know where Whitney had been Friday night and last night. "I hope you've had a chance to enjoy some festival activities while you're visiting the Grandsires. When did you arrive?"

"Late Friday. Penelope showed me around the town and the festival yesterday."

Late Friday wasn't precise enough to tell Val if Whitney had been in Bayport early enough to see Payton with Jennifer and then to mistake Fawn for Jennifer. "Did you happen to go to the corn maze last night? I saw someone there who looked a little like you."

"No, I was at the Grandsires' bash last night. Payton had to leave because Jennifer had a panic attack in the maze. She's a bit of a drama queen."

Compared to the cool Whitney, almost anyone would look like a drama queen. "Was Penelope upset that he left the party early?"

"It wasn't all that early. It must have been nearly ten when he went off. The party was winding down by then."

Penelope Grandsire and her son would have been missed if they'd slipped away from the party earlier. Whitney could have left without attracting notice, but this detached woman with a superiority complex didn't strike Val as someone who would lift a finger to harass a rival. On the other hand, unemotional people like her had been known to commit cold-blooded murder. And maybe Payton was the first thing Whitney had wanted in her life that money couldn't buy.

Whitney checked the small screen on her bike. "One minute left in my workout. Payton is level-headed. He must realize that Jennifer will hold him back. Once this weekend's over, he'll ease out of that relationship."

She sounded as if she was trying to convince herself.

Val arrived home at six fifteen. Her grandfather was in his favorite chair, a big grin on his face as he watched himself on the television.

He hit the pause button on his remote. "Hurry. You're missing my interview."

"I saw it live. You did a great job of putting the chef in his place."

"They showed that interview earlier. This is the one after I got the people's choice award."

Val sank into the worn tweed sofa and put two throw pillows behind her. "I'm ready. Roll 'em."

The same reporter who'd interviewed Granddad at his booth spoke into the microphone. "I've heard people rave about your winning dessert. Are you going to share the recipe for your chocolate fondue in an upcoming Codger Cook column?"

"I'm not planning on sharing my secret fondue

recipe . . . at least not yet. It may go into the cookbook I'm putting together."

Val stifled a groan. He'd mentioned this phantom publication previously, but this was the first time he'd put it out on the airwaves. "Your cookbook?"

"Shh."

The reporter smiled. "When can we expect the cookbook to come out?"

"I don't have a firm date yet."

"Or even page one finished," Val muttered.

The reporter took over the microphone. "I'm looking forward to the cookbook, so keep us posted. Now, on a less happy note, we understand that the young tourist who was strangled Friday night was staying at your house. Can you confirm that?"

"That's a question for the Bayport Police Department. Like everyone else in this town, I offer my condolences to the victim's family. We all hope the person responsible for this terrible crime is caught and brought to justice swiftly."

"Absolutely. Congratulations again, Codger Cook, on your winning dessert. This is Kayla King reporting from the Bayport Tricentennial Festival."

A middle-aged anchorman came on the screen. "Thank you, Kayla. We'll bring you up to date on that murder investigation later in the program, but first, the weather."

Granddad pressed the mute button on the TV remote.

"You're getting to be a real media personality, Granddad. I can't wait to try your winning fondue. Do you have any left over?" When he shook his head, she continued, "Then you'll have to make it again."

"I can't. When I made the fondue on Friday, I followed a recipe and used up just about all the brandy. I thought we had another bottle of it, but we didn't. There was plenty of similar stuff in the bar cabinet, so I grabbed a few bottles. People knew your grandmother liked liqueurs and brought them as gifts. I added a little of this and that until it tasted good."

"A little of this and that? Did you write down what you added?"

"I was in too big a hurry. I left the bottles out, so I'd know which ones I used. Then when I wasn't looking, your mother put them back in the cabinet."

Val didn't see that as an excuse not to make the fondue again. "The ones you used must be in the front."

"They would have been if your mother didn't rearrange the bottles and put them in alphabetical order."

Val laughed. "You made the most delicious fondue the world has ever tasted, and you can't duplicate it? Didn't you just announce on TV that the recipe would be in a cookbook you're writing? If you can't even list the ingredients for one recipe, how are you going to write a cookbook?"

He grinned. "*We're* going to put out a cookbook. Both our names will be on it."

"Uh-uh. I'm planning a cookbook of my own, with just one name on the spine." She held up her index finger. "And it's not yours."

"Did you ever win a cooking contest? No. Do you write a food column for a newspaper? No. You're an unknown, just another woman writing another cookbook. I'm a brand." He beat on his chest. "You can't do it without me. I can't do it without you. The book won't be a hit unless we work together."

She hated to admit he was right. The brand had more to do with the success of cookbooks than the recipes. But she couldn't give up without a fight. "By work together, you mean I cook and write the recipes for the book, and you sign your name to it? Oh, that sounds fair."

"I'll do more than that. I'll test some of your recipes. And you can use my title—*The Codger's Cookbook.*"

"*The Conniver's Cookbook* would be more accurate." She glanced at the TV. "The weather report is over. Turn on the sound."

The news anchor reported on a traffic accident that tied up Route 50 for several hours, with the footage showing bumper-to-bumper traffic.

The camera then focused on his female co-anchor. "Breaking news on the investigation into Friday night's strangling death of a young woman. Chief Earl Yardley of the Bayport Police Department has told us the police expect to interview a person of interest in the case. No details about when or where that interview will occur. We now turn to other area news."

Granddad muted the TV. "That's not big news. You know, it's a shame that Earl is tied up with this murder. We could have had him over to dinner while your mother was here. They haven't seen each other in a long time."

Val stopped slouching on the sofa. "I didn't realize Mom and the chief knew each other well." *Until yesterday.*

"They were sweethearts in high school. Your grandmother and I hoped they would get married."

Hmm. Gunnar might have been right about the mom-chief hug. "Why didn't they get married?"

"Your mother met your father and never looked back." Granddad took off his bifocals. "With him in the navy, we knew she wouldn't be living near us if she married him. That's why we were rooting for Earl."

"She didn't listen to you, I guess." So why should Mom expect Val to listen to her?

"We never pushed it with her. The more parents push, the more their children dig in. People have to marry who they want. It was her decision, and it turned out right."

"How did the chief take it?"

"He got over it. Your mother and Earl were friends before they were sweethearts, and afterwards. He'd come over and spend time here when she was visiting us with you and your brother."

"I remember. He used to bring me candy." Former sweethearts would hug in a different way than old friends, but that didn't mean they were current lovers. Val should have asked Granddad sooner about her mother and the chief, instead of letting Gunnar's interpretation of a hug bother her. Something else Granddad had just said surprised her. "It's hard to believe you didn't tell Mom about your preference in boyfriends. You're certainly vocal with me about your opposition to Gunnar."

"There's a big difference. Your mother had good taste in men, and you don't. Anyway, Gunnar's growing on me, though I'd rather you take up with that blond sheriff's deputy. What's his name again?"

"Roy Chesterfeld. I saw him today. He may be taking up with Bethany."

"Guess you missed your chance." Granddad wiped the lenses of his glasses on his sports shirt. "I figured, with your mother here, you'd ask Gunnar over this weekend. Everything okay between the two of you?"

Val shook her head. "Tony hugged me good-bye. Gunnar saw it and misinterpreted. I lost my temper." She didn't want to go into the details. "Where's Mom?"

"I sent her to the supermarket to pick up a nice piece of beef. I've been going without red meat a long time because of you and your healthy recipes. I deserve to celebrate today, and she agreed."

Oh, she agreed, did she? It was her idea to put Granddad on a healthy diet. Now she was swooping in to save him from the diet she'd mandated.

Val stood up. "I'm going up to my room—no, I'm not. It's still Mom's room for another day. I'll go sit on the porch." She wanted privacy when she called Gunnar.

Granddad leaned back in his chair. "And I'm going to stay right here and rest my eyes."

Val opened the front door and saw Jennifer and Sarina coming along the sidewalk. Jennifer toted two shopping bags from Main Street stores. Sarina started up the path to the porch as Val sat down in a wicker chair.

Jennifer held up the large bags. "I'll put these in my trunk." She kept walking toward her hatchback parked in front of the next-door neighbor's house.

Sarina went inside the house.

Jennifer dropped her bags on the ground and pointed at her fender. "What's *that*?"

Chapter 17

Val sprinted across the lawn toward the hatchback. What had Jennifer seen behind her car? Maybe another coiled rope. "What are you looking at?"

"My tailpipe. There's something orange in it." Jennifer crouched, reached into the pipe, and pulled out a round fuzzy object. "Oh. A stuffed bird." She stood up and brushed soot from the yellow-orange breast and the black wings.

Val recognized the bird. "It's a Baltimore oriole." The Maryland state bird made a good souvenir, but not for a tailpipe.

"It's cute. Why would anybody put it in there?"

To stop up the exhaust pipe? During a heavy snowstorm a few years ago, Val had heard warnings to clear snow away from the tailpipe or risk carbon monoxide seeping into the car. Hard to believe that a stuffed toy, a few inches in diameter, could cause the exhaust system to malfunction. But maybe it wasn't the only thing in the tail pipe.

Val glanced at Jennifer's keys. "May I use that flashlight on your key ring?"

Jennifer handed her the key ring.

Val leaned down, shined the LED light into the tailpipe and peered into the pipe. Five inches in, Val saw something black with a bit of red. The object conformed to the shape of the pipe, like the little oriole. *Another stuffed bird?*

She stood up and brushed away a pebble that stuck to her bare knee. Kneeling on asphalt was no fun. "There's something else in there."

"Let me look." Jennifer took back the flashlight and bent down. Wearing light yellow capris, she didn't go as far as putting her knee on the ground. "It's black. I can't tell what it is."

"I may be able to snag it." To pull it out, Val would need something long and narrow. "I'll go get a tool."

She ran to the house and returned a minute later with a fondue fork.

Sarina joined her and Jennifer at the curb. "What's happening?"

Jennifer held out her palm, cradling the Baltimore oriole. "This stuffed toy was in my tailpipe. It looks like something else is stuck in there too. Val's going to fish it out."

"Why bother?" Sarina said. "Just go to a garage and let a mechanic remove it."

Jennifer frowned. "It might be dangerous to drive with something in the tailpipe. What do you think, Val?"

"I think I can get it out." The trick would be to avoid pushing the object any further into the pipe.

If Val didn't succeed, Jennifer could call a garage and ask what to do.

Down on her knees again, Val guided the fork along the inner right side of the pipe until it was alongside the obstruction. She used the tines to maneuver the black object closer. Little by little, she worked it toward the end of the pipe until she could reach it with her fingers.

She pulled out a stuffed red-winged blackbird, about the same size as the Baltimore oriole Jennifer was holding. Did the tailpipe have more little birds in it? If it did, they'd be too far inside for Val to reach them with a fondue fork.

Sarina pointed at the blackbird. "That could be dangerous if it jammed up the pipe."

Val had initially taken the chase in the maze and the rope left there as serious threats to Jennifer. The birds in the pipe looked more like a prank, a playful reminder of Hitchcock, but frightening after the other threats. "The Baltimore oriole was visible. Whoever put it in there wanted Jennifer to see it. If she'd driven away without noticing it, it probably would have fallen out after a few road bumps."

Sarina folded her arms. "What about the other bird? It was farther in the pipe."

Jennifer turned toward a black sedan that was slowing down. "Here comes Noah. Let's ask him if I should worry about this."

Noah dismissed Sarina's concerns. "It's not a hazard. The exhaust would blow out anything that light. If something was really wedged in there, the engine would overheat after a while and the car would stop."

"You know that," Sarina said, "but how many other people do? It's a threat if someone intended to hurt you, Jennifer, whether or not the attempt could have succeeded."

Noah pointed at the stuffed birds. "Those are a threat for another reason. Why would anyone buy toy birds to put in a tailpipe, when rags would do just as well? Because birds are intimidating, after everything else that happened this weekend. A rope, a pursuit in a cornfield, and birds—they're all threats in Hitchcock movies."

Jennifer gasped. "Now you're scaring me. I'm going to call Payton and tell him what happened. He'll know what I should do." She opened her trunk and shoved her shopping bags in. She looked at her watch. "It's getting late. We'd better get dressed for dinner. We have to leave in half an hour."

"It's not going take me half an hour," Sarina said. "I'll be on the window seat upstairs waiting for the two of you."

After the wedding group went inside, Val rocked on the front porch glider. When had the birds gone into Jennifer's tailpipe? Probably last night in the dark when there was little risk of being seen. Who had put them there and why? Noah, the Hitchcock fan, made the likeliest tailpipe stuffer. By talking up the Hitchcock connection, he'd frightened Jennifer about something that wasn't in itself dangerous. Perhaps he'd hoped she would find the birds earlier today and leave town. Then he could protect her while her fiancé stayed behind partying.

Noah might also have chased her in the maze with the same goal in mind—to get her away from Payton and give himself an opportunity to prove his devotion. Good luck with that. Val rated Noah's chances against Payton as only slightly better than Tony's chances against Gunnar—nearly zero.

Val turned her thoughts from the wedding group's triangle to the one involving her. She'd chalked up Gunnar's reaction to her hug with Tony as jealousy and a faulty reading of body language, but maybe it wasn't so faulty after all. Gunnar had seen them hug the same way Mom and the chief had hugged. Two people powerfully attracted to each other in the past still felt that attraction, but wouldn't act on it. Gunnar had picked up on the attraction correctly, but had no way to know the full history, what had gone on immediately before the hug and long before it.

Val took her cell phone from her pocket and called him. Maybe he didn't go on duty as a zombie until sundown. She reached his voice mail.

"Hi, Gunnar. I was hoping we could talk before you turned into a zombie. If you're already out scaring people, let's talk tomorrow. Call me when you get a chance."

She turned her phone to vibrate and went inside. In the hall she heard voices coming from the upstairs alcove.

Sarina's words drifted down. "After that bird business, you have to go to the police."

"I'm not doing that now," Jennifer said. "We're all having a relaxing dinner at the inn. Then I'm going home with Payton."

"You *are?*"

Val was as surprised as Sarina sounded.

"Yes, I'm finally allowed to see the place," Jennifer said. "When I told Payton about the birds stuffed in the tailpipe, he said someone is trying to hurt me and knows where I'm staying and what kind of car I drive. He didn't want me here even one more night."

"His mother is okay with your staying there now, though she wasn't two days ago? What changed?"

"One of their guests left today, so she couldn't say they don't have room for me."

"That's great." Sarina's tone sounded more like sarcasm than enthusiasm. "What happens tomorrow?"

"Payton said he'd take my car to a mechanic to make sure it's safe before I drive it back to Washington. I'm so excited about seeing the house. I've got to go pack."

"Wait a minute, Jennifer. When are you going to tell the police that someone's stalking you?"

Val felt a jolt of excitement. If someone was stalking Jennifer, why hadn't she told the police already?

"I don't have a stalker." Jennifer sounded indignant.

"Telephone harassment qualifies as stalking. That includes text messages, like the one you got yesterday."

"I don't know what you're talking about. I have to pack for tonight."

A door slammed. Was Sarina wrong or was Jennifer in denial? She'd be crazy not to tell the police about a harassing message, especially after someone who resembled her was strangled. Val had known another woman who'd kept her suspicions of being stalked secret and failed to report vandalism to the police. And that woman had been murdered.

Val heard footsteps on the stairs and zipped into the hall bathroom. The creaking stairs allowed her to track the progress of the person coming down. She timed her exit from the room so that she'd "run into" whoever was descending to the main floor. It was Sarina.

"Hey, Sarina. Can I get you a drink? Coffee or tea?" *Or better yet, something that would loosen the tongue.* "How about a glass of wine?"

Sarina stood undecided on the bottom step, looking at Val intently as if contemplating painting her portrait. "Yes. A glass of wine sounds good. White or red, I don't care. Why don't you join me on the front porch?"

"Okay." Val figured Sarina wanted something from her besides a glass of wine. No problem, as long as Sarina gave something in return—preferably her reasons for believing Jennifer had a stalker.

Val tiptoed past her grandfather snoring in his easy chair, went into the kitchen, and found a cold white wine in the refrigerator. She crept back with two glasses and a bottle of tongue-loosener.

On the porch, she poured the wine and sat in a wicker chair that matched the one Sarina was in. They clinked glasses.

"Thank you." Sarina took a large gulp and stared straight ahead.

Up to Val to get the conversation ball rolling.

"How did you and Jennifer get to know each other?"

"In college. I started at James Madison University, took a year off, and then transferred to Virginia Commonwealth. Transfer students have a hard time getting into campus life. Jennifer took me under her wing and introduced me to people. We were roommates and, after graduation, we both ended up in the Washington area and shared an apartment for a few years."

"But not any more?"

"She left to live with a man she was seeing, a congressional staffer. By the time she figured out he had a wife and kid back in Kansas, I'd moved into an efficiency. I had no room for her." Sarina took another large swallow of wine. "This time, she exercised due diligence before committing to a man. Payton's a straight arrow, honest and scrupulous to a fault."

Amazing how Sarina made virtues sound like defects. Val poured her more wine. "So Jennifer has found the perfect man and she's planning the perfect wedding."

"Exactly. That's why it made no sense to me that she included a klutz like Fawn in the wedding party. You saw how she dropped strawberries in the fondue and onto the tablecloth. She would have tripped on her way down the aisle."

Given a choice between Fawn and Sarina as wedding attendants, Val would have chosen the klutz over the crab. Jennifer had put up with both of them. Could Sarina have been jealous of Jennifer's friendship with Fawn?

Val gave herself a mental shake to go back on track. She still hadn't learned anything about the harassing text message. "I'm sorry that Jennifer's weekend has turned into such a disaster. Hard to believe anything else could go wrong for her."

"Something else did. She's being threatened." Sarina swirled the wine around the glass. "I can't convince her to take it seriously and go to the police. Could you try to talk some sense into her? If you can't, maybe you can go behind her back and speak to your friend, the chief."

Val didn't mind doing that, but she would get more information from Sarina by stalling than by giving in. "How is she threatened? Noah said a clogged tailpipe wasn't dangerous. A neighborhood kid probably hid his sister's favorite toys in the tailpipe. My brother did things like that to me."

"I'd worry less if Jennifer found teddy bears in the tailpipe. As Noah said, the birds are intimidating because of the Hitchcock thing." Sarina tossed down more wine.

Val put on her skeptical face. "With intimidation, the threats usually progress, starting with something minor and ending with a bang. Here, it's the other way around. The murder came first, and the latest threat, if you can call it that, involves harmless toys. I can understand why Jennifer doesn't feel she has to go to the police." *Okay, Sarina, that's your cue.*

Sarina stared into her glass. "There's another reason she should go to the police. Yesterday morning we were sitting on the window seat upstairs, waiting for Noah. Jennifer got a text message. She turned white when she read it, started heaving, and rushed to the bathroom. She left the phone behind."

Val felt confident that Sarina had looked at the phone. "What did the message say?"

"I remember it word for word. 'On a day in May, you got your way. Is this the day when you will pay?'"

Not exactly a threat, but certainly unnerving. "I understand why you're worried. Do you know who sent it?"

"I tried replying to the text, but it bounced. An unknown number, probably from a disposable phone. When Jennifer came back from the bathroom, she said breakfast didn't agree with her. I suggested it was the text message that upset her. She wouldn't talk about it except to say that it made no sense." Sarina downed her wine. "I want her to go to the police so they can follow up on it."

"Don't count on them to do anything. I had a friend in New York who reported harassing messages to the police. They told her to contact the phone company." Val raised her glass to her mouth, but only wet her lips with the wine. She would save wine drinking for when she didn't need a clear head. "The police would act on a specific threat, like *I'm going to kill you tonight.* They might be interested in the text Jennifer received if it would help them track down Fawn's murderer. Do you have any idea what the text meant?"

Sarina added more wine to her glass. "No."

Val struggled to dredge up a memory. *Who had mentioned May this weekend?* Payton, when he talked about how he'd reconnected with Jennifer. A ripple of excitement ran through Val. "Payton told me about the double date the four of you went on. That was in May."

Sarina's eyes widened. "Really? Of course, the date would stick in Payton's memory more than mine."

"I'm surprised it didn't stick in your memory. From what I heard, the double date didn't turn out the way it was supposed to."

"It didn't turn out the way Noah and Payton expected." Sarina muttered. "When I said the date didn't stick in my memory, I meant the calendar date, not the event. I thought it was in April, probably because it wasn't long after Easter and the weather was cool. It could easily have been May."

Val paid no attention to the comments on the month and the weather, fixating on Sarina's first remark. The double date hadn't turned out as the two men expected, but maybe the women had anticipated the outcome. Was that the day Jennifer got her way, ending up with Payton, the hunky lawyer, instead of Noah, the homely one?

"I think the verse Jennifer received was about that double date," Val said. "Noah might have sent it because he was annoyed with Jennifer for dropping him in favor of Payton."

Sarina sipped her wine. "It happened five months ago. Why would he wait until now to show his annoyance?"

"Maybe he didn't wait, but sent similar messages previously. And Jennifer brushed them off, as she did this one, to avoid a confrontation with her fiancé's best friend."

"You're on the wrong track." Sarina stood up. "Thanks for the wine. It calmed me down. And forget about convincing Jennifer to talk to the police. I was overreacting to the birds in the tailpipe . . . and the message. Jennifer must have had indigestion like she said."

Not from my lemon ricotta pancakes.

Val would bet Sarina had changed her mind about notifying the police because she suspected Noah of sending that message and thought he was harmless—a man of words, not action. Yet the second line of the verse sounded like a threat. Why should Jennifer pay for getting her way and how would she pay?

Val followed Sarina into the hall, carrying the wine bottle and her half-filled glass. Sarina deposited her empty glass on the hall table and looked up at the sound of Noah's voice coming from the hall above.

"Why would you stay at the Grandsires' house with people who hate you?"

"Payton's parents don't hate me," Jennifer said. "They just don't know me. This is a chance for us to spend some time together and get acquainted."

"You're naïve if you think they'll ever accept you."

And Noah was naïve to think Jennifer would pay any attention to him. Granddad's words echoed in Val's mind—*The more parents push, the more their children dig in.* The Grandsires' opposition to Jennifer might make Payton all the more determined to marry her.

"I was supposed to stay at that house this whole

weekend." Jennifer sounded annoyed. "You're not going talk me out of going there on the last night. Better late than never."

She started down the stairs. Noah followed, carrying her massive suitcase.

"I didn't realize you were going to pack everything," Sarina said as Jennifer took the last step down into the hall. "That's why it took you so long."

"This isn't everything. I left some things in the closet and drawers." Jennifer turned to Val. "I'll come back tomorrow to pick them up."

"Enjoy your dinner," Val said as the three of them left.

Val glanced into the sitting room. Her grandfather was still snoring. Her cell phone vibrated in her pocket. She looked at the caller ID. Deputy Roy Chesterfeld. Maybe he had news about the murder investigation.

Chapter 18

Val went out to the porch to talk on the phone so she wouldn't wake up Granddad. She leaned against the porch railing and put her cell phone to her ear. "Hey, Roy. Good to hear from you."

"Hi, Val. I thought you might be interested in hearing about that rope you found in the maze. It was similar to the one the strangler used, but not an exact match for it."

No big surprise. Val was pretty sure the rope coiled under the corn stalks wasn't intended to strangle anyone but rather to create fear, like the birds in the tailpipe. "Any word on when Fawn died?"

"The medical examiner gave a two-hour range."

He wasn't going to give her the exact time, but maybe he'd answer a specific question. "Was she alive before the fireworks started, say eight to eight thirty?"

"That's at the outer edge of the M.E.'s time estimate. Witnesses saw her at the festival around that time."

One of those witnesses was Sarina, who'd reported seeing Fawn at eight near the bandstand. The chief had also mentioned someone who'd seen Fawn talking to a man as the fireworks were starting around eight thirty. *Was Fawn recognizable in her crab hat and could those witnesses be trusted?* If so, then Fawn had been alive when Jennifer was en route from the house to the festival for the fireworks. "I appreciate the information, Roy."

"You and your grandfather planning to act out the crime like you did last time?"

It hadn't crossed her mind, but why not? Reenacting the murder this time wouldn't take as long. "Are you going to help us again?"

"Count me in, as long as I don't have to play the victim again." He laughed.

"You can be the killer this time. Or the sheriff's deputy who arrests the killer. Can we do it sometime tomorrow?"

"My schedule's too tight tomorrow. Later in the week would work better."

By then, the suspects would have left town, and he'd have no chance of arresting the killer. "Let's hope the case is solved sooner than that. Thanks for calling, Roy."

Val tucked her phone away. The members of the wedding group would leave Bayport tomorrow, but they'd remain within reach of the local police if evidence against any of them came up. The same was true of Whitney and Chef Henri, who may have already left town, but that didn't mean he wouldn't return. He knew where to find the woman he blamed for ruining his life. Yet Henri made an unlikely strangler. He would use voodoo dolls, firecrackers, and words as weapons, but did he have the guts to commit an up-close murder? Probably not. A remote way of killing, like sending his victim a box of poisoned truffles, suited his style better.

Her mother's rental car turned into the driveway. Val helped carry the groceries inside. Her grandfather, still in his easy chair, opened his eyes as they passed the sitting room.

"Perfect timing, Granddad. The smell of red meat woke you up."

"I can hardly wait to grill that steak." He eased his chair into an upright position.

Mom held up her hand palm out. "Don't get up yet. We have to postpone dinner. I went by police headquarters and talked to Earl. Fawn's mother is going to stop by here soon. If she hasn't had dinner yet, I think we should invite her. She may not want to eat, but we should at least ask her."

Granddad nodded. "Poor woman. This is going to be bad enough for her. We don't want her going hungry. You got enough food?"

"I bought it before I found out she was coming. There's enough if we stretch it. I have mushrooms and lots of vegetables."

"Vegetables. Hmph."

"I could make beef stroganoff, Granddad. You like that, and I have an easy recipe."

"Don't cut that beef into pieces until we know she's staying for dinner and she eats meat. If she's a vegetarian, my steak is saved." He stood up. "How about appetizers since we have to wait for dinner?"

They adjourned to the kitchen. As they emptied the grocery bags, Val told them that Jennifer planned to spend the night at Payton's parents' house.

"One less mouth to feed in the morning," Granddad said. "Don't go giving her a refund on the room like you did on Fawn's room."

"It never crossed my mind." Val fetched the wine bottle and glasses she'd left in the hall.

"I'll have a glass of the red wine I just bought." Mom set out grapes and cheese on a plate. "You must have had a good nap, Pop. You look more rested than you did earlier today. I can't say the same for you, Val. You have dark circles under your eyes. It'll take more than a nap to get rid of those."

"I haven't noticed any dark circles, Mom. Then again, I've been too busy with the festival to look in a mirror." Val popped the cork off the wine. "I wish you'd picked a different time to visit when I didn't have so much to do."

"I'm here now, and I'm going to help. I want you to leave right after dinner so you get a good night's sleep at Monique's house. Your grandfather and I will handle breakfast for the guests. In the morning you can drive straight to the café, make the food for the booth, and take the rest of the day off. I'll stay at the booth and help your assistant."

With that offer, her mother redeemed herself, even for her interference with Tony.

"Thank you, Mom. I can use some downtime." *And free time for a murder reenactment.* She handed her mother a glass of the red wine. "With the festival winding down, the booths are closing at two. What time do you have to leave for the airport?"

"Five at the latest. I have to allow time to return the rental car." Mom sipped the wine. "By the way, Tony called to tell me he talked to you. That didn't turn out the way he hoped. He's on his way back to New York."

Granddad took a beer from the refrigerator. "Good riddance to him."

Mom put her wine glass down and crossed her arms, her lecturing stance. "I hear you're taking a private investigator course, Pop."

Granddad whipped his head toward Val. "You spilled the beans."

"No, Val's not the one who told me." Mom glared at her. "Though she should have."

"It must have been Ned. He never could keep his mouth shut."

Val sympathized with her grandfather. This wasn't the first time his buddy had tattled on him to Mom.

"Don't blame him, Pop. I ran into him at the festival. He naturally assumed you'd told me about this online course."

"Why should I tell you? If I want to take up a new career, that's my own business."

Her mother put a piece of cheese on a cracker. "I figured the course was a scam, so I asked Earl if an online course could possibly prepare someone to be a private investigator. He said that you can't be a P.I. in Maryland without five years of investigative experience."

Granddad looked thunderstruck. "They should have told me that before I plunked down good money for this course."

"Maybe you can get your money back for the rest of the course."

Val gave her mother a you-must-be-joking look. "Companies that run online courses would go bankrupt if they gave a refund to every student who doesn't finish a course."

Granddad flicked his wrist. "I'm no quitter. There's always a way around silly laws. I'll just operate without a license. Call myself a sleuth instead of a P.I. I won't be able to charge as much as a licensed investigator, but that's okay. I'll undercut the competition and give senior discounts." He popped a grape in his mouth.

Mom laughed. "Senior discounts go to customers who are seniors. You can't give your clients senior discounts because *you're* a senior."

"I expect my clients will be mostly seniors. They'll trust me because I'm one of them. Ned will talk me up at the retirement village."

"Go for it, Pop. You'll perform a real service if you can find lost bifocals and keys."

Val caught her mother's wink and smiled. They both knew Granddad had trouble finding his own glasses and keys. He wasn't good at finding much of anything . . . except trouble.

"The course isn't teaching me how to locate small stuff like that. It's a serious course. We had a unit on locating lost folks, even the ones who don't want to be found."

"That reminds me," Mom said. "Earl told me the Philadelphia police located the man Fawn was divorcing. He's in custody. I'm sure her mother will

be happy to hear her daughter's murderer is
behind bars."

"The murderer is behind bars?" Granddad
stroked his chin. "I wouldn't take that as gospel
truth yet."

Val picked some grapes off a stem. "Just because
he's in custody doesn't mean he's guilty of murder."

"The two of you egg each other on." The doorbell rang. Mom set her wine glass on the counter.
"I'll get it. That's probably Fawn's mother."

Her grandfather put down his beer. "I'm not
looking forward to this."

Neither was Val. "Let's make the best of it. We've
both been obsessing about who the strangler's intended victim could have been. But we know very
little about the actual victim. That's like cooking a
dish without a key ingredient." Understanding the
character of the victim had helped Val figure out
Bayport's other murders. Maybe it would help this
time too. "We can find out more about Fawn if her
mother can bear to talk about her."

"I've been to a lot of funerals. Talking about the
dead person is part of grieving. We'll hear about
Fawn, but only what her mother wants to remember about her."

They went to the sitting room to meet Fawn's
mother.

Mercy Schrank was in her late fifties, short and
plump with a round face. She had hair the color of
orange juice, except for gray roots. She apologized
for intruding, thanked them for their condolences,
and asked to see where her daughter had spent her
final moments.

Granddad took Mrs. Schrank through the kitchen to the backyard and, after a few minutes, returned to the kitchen. "She wanted to grieve alone. I invited her to stay for dinner, told her what we were eating, and she accepted."

"You know, she drove almost five hours to get here," Mom said, "and she's planning on driving back tonight. What do you think about offering her Jennifer's room?"

Val didn't like it. "Not without Jennifer's permission. She left some things in the room and said she'd come by for them tomorrow. I suppose I can call her and ask."

"Don't do it yet," Granddad said. "Jennifer will ask for her money back, and Fawn's mother may not even want to stay."

Mom finished her wine. "I'll go tidy the bathroom upstairs in case she does. We can change the sheets later if we need to." She left the kitchen.

Val put her grandfather to work making the salad while she cut up the onions and mushrooms for the beef stroganoff. "If Mrs. Schrank doesn't want to drive home tonight, maybe Monique will put her up. She has spare bedrooms because her children and in-laws aren't staying there tonight. I'd rather ask *her* for a favor than Jennifer."

Mom returned to the kitchen with a plastic trash bag. "I emptied the wastebasket in the bathroom and replaced the towels with clean ones."

Granddad grabbed the trash bag. "I'll take care of that." He headed out the back door.

Five minutes later Val glanced out the kitchen

window and saw him talking to Fawn's mother in the backyard. They returned to the kitchen together.

"It's so peaceful out there," Mrs. Schrank said. "I'm glad Fawn didn't die in some alley in a city. The police chief told me that Jennifer Brown, Fawn's friend from high school, is staying here. Is she around? I'd like to talk to her."

Granddad shook his head. "She's gone out for the evening."

Val's concern that Mrs. Schrank would find it too hard to talk about her daughter proved unfounded. Over dinner, she talked of nothing else besides her daughter and her husband, Gerald.

"Fawn's daddy left before she was even born. I married Gerald when she was about ten, and we moved to Franklin. He was good to her, even adopted her and gave her his name. That town was always too small for her. She was a restless girl, wanting to go places." Fawn's mother ate a bite of the beef stroganoff. "She had a beautiful voice. Sang solos in the choir when she was fourteen or fifteen. But then she decided to be a pop singer and quit the choir. Gerald did not like that at all, or the people she was hanging out with at school. He said they were leading her down the road to perdition. She didn't take kindly to his scolding."

Val suspected that Gerald didn't give his wife much chance to talk and she was making up for it now. She paused in her monologue only long enough to take a bite and wash it down with water. No wine, beer, or even iced tea for her. Gerald didn't approve of alcohol or caffeine. Mrs. Schrank had perfect timing, forking food into her mouth only when Val's mother, the one person at the table who might want to change the subject, was busy chewing.

"Fawn went to Blue Ridge Community College. She finished there and was going to transfer to a university, but then she took up with a rock band. Gerald said they were all taking drugs. Fawn ended up marrying the guitar player, Bo Finchley. Gerald said Fawn would regret it." Mrs. Schrank paused for a drink of water. "Bo made her sign on to loans he took out. She took out loans, too, so she could finish her degree online. Then Bo went on the lam and left her to pay all his debts. Even then, she wouldn't come back home. Just wouldn't admit she was wrong and Gerald was right."

Val took advantage of a pause in the monologue to divert the meandering stream of words in a direction she wanted it to go. "Were Fawn and Jennifer good friends in school?"

"They were in the drama club together. Fawn got the good parts in the musicals because of her voice. Jennifer designed the sets for all the shows. They were two of a kind, Fawn and Jennifer, both of them itching to leave their small town and make a splash in a bigger pond."

Val could sympathize. After graduation from college, she'd found the big pond alluring too. "Did you know Jennifer's parents well?"

"Just to say hello to. Jennifer's family had more money than we did. They lived in a better part of town. Jennifer had more freedom than Fawn. She got to use the family car on weekends. Gerald always said high school kids were too young for cars. Jennifer used to give Fawn a ride to parties and such. Lucky for her Fawn was there when a young fella on a bicycle shot out in front of the car."

Val snapped to attention. "Why was it lucky?"

"Fawn saw the whole thing and told the police what happened. They might not have believed Jennifer without a witness."

"I hope no one was hurt badly," Granddad said.

"The man on the bicycle died right there. Cracked his head open. No helmet. Jennifer had the right of way and wasn't speeding or anything. The police tested her for drink and drugs, but she was clean, thank the Lord. Still, it was a mighty bad thing, right before graduation. Jennifer and Fawn were so sad about it. They didn't even enjoy their graduation parties."

Val glanced across the sitting room toward the study, wishing she were sitting there in front of her computer. That accident was worth researching. Mrs. Schrank had made her daughter into a heroine who'd vouched for her friend's version of the accident, but something different might have happened. Maybe Fawn was driving, perhaps without a license, and prevailed on Jennifer to lie about who'd been behind the wheel.

Val tuned her mental dial back to the Mrs. Schrank station.

"Fawn and Jennifer lost track of each other for a long time. And now, after they just found each other and Fawn was going to be part of Jennifer's wedding, another terrible thing happens." Mrs. Schrank's eyes glistened with tears. She rose abruptly from the table. "It's time I got on the road. Thank you all for dinner."

Granddad stood up. "You're welcome to spend the night."

"I couldn't do that. Gerald wouldn't like it if I didn't come home tonight. Tell Jennifer I'm sorry I missed her."

Val and her mother cleared the table while her grandfather saw Mrs. Schrank out.

Granddad joined them in the kitchen. "I feel sorry for that woman, losing her daughter and going home to Gerald, but I'm glad she's not staying here. She would have kept us up half the night with her chatter."

The three of them barely spoke as they cleaned up after the meal. Val appreciated the silence, still shell-shocked from Mrs. Schrank's volley of words.

When Mom went upstairs to grade papers and Granddad took out the kitchen trash, Val went into the study. She fired up the computer, convinced that she could find details about the accident Fawn's mother had mentioned. Long simmering anger over the accident might have led someone in the bicyclist's family to go after Jennifer, or both Fawn and Jennifer, believing they'd lied about the accident.

Payton had said he met Jennifer ten years ago when she was still in high school. That would have been around the time of the accident. Val looked up Franklin, Virginia. The town near the North Carolina border had a population of less than a thousand, smaller even than Bayport. Val's online search turned up nothing about the death of a bicyclist in the vicinity of Franklin, Virginia, ten years ago . . . or at any time.

A creaking noise from the floor above made her look at the ceiling. Jennifer's room was above the study. Val listened intently. No other noise. The old house did give off random noises now and then. She continued her online search, expanding it to include adjacent counties and nearby cities—Petersburg, Richmond, and as far away as Charlottesville, where Payton and Noah had gone to law school. No results from that. Ten years ago, not every local newspaper posted every article online.

The floorboards above creaked again. Someone was definitely in Jennifer's room.

Chapter 19

Val left the study and crept up the creaky stairs. Someone could have slipped into the house, possibly while she was in the kitchen with Mom and Granddad, cleaning up after dinner. Maybe Jennifer had returned for an item she'd forgotten to pack.

Her bedroom door was ajar. Val pushed it open wider. Granddad, wearing rubber gloves, was rooting in the wastebasket. "Get out, Granddad. You can't go poking around in a guest's room. It's an invasion of privacy."

"Shh. Your mother will hear. I'm finished and I'm leaving."

Val eyed his gloved left hand. He was clutching something small. "What are you taking?"

"I'll show you. Come on downstairs." He removed a key from his pocket and locked Jennifer's door behind them as they left.

It was probably illegal for a property owner to unlock a room he'd rented and snoop in it. Though

Val didn't approve of what he'd done, she was curious about his find.

Once they were downstairs, she motioned him into the study and closed the pocket doors that shut it off from the sitting room. "I hope you haven't found evidence related to the murder because it probably can't be used in court now that you've removed it."

"This isn't evidence of murder, but you got to follow every lead. That's what they teach in my investigator course." He showed her two tags snipped from items bought at Bayport Outfitters on Main Street. "They used to carry only ladies clothes there, but now they sell other things too."

"I've seen souvenirs, kid's clothes, and small toys there. Let me see the tags." She looked at them. "They have product codes on them, but I don't know how to decipher them."

"Can you take these tags to the shop tomorrow and find out what she bought? I'd do it, but you can come up with a better cover story for a shop like that. Dollars to doughnuts Jennifer bought clothes there."

"That's a safe bet." It dawned on Val why he'd grabbed the garbage bag from her mother before dinner. "Did you find anything in the trash from the upstairs bathroom?"

"Sure did. Band-Aids with blood on them. I saved them."

"Why? To prove that Jennifer or Sarina cut herself?"

"Or Noah. The hall bathroom isn't locked. Maybe

he couldn't find a bandage in his bathroom, so he looked in the hall bath."

"You have sales tags and Band-Aids, Granddad. That's not much to show from pawing through trash."

"I'm not finished yet. I still have to check the trash in Sarina's and Noah's rooms. I need you as a lookout. I figured I was safe in Jennifer's room because she wasn't coming back here after dinner, but the other two might. You just park yourself at the window seat upstairs and watch. If you see any of them, come and get me."

That would make her an accessory to his snooping. "It's not worth doing. You expect a murderer who left no traces at the crime scene to drop something incriminating in a wastebasket? Dream on."

"Our murderer might get sloppy, figuring he or she got away with it. In the garbology unit of my course, we read about cases cracked because of things that turned up in the trash."

If Val didn't help him, he would snoop on his own without a lookout . . . and risk getting caught. She trudged upstairs after him and took up her post by the window seat. From there she had a good view of the street. No cars or pedestrians in sight.

Granddad waited at the top of the staircase, a key in his hand, until she gave him a nod. Then he hurried toward Sarina's room.

Two minutes later, he joined Val by the window seat. "Nothing but used tissues in Sarina's trash. Maybe I'll have better luck in Noah's room."

A car slowed down in front of the house. Val

couldn't see who was driving, but the car looked like Noah's sedan. "It's too late, Granddad."

They waited until they saw Sarina open the sedan's passenger door.

Granddad pulled Val away from the window. "Let's take the back staircase. They won't even know we were up here."

Once downstairs, she said goodnight to him and took the side door to the driveway, avoiding Noah and Sarina who were coming in the front door.

On the way to her cousin's house, Val kept her eye on the rearview mirror, but saw no cars following her.

The house was dark except for a light in the hall. Val crept through the kitchen-family room and looked out the sliding door in case the prowler had returned. Everything outside was still. She went to bed.

Val woke up at the same time she had on the previous two mornings at her cousin's house. Today, though, she didn't have to fix breakfast for Granddad's guests. He and Mom would take care of it. Val packed the small suitcase she'd brought on Friday night and stopped in the kitchen where Monique was pouring coffee. "Thanks for putting me up this weekend. Did you check the backyard this morning for signs of a prowler?"

"Yes, and I didn't find anything." Monique handed Val a mug of coffee. "I have some photos to show you on my big monitor."

She took Val to a tiny room off the hall. A thirty-inch monitor dominated the space Monique used as an office.

Val perched on a stool next to her cousin's desk chair. "Are these photos from the festival?"

"They're from Friday evening when I walked around the historic district taking pictures of people shopping and eating. I'd like you to look at some pictures I took around six thirty." Monique moved her mouse and clicked to open a photo of a man at a small outdoor table, wearing a crab hat. People were eating at similar tables around his, but none of them wore the souvenir hat. He sat alone, holding a phone, his thumbs in a position to punch buttons.

The crab hat and the angle of the man's head made it hard for Val to see his features. "Who is he?"

"My face-recognition software says it's this man." Monique brought up a headshot of Noah. Then she zoomed in on the face of the man sitting alone at the table.

Val saw the resemblance. "Yes, that's Noah. Based on this photo of him at the table, your software found his headshot among your photos?"

"The other way around. I started with the photos I took of the wedding group. The software derived the characteristics of each face and then looked for matching faces in the set of photos I took over the weekend. It didn't find many matches, but I thought this shot from Friday evening would interest you."

Val studied the objects on the table in front of Noah. "A glass of wine, utensils, no food. The table is set for one person. He's waiting for dinner.

What's that small, rectangular thing near the folded napkin?"

Monique zoomed in on it. "It looks like a phone to me. He has one phone in his hand and another one on the table."

"The one on the table could be the smart phone I've seen Noah using at the house. I can barely tell that the thing in his hand is a phone."

Her cousin magnified Noah's hand. "He's cradling it. It's not a fancy phone with a large display. Some people have one phone for business and one for personal use."

"And some have phones that can't be traced back to them." Val remembered Sarina's remark that Jennifer's harassing message had probably come from a disposable phone. "The one he's holding could be a burner phone, to use when he doesn't want someone to know who's calling or messaging. Where was he when you took this picture?"

"On the patio at the Bayport Bistro."

Val hadn't tried the recently opened bistro, though she'd walked past it. It was at the corner of Main Street and Locust Lane, with its patio facing the lane. *Aha.* "Right across from the Bugeye Tavern. Payton and Jennifer had dinner there on Friday night. Now I understand why Noah's wearing a crab hat. He didn't want them to see him there. If they were sitting in the glassed-in porch at the tavern, he could have watched them."

"And I watched him. He finished thumbing his text message as his dinner arrived. He ignored his food and stared at the tavern's enclosed porch. I wondered what interested him so much,

so I snapped a picture of the people seated there."
Monique switched to displaying thumbnails of
photos. She selected a photo showing tables near
the floor-to-ceiling windows on the tavern's porch.

Val scanned the women at the tables near the
window. "I can't see all the faces clearly, but no one
there has hair like Jennifer's. Maybe she and
Payton ate in the tavern's back room."

Monique pointed at a man whose face was turned
away from the window. "This guy was reaching into
his pocket when I took this picture. He pulled out
his phone and looked at it for a long time. I took
pictures of him from a different angle and used my
telephoto lens." She brought up the next photo in
the set.

Val recognized the profile. "That's Payton. But
where's Jennifer?"

"You'll see. These are the next few photos I
snapped. I took the whole set within a minute."

Val studied the series. Payton put his phone into
his pocket. A smiling Jennifer approached the
table. He sat back, his arms crossed. She leaned
toward him, now down in the mouth. The couple
huddled over the table, apparently in a serious
discussion.

"I wish I could have heard their conversation,"
Val said.

"Judging by the next picture I took, Noah wished
the same thing." Monique enlarged a thumbnail
shot of Noah gazing across the street. "The time-
stamps on the photos indicate that two minutes
have passed since the server delivered the food,
and Noah still hasn't touched it."

"Maybe he wanted to see the effect of his text message." Val could now understand why Noah had discouraged Fawn from joining him for dinner. He couldn't have watched Jennifer and Payton so intently if Fawn had been there. "It's possible Payton was reading a message from someone other than Noah."

"Anything's possible, but how likely is it that Payton got a text from someone else at that exact moment? Noah stopped thumbing and put his phone down only seconds before Payton took out his phone and studied the display."

Val leaned toward the monitor to peer at the thumbnail images. "Did you take any other photos on Locust Lane?" When Monique enlarged the pictures, Val looked for anyone resembling Fawn, Sarina, Payton's ex, or his mother. No luck. "Some people walking on the lane wore crab hats. Noah's the only person wearing a crab hat at a restaurant. Eating with those claws hanging down wouldn't be easy."

"It's creepy to think about the best man stalking the bride and groom. Is he jealous?"

"Probably. He was going out with Jennifer before Payton replaced him." Val stared at the photo of Noah watching the engaged couple. If they'd looked out the window, they could have seen him, but not necessarily recognized him. "I just realized something that should have occurred to me earlier. All along, I've thought that the crab hat could have obscured the victim's identity from the strangler. Now I know that a crab hat could also disguise a stalker . . . and even a murderer."

Chapter 20

As Val drove from her cousin's house to the Cool Down Café, she thought about the advantages of a crab hat as a disguise. With so many people wearing the souvenir hats on Friday night, the killer could have blended in with the crowd at the fireworks and trailed Fawn to Granddad's house. If Fawn had glanced behind her, the combination of darkness and a face-obscuring hat might have kept her from recognizing someone she knew. No one along the route would pay close attention to one crab-hat wearer walking behind another one.

After the murder, Granddad had asked the wedding group if they'd worn crab hats. What Val had learned since that night gave her a new perspective on the wedding group's responses to that question.

Sarina had said she hadn't worn the hat, intending it as a gift. The next day she refused to don the souvenir hat even briefly for the wedding group photos Monique had taken. Maybe Sarina realized that a photo of her in a crab hat might jog the memory of someone who'd seen her wear one the night of the murder.

Noah had also said he was saving the hat as a gift. Yet he'd worn the hat while eating dinner across the lane from Jennifer and Payton, just hours before the murder.

According to Jennifer, she'd worn the crab hat, removed it for her dinner with Payton, and put it on again afterwards because it was easier to wear than carry. That story had sounded believable on Friday night, but now that Val knew Jennifer had gone back to the house with Payton, the last part of the story rang false. Jennifer could have simply left the crab hat at the house. Instead, she'd worn it to the fireworks. Because she'd gotten into the festival spirit? Or because the hat would make her hard to recognize?

Other people might have wanted to disguise themselves that night. Payton's ex-girlfriend, Whitney, could have worn a hat to spy on him and later lie in wait for Jennifer at the house. And Whitney was the likeliest person to mistake Fawn for Jennifer. Finally, Chief Yardley's favorite suspect, Fawn's husband, could have donned a hat to keep Fawn from recognizing him when he followed her back to the house after the fireworks.

Whether or not the killer had worn a crab hat as a disguise, Val still had no answer to the question that had occurred to her immediately after the murder—who was the intended victim? Fawn, if her husband had been the strangler. Jennifer, if Whitney had been the strangler. As for the others in the wedding party, Val could only guess at their motives for wanting either woman dead.

She parked in the lot at the racket and fitness club and walked quickly to the entrance, catching up with a woman headed in the same direction. "Hi, Yumiko."

"Happy to see you, Val." The club's tennis manager smiled broadly. "The doubles group wasn't the same without you and Monique playing with us on Saturday. I heard many people say they were sorry the café was closed this weekend. I missed your coffee and muffins."

"I'll make coffee and put out some nibbles, if you want to stop by. Tell anyone who asks about the café to drop in. I'll be there for another hour or two."

Over the past two days Val had made four times as much at the booth as she earned on an average weekend, but she'd missed the conversation and camaraderie that made her work at the café so enjoyable. Most of the people she'd served this weekend had been strangers. They'd walked away from the booth after picking up their food. It wasn't the same as serving food to the café regulars, her friends and tennis teammates, who hung around to talk.

For the tourists and the locals involved in the festival, this was the last day. For the locals not involved in the festival, this was Monday. They had regular tennis games scheduled, aerobics sessions, and yoga classes.

Val preheated the oven, made coffee, and ate a pecan mini muffin left over from yesterday. She put the remaining ones on a plate as freebies for anyone who stopped by.

As she made the dough for today's muffins, a bartender who worked out regularly at the club came into the café for coffee. He told her that the chef who'd judged the cook-off had spent Friday night in the bar, drinking and ranting about how she'd destroyed his car and nearly killed him.

"How long was he there?" Val said.

"All night. From seven 'til ten or ten thirty. He drank so much he had trouble walking."

Earlier Val had all but crossed Henri off her list of murder suspects. Now she could do that with certainty. He'd been occupied with alcohol while Fawn was strangled. Val still held him responsible for the voodoo doll and the firecrackers, though she had no proof he'd played those juvenile dirty tricks.

While the muffins baked, she chopped fruit and vegetables for the salads. The bartender left, and two women from her tennis team dropped in for coffee before going out on the court. The pace this weekend reminded her of the hectic life that she used to lead in New York . . . and that she could return to. But why would she want to? She could come up with only one reason—to redeem her reputation as a cookbook publicist. She'd left under a cloud and now she could return triumphant, but was that ego boost worth giving up her friends and family here?

Val sensed someone at the counter behind her.

"I'm glad I found you alone, Val."

Gunnar. Her heart leapt. She turned around.

He wasn't smiling the way he usually did when he saw her. "I'm really sorry for being a jerk. I was wrong."

She released the breath she'd been holding. "No, I was wrong. I shouldn't have lost my temper. And you're not a jerk."

He sat at the counter. "I acted like one. I had trouble believing you'd prefer me to Tony. He's like the star of the show, and I'm the understudy who'll never get a chance to take his place."

"I felt the same way about your ex-fiancée when I saw her." Val walked around the counter, sat on the stool next to his, and reached for his hand. "The only thing that matters is that we're stars to each other. By the way, I decided to turn down the job offer in New York."

He studied her face. "Are you sure? I'd like you to stay in Bayport, but if that's the right job for your career, you should take it."

"It's not the right job for me *now*. It would be a step back. I enjoy what I'm doing here better."

Yumiko and the reception desk manager came into the café. Val went behind the counter, poured coffee for them and Gunnar, and passed the muffins around. She took out the ingredients for apple turnovers—the dough she'd thawed overnight, the filling she'd made yesterday.

"Anything new on the murder?" Gunnar asked when the club staffers left.

As Val cut the dough into squares, she told him about the intimidating text message Jennifer received and about Noah spying while wearing a crab hat.

"You figure Noah's hung up on Jennifer?"

Val put apple filling in a dough square and folded the dough into triangles. "Yes, and I've been hung up on triangles all weekend. Not just Jennifer, Payton, and Noah, but also Payton, Jennifer, and Whitney. She's Payton's ex-girlfriend. A Noah-Fawn-Sarina triangle also occurred to me, but Sarina doesn't show a lot of interest in Noah. Of course, she'd want to hide her interest for a while if she eliminated Fawn as a rival."

"It's hard to escape a pattern once it settles in your mind. It pops up everywhere."

Val stopped making dough triangles and looked into his eyes. He was talking about the triangle that had obsessed him this weekend, the one involving her, Tony, and himself. "Not everything, or everyone, fits into a three-sided box. You and I don't, and neither do my mother and the chief."

"I know that now. I'm throwing out all my three-sided boxes."

The smile that transformed his face warmed her all over. Too bad she couldn't act on the stirrings she was feeling inside. *Too many other things to do now. Focus on the strangling.* "I'm not ready yet to throw out the three-sided boxes the wedding group fits into, though last night I heard a story that gave me a new angle on the murder." She told him what Fawn's mother had said about the death of a bicyclist beneath the wheels of Jennifer's car.

Gunnar raised a skeptical eyebrow. "That happened ten years ago. How does it explain a murder here and now?"

Val rearranged the turnovers to fit more of them

on the baking sheets. "It doesn't, unless this is the anniversary of the accident. Maybe someone's been brooding on it and finally sprang into action. Unfortunately, I couldn't find anything online about a car hitting a bicyclist near Franklin, the town where Jennifer and Fawn were high school friends. I also checked the surrounding counties and nearby cities. Nothing turned up."

"You could have been looking for information in the wrong part of the state. Indiana has two towns named Franklin. Virginia might have more than one Franklin."

"I'll look into that. It's also possible Fawn's mother forgot the details and called a motorcycle a bicycle. I was too tired to do a thorough search last night, but I should have time later. Do you have any free time today? My mother is taking my place at the booth."

"I have a meeting with a new accounting client at noon. Otherwise, I'm at your disposal." He wiggled his eyebrows suggestively. "What do you have in mind?"

"Chocolate fondue. In Granddad's backyard. I want to run through what happened the night of the murder."

"That's really romantic."

Val laughed and glanced toward the café entrance. "Here comes Bethany. Time for us to go into high gear on making the food for the booth."

Gunnar stayed at the counter, talking with her and Bethany for ten minutes. Then he stood up. "I'll see you later, Val. What time do you want me at your grandfather's house?"

"A quarter to eleven." That would give her time to make sure the booth was operating smoothly before leaving it in her mother's and Bethany's hands. And he'd have plenty of time to make his business meeting.

Five minutes before Gunnar was due to arrive at the house, Val chopped up a bar of dark chocolate. She reversed the cooking tradition in the house and simplified Granddad's recipe, melting the chocolate with cream in the microwave for a fast fondue. Granddad shook his head in disgust and told her it wouldn't turn out right if she cut corners. How often had she said the same thing to him when he pared down her recipes to five ingredients?

She stirred the melted chocolate. "This isn't going to be a gourmet experience. It's a prop for a crime reenactment Gunnar and I are going to do in the backyard."

"Hmph. You didn't have to waste good chocolate on that. And why do you need him anyway? You and I could have recreated the crime without an actor."

"Sarina and Noah are still upstairs. Payton and Jennifer may show up here. You have to keep them all away from the back windows. I don't want them to see what we're doing." Fortunately, only the kitchen and her bedroom above it had windows overlooking the backyard.

Granddad looked less grumpy, now that he had a role to play. "I'll make sure your mother locked your bedroom door from the outside when she left. Then no one can go in there and watch what you're doing from the window." He went up the staircase by the kitchen and came down a minute later, carrying the barking motion detector. "The door's locked. Here's my plan. I'm going to hang around the front hall. If Noah and Sarina come downstairs or if Payton drives Jennifer back here, I'll keep them away from the back of the house. I'll also set up RoboFido at the base of the staircase here. If anyone sneaks down, Fido will bark to alert me."

"That'll certainly scare away whoever is coming down the back stairs." She laughed as she poured the melted chocolate into a bowl. "By the way, you can stop worrying about Chef Henri coming after me. He didn't mistake Fawn for me and strangle her. He was drinking at a bar Friday night."

"I stopped worrying about him yesterday. He checked out of his hotel and drove north."

"How do you know?" She scraped the chocolate from the pot with a wooden spoon.

"I got Ned to tail him."

Val dropped the spoon she was about to offer Granddad to lick. Chocolate splattered on the counter. "You involved Ned in your sleuthing again?"

"He offered to keep an eye on the chef. Ned's very fond of you. He lost the chef for a while on Saturday, but he stuck with him on Sunday."

The doorbell rang as Val was wiping the chocolate off the counter. "That must be Gunnar. I'll get it."

She brought him back to the kitchen. Granddad gave him a more cordial welcome than usual. Chocolate wasn't the only thing melting in the kitchen.

Now might be a good time to mention her mother's plan. "Mom wants to takc all three of us to lunch when the booth closes at two. Can you make it, Gunnar?"

He nodded. "I'm looking forward to meeting her."

"And I'm looking forward to eating steak," Granddad said, "since I didn't get it last night."

"Don't get your hopes up, Granddad. Mom's planning lunch at the crab house."

"That's okay too. Crabs are even better than steak."

Granddad set up the barking sentry as Gunnar and Val adjourned to the yard to reenact Fawn's final fondue.

Chapter 21

Val put a plate of strawberries, a bowl of melted chocolate, and a fondue fork on the picnic table in the backyard. She gave Gunnar an old clothesline she'd found in the shed. "Can you make a rope that looks like the one we saw in the maze? I know the clothesline is thicker than that rope, but it won't matter for this purpose."

Gunnar took out a pocketknife and cut a length of rope. Then he looked up. "We'd better make this fast. It looks like a storm is coming."

She watched the clouds race across the sky. "It might blow over." She pulled a bench close to the table. "Before you arrived, I went online to look for another Franklin in Virginia. No luck. Then I realized no one had actually said the town was in Virginia. I'd assumed it because Jennifer and Fawn both went to college in Virginia. I found a Franklin in West Virginia, close to the Virginia border."

"Any hits on an accident that killed a bicyclist there?"

"None. I checked a map to see where two teenagers from Franklin, West Virginia, might go for a party. James Madison University in Harrisonburg, Virginia, is an hour east of Franklin. *That's* where the accident Fawn's mother described happened. The driver was a minor whose name was withheld. The bicyclist was a student at James Madison. Emilio Alvarez."

Gunnar tied a bowline on one end of the rope. "You don't know for sure Jennifer was the driver."

"Right, but everything else fits. Ten years ago. A passenger in the car. The driver absolved of any fault. The bicyclist had entered the intersection without having the right of way." Now for the exciting part she'd been bursting to tell him. "Someone came forward who'd received a text message from the driver shortly before the accident occurred. But that was discounted as a factor in the accident because the passenger texted the message, using the driver's cell phone."

Gunnar finished tying the second knot. "Who got the message and what did it say?"

"That will take more digging. I ran out of time, but I'll go back online when we're finished here. Payton may be involved somehow. That's around the time when he met Jennifer. He and Noah were in law school then at the University of Virginia, less than an hour from James Madison University."

"Just tell the police what you found out. They'll do the digging."

"They think they have the culprit—Fawn's husband. If I'm going to convince them otherwise, I'll need something more concrete. Everyone in that wedding group is holding back something. The question is how to get them to talk."

He slipped his hands through the loops he'd made in the rope. "What do you expect to learn from acting out the murder?"

"I just want to make sure I haven't missed anything." She sat down on the bench, with her back to the house. "I'll dip a strawberry in the chocolate and eat it. Meanwhile, you creep around the side of the house and come up behind me, put the rope over my head, and tighten it as if you were going to strangle me."

She had just swallowed the last bite of a chocolate-coated strawberry when he took her by surprise. She flailed, dropped the fondue fork on the ground, and then slipped her index finger under the rope."

"No fair," Gunnar said. "You can't get your finger between the rope and the neck if I'm pulling it tight enough to strangle you."

"Okay. We need another take. So far, we've proven that Fawn wouldn't have heard anyone sneak up behind her. I didn't hear you even when I expected you to come." Val speared another strawberry. "Let's run through it again from the top."

"Are you sure this isn't an excuse to gorge on chocolate fondue?"

"Of course it is."

This time Val had finished eating a strawberry and put down her fondue fork by the time he threw the rope over her head. She grabbed the fork, whipped it behind her, and poked him in the leg with the blunt side of it.

"Ow!" Gunnar rubbed his leg. "I saw that coming a second too late to get out of the way."

"Fawn's strangler wouldn't have seen it at all in the dark. To hit you with the fork's wood handle, I twisted my wrist outward. Fawn just had to reach back and stab her attacker with the business end of the fork." Val mimicked the action and touched her finger to the tips of the two prongs. "They're sharp."

"Assuming Fawn succeeded, the strangler would have puncture wounds. If I'd been stabbed while strangling someone, I might loosen up on the rope for a second when the pain hit, but then I'd be really mad and jerk the rope even tighter."

"And you'd have blood running down your leg." The strangler's blood might be on the bandages Granddad had fished from the trash, but there was no way to prove that the blood on them came from a wound made by a fondue fork. Val stood up. "Show me where I hit you."

He pointed to a spot on the outside of his right leg just above the knee.

She moved her leg next to his to see where the fork would have hit someone shorter. "Fawn would have stabbed me or Jennifer a third of the way up the thigh. Sarina and Noah would have puncture wounds a few inches below that. Payton's ex, Whitney, has long legs. The fork would have hit her about where it hit you."

"If Fawn stabbed the strangler, the fork would have DNA on it."

Val felt a tingle of excitement. "That's why it disappeared the night of the murder. The killer must have taken it to wash the blood off. It still hasn't turned up."

"Bleach could have removed the blood and the DNA from the tines. Is this fork like the one that's missing?" At Val's nod, Gunnar picked up the fork she'd used and pointed to the place where the metal was set into the wood handle. "Even a droplet of blood can leave a trace in a place like this or in one of these scratches on the wood. If the killer knows that, you'll never see the fork again."

"It's not easy to dispose of a ten-inch long fork. You can't just put it in the trash and expect no one to notice." *Especially with Granddad practicing his garbology.*

"You can throw it in the river or bury it in the ground, but someone might see you do it."

"It's not necessary to find the fork. If Fawn managed anything deeper than a scratch, her killer may still have tine marks on the leg. Wait much longer, though, and the wound will heal without leaving a trace. That's why the police need to identify the murderer fast."

"They can't ask your guests to roll up their pants or raise their skirts based on your speculation that one of them has a fork wound. But you can try strip poker and hope the strangler loses."

She laughed, sat down on the bench, and pointed to the strawberries and the bowl of chocolate. "Have some. Did you know that the original chocolate fondue was made from triangular-shaped chocolate bars? Swiss chocolate in the shape of a mountain."

He sat next to her and took a strawberry. "I didn't know that, but I'm not surprised. There are triangles everywhere this weekend."

"And text messages. Five texts in all, counting the one sent ten years ago from Jennifer's car. On Friday afternoon Jennifer texted for directions to the house. That evening Fawn texted Noah, asking to have dinner with him, but he turned her down. Then Payton received a text in a restaurant, shortly after Noah sent one. On Saturday morning Jennifer got an intimidating verse in a text." Val took a strawberry. "I want to know who sent the text to Payton, what was in it, and who texted the verse to Jennifer. I suspect Noah has the answers."

"Don't corner him in a dark alley and grill him."

"I won't, but I wish the police would take him into the grilling room."

Gunnar's cell phone dinged. "That's a message from my calendar, reminding me about my appointment. I have just enough time to walk home and put some papers together for my pitch to a client."

"Thanks for helping."

"See you later." He kissed her and left by the side yard.

Val took her props to the kitchen and found Granddad there. "Are Noah and Sarina still in the house?"

"They just left with Jennifer and Payton. They were going to walk around town and get some lunch before the parade. They may be back if it starts raining. Why don't you go to Bayport Outfitters and ask about those tags I found in Jennifer's trash? Find out what she bought."

Val couldn't imagine it would matter. She had the impression he was trying to get rid of her. "Don't you even want to hear about the crime reenactment?"

"Not unless it told you who murdered Fawn." He pointed out the window. "You'd better get going or you'll get caught in a downpour."

She'd rather do more online research into the accident, but he wouldn't give her any peace until she went to Bayport Outfitters.

A ten-minute walk brought her to the shop. Despite not much frontage on Main Street, the shop had a large sales floor because the building was deeper than most of the older structures in the historic district.

Val approached a middle-aged salesclerk. "A friend who was visiting this weekend bought some things here and really liked them. She was sorry she hadn't bought more. When I found the tags, I decided to surprise her and buy them for her as gifts. Can you tell me if you have more of these?"

The clerk looked at the tags Val gave her and held one up. "This is a tag for our skinny capri pants. They're popular this weekend because the weather is warmer than most people expected for October. I'll check if we still have them in the size your friend bought."

Val followed the clerk to a clothing rack along the wall. Hanging there were yellow capris like the ones Jennifer had worn Saturday afternoon and yesterday. Val pointed to them on the rack. "Those are the ones she liked."

The clerk checked the tags on the ones hanging on the rack. "They're the right style, but we don't have any more in her size in any color. We have a similar style here somewhere." She flipped through the hangers.

"I'd rather stick with what I know she'd liked. What about the other item?"

"That's a skirt. Let me see if we have another one like it." The clerk moved to a different rack. She held up a pencil skirt in a length that would skim the top of Val's knee and a width that would cling to her hips and thighs like elastic wrap. "The tag you showed me is for this skirt in electric blue. Here it is in an eight. That's the size your friend bought."

"I'm not sure she'd want another skirt in that bright blue. Does it come in other shades?"

"We sold out in the other colors. You might like this skirt for yourself."

"Not my style." Val gestured toward her loose khaki skirt with patch pockets. "But thank you for your help." She'd learned one thing here—however many clothes Jennifer had packed into her massive suitcase, they hadn't sufficed for her weekend in Bayport.

The clerk gave back the clothing tags and hung up the skirt. "If you see anything else that interests you, let me know."

"Thanks. I will." Val stopped to look at the sweaters folded on the shelves lining the wall. Then she ambled toward the rear of the shop and poked through a rack of sale items. Even at clearance prices, the clothes in this shop were no bargain. The prices would decrease in another month, when the tourist season wound down.

As she was about to make a U-turn and retrace her steps, she came to the children's section. Stuffed critters sat on shelves along the back wall. Birds perched on one shelf, including a red-winged blackbird like the one she'd fished out of Jennifer's tailpipe. Val picked up the blackbird and stroked its wings. It looked and felt exactly like the one in the tailpipe.

She forced herself to keep an open mind. Just because Jennifer had shopped for clothes in this store didn't mean she'd shopped for stuffed birds too. Val shifted the stuffed toys on the shelf, looking for a Baltimore oriole, the bird Jennifer had plucked from the tailpipe. No luck.

Val approached a young woman who stood behind the cash register counter. "I was looking at your little birds over there." She pointed to the shelf. "Do you happen to have a Baltimore oriole?"

"I'm sorry. I sold the last one this weekend. We'll be getting more in stock, but I don't know exactly when."

"I was hoping to give it to an avid bird watcher who's particularly fond of orioles." Val chose her words carefully to avoid saying whether her friend was male or female. "Maybe my friend bought your last one. Do you happen to remember the person you sold it to?"

The clerk frowned in concentration. "Sorry. There were so many people here this weekend."

Val regretted not having taken the wedding group's photos Monique had printed for Granddad. Seeing a picture of the customer might have jogged the clerk's memory. On the other hand, whipping out photos and asking the clerk to identify the buyer of a stuffed bird would have been decidedly weird. Val had enough information to draw tentative conclusions without a positive identification.

She left the shop and weaved through the crowd on Main Street. Probably Jennifer had bought the birds and stuffed them in the tailpipe. Did that mean she'd lied about someone running after her in the maze? Not necessarily. She'd seen how promptly Payton had left his parents' party to join her when he believed her threatened in the maze. Maybe she decided to trump up another threat to get more attention from him. The birds in the tailpipe convinced him she wasn't safe anywhere but in his parents' house. She finally got her way.

The phrase reminded Val of the verse someone sent Jennifer. If her sole purpose had been to persuade Payton she was in danger, why did she brush off the intimidating text message? She'd passed up a chance to reinforce the idea that someone was targeting her. Payton might have whisked her away even sooner to his parents' house if he'd known about that message.

Val turned onto a side street. Fawn's death gave the threats against Jennifer a force they wouldn't have otherwise had, but was the murder related in any other way to the threats? Val was back to the question she had from the start—who was the intended victim?

Her phone chimed. She pulled it from her bag. The caller ID displayed the number of her grandfather's cell phone. Either he was on the road or he didn't want someone in the house to overhear him talking on the hall phone.

"Hey, Granddad. Where are you?"

"Home. Get the police. Quick!"

"Why?"

Val heard only silence on the line.

Chapter 22

Val lengthened her stride and scrolled through the contacts on her phone. She found Chief Yardley's cell phone number, phoned him, and told him her grandfather needed help. "I don't know why he asked me to call you instead of phoning you himself. He didn't ask for an ambulance, so I don't think anyone's hurt."

"I'm on my way," the chief said.

He was responding in person to this plea for help, maybe because of the murder at the house or because of his close relationship with Granddad . . . or both.

Val sprinted, running along the curb instead of on the brick sidewalk. A police siren wailed and, when she was half a block from Granddad's house, a squad car pulled into his driveway. She went in the front door ten seconds behind Chief Yardley and Officer Wade.

She heard male voices upstairs and took the steps two at a time. Panting, she joined the four other people standing in the upstairs hall.

Granddad was blocking the doorway to Noah's room, his arms out like a school crossing guard. The two policemen were in the hall and so was Noah, red-faced and baring his teeth.

He swept his arm toward Granddad. "He won't let me into the room I paid for. He's ranting that I'm going to destroy evidence. I don't know what he's talking about. I want to pick up something that belongs to me."

Granddad didn't budge, blocking the door next to the *Rope* poster. "I know what you want to get. The rope you hid in the magazine basket. It matches the one you used to strangle Fawn."

After finding the plant hanger that was missing two lengths of rope, Granddad would recognize the matching rope when he saw it. Obviously, his search of Noah's room had gone beyond poking in the trash.

"I didn't put any rope in any basket." Noah glared at Granddad. "You were in the room. You must have put it there."

Val stepped toward him, seeing a chance to turn Noah against his friends. "Why would my grandfather plant a rope in your room? He doesn't have a reason to frame you, but someone else staying here might want—" She broke off as the front door slammed.

Sounds came up the stairs from the hall below—Jennifer's breathy voice, Payton's clipped syllables, and Sarina's grating tones.

Chief Yardley motioned his junior officer toward the staircase. "Keep them downstairs, Wade. Everyone here, follow Officer Wade downstairs, please."

Val lingered until Granddad and Noah had started down the stairs. Then she turned to the chief and kept her voice low. "One of the people in the wedding group killed Fawn. I can't prove it yet, but I might get them to turn on one another. That's the fastest way to find out the truth before they lawyer up."

His eyes narrowed. "Do you know something I don't?"

"Uh-huh. On Saturday Jennifer received an intimidating text message. On Sunday someone messed with her car. Noah spied on her before the murder Friday night. I know you don't think she was the strangler's target, but—"

"I haven't ruled it out. Fawn's husband came up with a solid alibi for Friday night. Right now, I have no other suspects in her murder and no reason to detain any of those folks downstairs. You gonna give me a reason?"

"I'll try my best."

He pressed his lips together and gave a curt nod. "Okay, but I'll cut you off if you go too far. I don't want the case compromised."

They went downstairs. He stopped halfway down the staircase and addressed the group gathered in the hall. "Would you mind going into the sitting room, folks? There are new developments in the investigation into your friend's death."

Val waited in the archway between the hall and the sitting room while the guests filed into the sitting room. Sarina sat at the end of the sofa near Noah's armchair, Jennifer next to her, and Payton on

Jennifer's other side. He sank into the old sofa, the bent knees of his long legs higher than his backside.

Val checked out the other knees in the room—Jennifer's exposed below the hem of her Bayport Outfitters skirt, Sarina's hidden under the gaucho pants she'd worn all weekend, and Noah's visible beneath his cargo shorts, but only on the left side. Val would have to squeeze between the sofa and the bay window for a view of his right side. From where she was standing, she couldn't see marks from a fondue fork on any of them.

Officer Wade set two dining-room chairs beside the fireplace. He caught Val's eye and silently offered her one of them. She shook her head.

The chief stood in front of the fireplace. "Val has some information to share. Let's start with that." He nodded to her and sat in the chair next to Wade, facing the group on the sofa.

She felt the eyes of everyone in the room on her as she stepped into the place the chief had vacated in front of the fireplace. "On Friday night, when we found out that Fawn had worn a crab hat, I wondered if the strangler might have mistaken her for someone else because the hat hid her face. Jennifer and I are about Fawn's height and we both wore crab hats. I was worried I might have been the intended victim. Did you think the same thing, Jennifer?"

The bride-to-be hesitated. "Not at first, but when someone ran after me in the maze, I was afraid of that."

"But what happened in the maze could have been a random prank," Val said. "Teenagers chased people in the maze, trying to scare them. So did maze employees in monster costumes. If you'd been with other people when someone chased you, you wouldn't have been scared."

Jennifer nodded. "That's true."

"So what happened to Jennifer in the maze doesn't prove someone intended to kill her." Val decided not to mention the rope she'd found on the ground there. No way to know who'd dropped it, and talking about it would just muddy her argument. "But the next day, when Jennifer found birds in her tailpipe, it was clear that someone was specifically targeting her."

The chief and Granddad looked at each other, puzzled. Val told them about the incident.

Granddad sat up straight. "A blocked exhaust pipe isn't really dangerous, but—"

"The intention matters, not the act," Sarina said.

"The target matters too." Val said. "It's easy to blame pranksters for what happened in the maze. Shoving things into a car's exhaust pipe looks like a prank too, but if the car belongs to the same person who was chased in the maze, you have an impossible-to-believe coincidence. Those couldn't have been random pranks. They were intended to threaten . . . or to look threatening."

Granddad piped up. "Don't forget the common thread. Murder by rope, pursuit in a cornfield, and threats by birds occur in the Hitchcock movies shown in the posters upstairs."

Payton gaped at him. "Are you saying some Hitchcock nut went after Fawn and Jennifer?"

Val jumped in before her grandfather could respond with the wrong answer. "Not necessarily.

The murder and the intimidation may not be the work of the same person, though the murder could have inspired what happened later." Val glanced out the bay window behind the sofa. The continued darkness told her that the storm wasn't going to blow over. She'd better hurry or her outdoor demonstration would be rained out. "If we pool what we each know, I think we can figure out whether Jennifer was the intended target. First, let's go to the backyard and see where and how Fawn was killed."

She rushed to the kitchen for props. While the others walked through the dining room, the butler's pantry, and the kitchen en route to the back door, Val dumped yogurt into a small bowl to substitute for the chocolate she didn't have time to melt. She put the bowl in the middle of a plate of strawberries and grabbed the other items left over from this morning's murder reenactment—a fondue fork and the clothesline, still with the loops that Gunnar had tied at each end.

She led the group to the picnic table flanked by two backless benches as the swirling wind blew her hair around. "I found Fawn dead near this table. She was strangled while sitting here, eating chocolate-dipped strawberries, leftovers from the fondue we'd served earlier."

Sarina arched one eyebrow. "She went into the kitchen and helped herself to the food?"

Jennifer flicked her wrist. "Typical of Fawn. She was a moocher."

She hadn't spoken ill of the dead Friday night. No longer the case by Monday noon.

"The yogurt is standing in for chocolate." Val

dipped a strawberry into the yogurt with her fingers. She didn't use the fondue fork, hoping her audience would forget it was there. "I'm going to play the role of Fawn. Who wants to play the strangler?"

No one jumped at the chance. The chief, Officer Wade, and Granddad stood apart from the wedding group, watching intently.

Jennifer stepped forward. "Okay. Tell me what to do." She took the rope from Val and held it away from her body as if it were a poisonous snake.

"Put one hand into each loop. That will give you a tight grip on the rope." Val sat down on the bench in front of the food, her back to Jennifer. "Now slip the rope over my head and tighten it."

Jennifer encircled Val's neck with the rope and pulled it straight back. "Like this?"

"You can't strangle me holding the rope that way. I'll just reach back and pull it away." Val grabbed it to demonstrate. Then she returned the rope to Jennifer. "You're going to have to start with your hands crossed to make a loop and throw it over my head."

Payton folded his arms. "This is sick."

Jennifer slipped the loop over Val's head and pulled on the ends to make it less slack, though she didn't come close to how tight it would have to be to strangle someone.

"Wait." Sarina held up her hand as if stopping traffic. "The strangler would have had a harder time getting the rope around Fawn's neck. Wasn't she wearing a crab hat? The claws hanging down would have gotten in the way of the rope."

But was Fawn wearing a crab hat at that point?

Val caught the chief's eye and shook her head to signal she wasn't going to mention the hat she'd seen near the body. "Fawn had gone inside the house already and she'd spent time in the kitchen. She cut up strawberries and warmed up leftover chocolate for her fondue snack. It would have been odd to keep a hat on her head all that time."

"If she wasn't wearing the hat," Sarina said, "then she would have been more recognizable as herself."

Val felt a drop of rain and wished Sarina would stop delaying her. "Without a hat, Fawn's face would have been more visible. But the strangler approached her from behind. Her hair and Jennifer's would have looked similar in the dark." Val glanced up at the clouds. *Go away. I need a few more minutes.*

Jennifer also looked up. "We're going to get wet if we stay out any longer." She led a rush to the back door, seconds before a curtain of rain descended, prematurely ending the outdoor scene.

Now Val wouldn't get to see the reactions from the wedding group when she used a fondue fork to defend herself. Taking the time to recreate the scene in the house wasn't worth it. This delay would make the killer's reactions less spontaneous, and her audience was losing its patience. She'd have to rely on words to expose the strangler.

Chief Yardley shepherded everyone out of the kitchen as Val brought her props inside and left them on the counter. She hurried into the sitting room for the last scene.

Chapter 23

Instead of standing like an emcee at the fireplace, Val sat where she had Friday night after the murder—on the ottoman she'd moved near Granddad's chair. *Now to make some truth soup, like the stone soup in the folk tale.* She was like a hungry stranger in the folktale, trying to trick the villagers into contributing the food they were each hoarding. Everyone in the wedding group had something to add to the soup pot and a reason not to share it. Her goal was to coax the necessary ingredients from them.

Noah chewed the inside of his cheek, obviously nervous.

Sarina made a show of consulting her watch with its thick leather strap. "I hope this doesn't take much longer. We have a lunch reservation in half an hour. Did we learn anything by going outside?"

Not as much at Val had hoped. "We've established that the strangler could have mistaken Fawn for Jennifer. The question remains whether the strangler targeted Jennifer after the murder. She went into a crowded maze with her friends. No one could depend on her being alone there and vulnerable. But two people knew exactly when she was alone." Val saw Noah and Sarina exchange wary looks. "The path where Jennifer was running intersected with the ones Noah and Sarina took when they separated to search for her. It would have been easy for one of them to have followed her."

Everyone in the wedding party looked astonished.

Payton raised a skeptical eyebrow. "Why would they?"

Val welcomed the question, especially from him, so she could answer it bluntly. "Maybe as payback for the double date when you and Jennifer treated your best friends badly."

Noah flicked his wrist. "We're over that."

His spying on Payton and Jennifer Friday night suggested otherwise, but Val didn't want to bring that up . . . yet. "One of you isn't over it. Jennifer got a text message yesterday, a little verse. *On a day in May, you got your way. Is this the day when you will pay?*" She recited it slowly as Officer Wade wrote in his notebook.

Payton frowned at his fiancée. "You didn't tell me about that message."

Jennifer glared at Sarina. "I don't know why you told *her* about it." She pointed at Val. "Some nut job sent me that text by mistake. It made no sense."

Val tapped her index finger on her forehead. "It made sense to me, Jennifer. You were going out with Noah and threw him over for Payton during a double date in May." She shifted her gaze from Jennifer to Noah. "Revenge is a dish best served cold. Combined with jealousy, it makes a powerful motive for murder."

"You're accusing *us* of wanting to murder Jennifer?" Noah's voice rose in outrage.

Sarina picked nonexistent lint from her pants. "I was with Jennifer when that verse popped up. Noah was in his room."

Noah couldn't have looked more surprised or angry if Sarina had smacked him. "That proves nothing. You can schedule a delivery time for a text." The gloves were off. He wouldn't be using *us* for himself and Sarina anymore.

Sarina gave him a steely look. "I had no reason to be angry or jealous because I wasn't ever supposed to end up with Payton. Jennifer had kept tabs on him for years. She went out with you because you were an avenue to him. You were the only one who got the shaft on that double date."

Better than Val had expected. She felt a surge of triumph. The fragile bond between the best man and the maid of honor hadn't been hard to break. How long would it take Jennifer's alliances to collapse?

Payton leaned away from Jennifer, looking askance at her. "Is that true?"

"Of course not. Sarina misunderstood," Jennifer said through clenched teeth. Her face relaxed when she looked into Payton's eyes. "I was attracted to you when I met you years ago. I never expected us to meet again. When Noah said he had a friend named Payton, I hoped his friend might be the handsome law student who helped me." She turned to Noah. "I should have told you that I had a crush

on someone named Payton years ago, but I had no
reason to think he'd remember me or that we'd
click. I'm sorry, Noah."

He stared stonily ahead.

Sarina scowled at Jennifer. "I did *not* misunder-
stand. Your campaign for Payton started long before
that sham double date."

"And it continued this weekend," Val added,
"with a campaign to breach the Grandsire fortress.
Jennifer took the first step in the campaign at the
maze when she slipped away from Noah and Sarina."

Jennifer's eyes blazed. "I didn't slip away. A bunch
of people stampeded us and we got separated. Then
someone chased me. What was I supposed to do?
Stand still? After Fawn was murdered, I wasn't taking
any chances."

Five minutes ago, before Jennifer's scheme to
snare Payton came to light, her friends would have
defended her, but not now.

Val forged ahead with a direct accusation. "Your
story of being pursued got you some attention from
Payton, but not the invitation you'd hoped for. So
you added the birds, which you bought in the same
Main Street shop where you bought clothes this
weekend."

"Bayport Outfitters," Granddad announced, delighted that his garbage picking had paid off.

Val pointed toward Granddad, but kept her eyes
on Jennifer. "Even my grandfather knows where
you got the birds. That's life in a small town. The
salesclerk remembered selling those birds this
weekend. She can identify you from a photo."

Jennifer wet her lips. "Okay. I bought the birds." She glanced at Payton, who squirmed in his seat, and then at Sarina, who looked askance at her. "I was really scared after someone chased me in the maze. I didn't want to be a sitting duck, here or in my apartment, where I'd be alone. I figured I'd be safer with you, Payton."

Words at odds with her actions, and Val wouldn't let her get away with it. "If you were really worried about your safety, why didn't you tell the police about the text with the intimidating verse? That would have convinced Payton fast enough, especially after the text he received Friday night in the restaurant." A stab in the dark that Val hoped would cut deep.

Payton eyed her with suspicion. "I tried to text back to the sender, but the number didn't work. What do you know about that text? Did you send it?"

"No, but I'll tell you who did send it, if you tell me what it said." Val focused on Payton, resisting the urge to watch Noah. She didn't want Payton following her gaze and drawing his own conclusions about the sender, at least not until she knew what was in that message.

Payton shrugged. "The message contained a calendar date, not a recent one, and a question— *What really happened that night? You don't know, but your fiancée does. Demand the truth from her.* It meant nothing to me or Jennifer."

Not recent. Val's pulse quickened. "Was it a date from ten years ago?"

Payton looked thunderstruck. "I thought you didn't know what was in the message."

"I had a hunch." But it had just come to her, along with the realization that she'd misinterpreted the verse sent to Jennifer. "What was the month and day?"

"I'll check." He whipped out his phone. "May 29th."

A key ingredient had just gone into the pot. Val wondered how she'd missed it in the online article about the bicyclist killed ten years ago. The first article she'd located had a June publication date, but it reported on an accident that had happened a few days prior to that. In her hunger for details about the driver and passenger, she hadn't taken the time to research the precise day of the accident.

"Who cares about a stupid anonymous message?" Jennifer pointed out the bay window behind the sofa. "It stopped raining, but it might start up again. Let's get to the restaurant before it does." She stood up, smoothing her skirt.

Payton reached for her arm and pulled her back down on the sofa. "We're not going anywhere until Val tells me who sent that message."

Val waited, hoping Noah would speak up. She'd never tattled as a kid. She hated to do it now, but she'd made a bargain with Payton and would keep it. "A man was sitting on the patio at the Bayport Bistro, across the lane from the Bugeye Tavern, where you and Jennifer ate Friday night. If the man hadn't been wearing a crab hat, you might have recognized him. Face recognition software had no trouble identifying him from a photo taken while he was sitting there. He was tapping out a message seconds before you read the text in the restaurant."

"Who was he?" Payton said. "And how do you know all this? Are you some kind of private detective?"

"Actually," Granddad piped up, "I'm a private detective . . . in training. She's learned a lot from me."

His aside gave Val an opportunity to stare down Noah and make it clear she would speak up if he didn't.

He crossed his legs, his eyes on Payton. "That was me at the bistro. I ordered dinner before I realized you two were at the restaurant across the way. I put on the crab hat because, if you saw me, it would have looked as if I was following you. But I didn't send you a text message."

Val didn't believe him, but the others might. *Add some spice to this soup.* "Well, then who else might have sent it, Payton? That day ten years ago was around the time you met Jennifer and Fawn. You were almost finished with law school. The bio on your firm's website says you worked in legal aid then."

Payton slapped his forehead with the palm of his hand. "May 29th! I remember now. Fawn must have sent it."

Val reared back in exaggerated surprise. "That message read like a poison pen letter. She didn't strike me as the kind of person who'd write something like that."

Granddad nodded vigorously. "Cute girl. Sweet disposition."

Jennifer put her hand on Payton's thigh. "We'll

never know if she sent it. It doesn't matter anyway now."

"That message matters, because it led to Fawn's murder." Val's statement had the dramatic effect she'd hoped. Payton gasped, Sarina's jaw dropped, and Noah recoiled. Val glanced at the chief. Judging by his raised eyebrows, she'd surprised him too. She continued, "There *is* a way to tell if Fawn sent that text to you in the restaurant. Do you still have the message, Payton?"

He pulled out his phone, poked and scrolled, and held it out to her.

She took the phone and read the message. "Pay attention to the wording. *What really happened that night? You don't know, but your fiancée does. Demand the truth from her.* The person who sent this is a careful writer. Full sentences. Correct punctuation. No typos, spelling errors, or even common texting abbreviations. But the message Noah received Friday night from Fawn, asking to have dinner with him, wasn't like that. When you showed it to the chief, Noah, he had trouble figuring out what it said."

The chief nodded. "Full of mistakes and quirks, barely readable."

Payton stood up, his hands fisted. "You sent me that text in the restaurant, Noah. Why?" With two long strides, he went around the coffee table and halfway to Noah's chair.

The chief sprang up and blocked him. "Sit down, Mr. Grandsire." He waited until Payton retreated and then moved closer to Noah, towering over the seated lawyer. "Did you send the message to Mr. Grandsire at the restaurant?"

Noah nodded. "I thought you'd recognize the date, Payton. It's when Jennifer and Fawn were in the car that killed the bicyclist. Jennifer was driving and texting. Fawn covered for her."

Jennifer's jaw dropped. "Did Fawn say that? It's not true. She was always a liar. Everyone thought she was so nice, but she was a bla—it doesn't matter."

Val wondered what Jennifer had started to say. Blabbermouth? Blackmailer?

Noah wiped sweat from his brow. "Fawn didn't say anything to me about the accident. Ten years ago, Payton told me about two attractive girls who'd come to the Legal Aid office for advice about an accident. I researched the incident and interviewed a frat boy who'd received a text sent from Jennifer's phone right before the accident. I still have a transcript of that message."

Sarina snorted. "After ten years?"

Noah shrugged. "I save all my paperwork. I dug up my notes about the accident when Jennifer and Payton got engaged. On Friday night, when Fawn sent me that message with all the mistakes in it, I realized she couldn't have texted from the car before the accident. The text from the car was errorless, standard English, like Jennifer's writing. I realized then that Jennifer was texting while driving and killed someone because of that."

Jennifer jumped up. "It's a lie. People don't always text the same way."

"Sit down, Ms. Brown," the chief said. "The truth will come out, but not by shouting."

Noah leaned forward in his chair, his hands folded. "After I read Fawn's text Friday night, I fired off that message to you at the restaurant, Payton. I was rattled to find out that Jennifer had hoodwinked you about the accident ten years ago. I should have waited to tell you the next time I saw you, but I thought you should know."

Noah had made it sound as if he'd acted out of loyalty to his friend, but Val suspected self-interest had motivated him. If Payton knew the truth, he might end his engagement to Jennifer, and Noah would be there to comfort her. The text Noah sent Payton in the restaurant didn't produce the effect Noah intended, so he tried again.

Val gave him a hard look. "You also texted Jennifer a verse on Sunday morning—*On a day in May, you got your way. Is this the day when you will pay?* I was wrong when I guessed that it referred to the double date the four of you had. You sent that verse to pressure Jennifer into telling the truth about the accident."

"I didn't have any idea what that verse was supposed to mean." Jennifer extended her hands, palms up, in an appeal. The others in the wedding group didn't respond to it.

Val looked straight at Jennifer. "This weekend you went to great lengths to suggest someone was threatening you. That verse would have proved it. Yet you kept quiet about it. Why? Because it was tied to your motive for murdering Fawn."

Payton and Sarina protested.

Jennifer's eyes blazed at Val. "You're crazy. You know nothing about it."

"I know you were doing well financially. Fawn wasn't." Val had surmised the rest. "Fawn did you a huge favor ten years ago, lying about who'd typed the text in the car right before the accident. After she ran into you last month, she demanded favors in return. You had to include her in your wedding so she could hobnob with Payton's rich friends. You had to cover the cost of her room this weekend. Maybe you even gave her money to pay her bills. If you'd refused, she might have told Payton and the police what really happened that night."

"I didn't murder her. You can't prove that I did."

Val returned Jennifer's defiant look. "Fawn had only one weapon to use against her strangler—a fondue fork. I think she stabbed her killer with it. I played the role of victim earlier today and hit the mock strangler in the thigh with the fondue fork." She glanced at the chief. Did he now have grounds to check Jennifer for tine marks?

Payton reached out to Jennifer as if to hold her hand. In a sudden move, he tugged up her skirt and ripped off a Band-aid. Two scabs, half an inch apart, marred her lovely leg.

Chapter 24

The sun was shining by the time Val joined Granddad, Mom, and Gunnar at the crab house for a late lunch. They ate on the deck of the restaurant overlooking the river, with water lapping against the piers as background music. Keeping her voice low so the other diners couldn't hear, Val told Mom and Gunnar the strangler's identity and the motive. She answered their questions until Granddad quashed further talk about the murder, saying he wanted to forget about it and enjoy his meal.

After lunch, Val picked up the food she'd need for the café the next day, Mom returned to the house with Granddad so she could pack, and Gunnar went to buy ingredients for the dinner he insisted on cooking for Val that night.

Four hours after Chief Yardley escorted Fawn's murderer to police headquarters, Val was giving her mother a good-bye hug in the driveway.

"I'm so glad I got to meet Gunnar," Mom said. "He's a keeper. Don't you think so, Pop?"

"He's all right."

Val hid her astonishment. What had Gunnar done to merit such high praise from Granddad?

Mom started up her rental car and rolled down the window. "I meant to ask you about Bethany, Val. She ate baby food for lunch. Does the poor thing have digestion problems?"

"No, Mom, she has body image problems. She tries on wacky diets for size. She'll give up this one by tomorrow or the next day." But the protein bar diet might replace it. Val turned to Granddad after her mother drove off. "Now I'm going to unpack the big suitcase I filled up three days ago."

He joined her in her bedroom, carrying an armful of her clothes on hangers. "Here's some stuff you put in my closet."

She took the clothes from him and hung them up. "I'll bring up the rest later."

"Okay." He went over to the table and chair by the window and sat down. "Too bad the rain washed out your murder demonstration in the backyard. Were you planning to poke Jennifer with a fondue fork?"

"With the handle, but she couldn't count on that. Once stabbed, twice shy. If she jumped out of the way of the fork, I would have been positive she'd killed Fawn. As it was, I was ninety percent certain."

"I sure didn't see her as the murderer. She couldn't make up her mind about the smallest thing without asking for advice. I figured she'd take a poll before she murdered anybody, but she acted fast Friday night."

Val moved her athletic shorts from the suitcase to the bottom drawer of her dresser. "Jennifer only pretended to be indecisive. She was never going to leave Bayport unless Payton went with her. She asked people for their opinions and then took the advice that matched what she'd already decided."

"What made you think she was guilty?"

Val held up her hand and ticked off the clues on her fingers. "The fondue fork, her new clothes, the crab hats, the ropes, and the texts. They don't mean much in themselves but when you string them together, they tell a story."

"You gotta give me some credit. You figured out that Fawn used the fondue fork on the strangler because of the bloody Band-Aids I found."

Partly. "Yes, but I didn't know whose blood was on them. Jennifer's clothes gave it away. Before the murder, she wore really short skirts, showing off her legs. The morning after the murder, she wore blue jeans, probably the only long pants she'd packed. As soon as she could, she went shopping for a skirt and pants that would cover her legs above the knee."

"But she couldn't keep Payton's hands off her thighs."

"So he knew she didn't have a Band-Aid on before the murder and she did afterwards." Val took T-shirts from the suitcase and stacked them on the bed. "Hiding her wound was only one of Jennifer's problems after the murder. Apart from Fawn's husband, she was the likeliest strangler because she knew Fawn. So Jennifer had to convince people that the strangler really intended to kill her."

Granddad pointed to the crab hat Val had left on the table. "Those hats helped her do it. She could have left her crab hat here when she came back to the house before the fireworks. But she wore it to play up her resemblance to Fawn."

"And she dropped a hat near the body so everyone would think Fawn was wearing it when she was strangled."

Granddad rubbed his chin. "What do you think happened to your favorite knife? We haven't seen it since the murder."

Val had given up hope that the knife would turn up in the house. "Jennifer probably grabbed it when she stopped at the house before the fireworks Friday night. It would have fit in that long, narrow purse she was carrying this weekend. Maybe she intended to stab Fawn, but on her way to the fireworks, she saw the rope plant hanger and decided to strangle Fawn instead."

"No blood to get her clothes dirty. She took a second piece of rope to plant on a scapegoat. After I found the rope in Noah's room, I was sure he was the strangler." Granddad rested his chin on the palm of his hand. "I wonder what she did with the fondue fork."

"She might have put the fork, the knife, and Fawn's phone in the portable johns at the festival. Jennifer told me she visited them early Saturday while they were still clean."

"I don't want that fork back if that's where it went." Granddad grimaced. "It's a good place to ditch incriminating evidence. The folks who vacuum out those things have found guns in the muck. Do you know why Jennifer took Fawn's phone?"

"I guess to keep the police from finding any texts about the accident. She assumed Fawn had sent the text to Payton in the restaurant Friday night. So she got rid of Fawn to make sure Payton didn't find out the truth about the accident." Val paired up the socks jumbled in the suitcase. "The next morning, when Jennifer got the rhyming text, she realized that killing Fawn hadn't solved her problem. No wonder she got sick when read that verse."

"Noah didn't commit the murder, but he's partly guilty. If he hadn't sent those texts, Fawn would be alive. He should have taken Payton aside and told him Jennifer lied about the accident."

"But then Jennifer would have blamed Noah if her marriage plans fell through. He sent the texts to push her into telling the truth, hoping Payton would then break off their engagement." Val moved the socks to her dresser. "If Payton's as scrupulous as Sarina says, he wouldn't have excused Jennifer's lie. He might even correct the record about that accident."

"Jennifer could be prosecuted for manslaughter, but that's better than first-degree murder. You remember the two old movies Noah talked about when he arrived on Friday, the first Hitchcock talkies?"

Val nodded. "*Murder!* and *Blackmail.* Who knew the weekend would involve those two things?"

Granddad stood up and gazed out the window overlooking the backyard. "Fawn really had me fooled. She was like a sour grape dipped in chocolate fondue, sweet only on the outside."

"She was desperate for money, but she probably wouldn't have done anything if Jennifer had stood up to her. After all, Fawn had lied about the accident too." Val zipped up the now empty suitcase. "This whole weekend was about dealing with the past. For the wedding group. For me, with Tony and Chef Henri." And the job offer she would turn down tomorrow. "Even your dessert came from the past."

"I'll never make it again. From now on, I'm all about the future." He walked toward the door of her room and then turned back with a mischievous grin. "There's one mystery you didn't solve this weekend. You never figured out who was in Monique's backyard."

Val couldn't remember telling him about the prowler. Why was he looking so pleased with himself? Light dawned. "*You* were there? You frightened Monique's mother-in-law. She took the kids away for the weekend."

"That's better than the chef storming the place to get at you. The police wouldn't protect you. I had to do it myself, with a little help from Gunnar. He relieved me Saturday night just before midnight. I told him to keep watch until dawn."

"*What?* He stayed up all night?" No wonder he'd been so irritable about Tony. Lack of sleep would make anyone testy . . . and spacey enough to do something out of character, like leaving litter behind.

"I tested him to see how much he really cared for you. And he passed the test."

"I'm glad he finally met your high expectations." Despite her dry tone, she really was delighted. "By the way, I'm going over to Gunnar's place now. Don't wait up for me."

Granddad frowned. "What about my dinner?"

"You had a big meal at the crab house. I brought home the leftovers from the booth. There's plenty to eat in the fridge."

"I figured you and I could work on *The Codger's Cookbook*."

"I'm taking the night off, Granddad."

"Well, then I'll finish my detective lessons. After that, I may take a course in viral marketing. I have to do a media campaign for *The Codger's Cookbook* and my sleuthing business."

Val put her arm around his shoulder. "You can't teach an old dog new tricks—that doesn't apply to you."

"Sure doesn't." He pointed to his chest. "This old dog teaches himself new tricks."

Acknowledgments

I'd like to thank those who contributed the essential ingredients to make *Final Fondue*: subject-matter experts, writing partners, beta reviewers, and the publishing team.

Thank you to D. P. Lyle, M.D. for information that helped me create the crime scene. I'm grateful to my son, Paul Corrigan, who provided a Gen-Xer's perspective on technology and terminology. Thanks also to my friend Susan Fay, who contributed a key idea for the murder scenario.

Thank you to my writing partners, mystery authors Carolyn Mulford and Helen Schwartz, who gave me helpful advice during our weekly meetings. Their suggestions on the first draft through the nearly final version of this book were invaluable.

I'd also like to thank everyone who read the book in its late stages for their helpful feedback: Joyce Campbell, Paul Corrigan, Toni Corrigan, Susan Fay, and Elliot Wicks. As always, I'm grateful to Mike Corrigan for his support through the long process of writing a book and his comments on the manuscript. Special thanks to him for acting out several variations of the crime scene with me and for accepting whichever role I assigned to him, murderer or victim.

I'm grateful to the team who worked on *Final Fondue* at Kensington Books: my editor, John Scognamiglio, the cover designer, copy editors and proofreaders, and the marketing and sales team.

Finally, there would be no *Final Fondue* without readers who enjoy mysteries. Thank you.

The Codger Cook's Recipes

FIRST FONDUE

The first chocolate fondue in recorded history was made with triangular-shaped Toblerone chocolate bars, which contain honey and nuts.

½ cup heavy cream
3 3.5-ounce bars of Toblerone milk chocolate, chopped into small pieces
1 tablespoon cognac or kirsch

Heat the cream until hot in a heavy saucepan over medium heat. Remove the cream from the heat, add the chocolate, and let it stand 3 minutes. Stir when the chocolate is melted. Thin the mixture slightly with liqueur, whisking it into the chocolate.

Pour the chocolate into a small fondue pot on a stand over a lit candle.

Serve with your choice of fresh fruit and angel food or pound cake.

Serves 6. Reheat leftover fondue in a heavy pan over medium heat, stirring until warm.

FAST FONDUE

Cut up the fruit and cake before you start making this recipe. With a microwave, the fondue is ready within minutes.

¾ cup heavy cream
12 ounces of semisweet or bittersweet chocolate, chopped fine
1–2 tablespoons cognac, liqueur, or rum.

Mix the cream and the chopped chocolate in a microwave-safe bowl. Heat the cream and chocolate at half-power for 2 minutes, stopping the microwave every 30 seconds to stir the mixture. Whisk in the liqueur.

Pour the chocolate into a small fondue pot on a stand over a lit candle.

Serve with your choice of fresh fruit, dried fruit, angel food or pound cake, ladyfingers, cream puffs, cookies, or marshmallows.

Serves 6. Reheat leftover fondue in the microwave at half-power, stirring every 30 seconds.

SCRUMPTIOUS SHRIMP

It's harder to say the name of this recipe fast five times than to make it for dinner. Serve it as a first course, or add crusty French bread and a salad for a main dish.

    1 pound of large shrimp, shelled and with veins
        removed
    2 tablespoons olive oil
    2 large cloves of garlic, chopped fine
    1 14.5-ounce can of diced tomatoes
    3 ounces feta cheese, crumbled into small
        pieces

Heat the oil in a 10- or 12-inch skillet over medium-high heat until the oil is hot, but not smoking. Add the shrimp and garlic to the pan. Cook for a minute, stirring the shrimp around.

Add the tomatoes with juices and stir to loosen any brown bits in the bottom of the pan. Cook until the mixture is hot, turn the heat down low, and simmer until the shrimp are cooked through (around 3 minutes, longer for jumbo shrimp).

Stir in the cheese and serve the shrimp. If you want the cheese to melt into the shrimp mixture, keep stirring over low heat before you remove it from the skillet.

Serves 4 as an appetizer or 3 as a main course.

STRESSLESS STROGANOFF

This dish doesn't put stress on your teeth or your time. It uses beef tenderloin tips, a less expensive cut than filet mignon, but just as tender. If you want to give your choppers more of a workout, you can make this dish with sirloin.

- 1–1¼ pounds boneless beef tenderloin tips, sliced into ¼-inch thin strips
- 2 large onions, thinly sliced
- 12 ounces mushrooms, thinly sliced
- 4 tablespoons olive oil, divided (2 tablespoons for the vegetables and 2 for the meat)
- 1 cup sour cream
- Optional: 1 tablespoon Dijon mustard. Salt and pepper to taste.

Cut the beef into strips ¼-inch thick and set it aside.

Heat 2 tablespoons of olive oil in a heavy 12-inch skillet until the oil is hot, but not smoking. Put in the onion slices and stir to break them up. Cook until they're soft and translucent. Then add the sliced mushrooms. Cook the mixture over medium heat for about 3 minutes. Empty the mushrooms and onions into a large strainer set over a bowl to catch the juices. Keep the juices handy in case you want to add them later.

Wipe out the skillet with paper towels. Heat 2 tablespoons of oil until hot. Pat the beef strips dry with a paper towel to make sure they brown well. Add the beef to the skillet. Cook over high heat until the meat is browned all over, about 2 minutes.

Turn the heat to medium. Dump the mushroom and onions into the skillet. Mix in the sour cream (and the mustard for a spicier dish). Heat the mixture through, and taste it. Add the juices from the vegetables if you prefer a thinner mixture. Season to taste with salt and freshly ground pepper. Serve with rice or noodles.

Serves 3-4.

SLEEP-ON-IT CASSEROLE

You assemble this casserole and then put it in the refrigerator to rest. You can sleep on it all night or take a nap while it's in the fridge. The ingredients listed are for a vegetarian casserole. You can make a meat version by changing one ingredient. See the directions below.

Preheat the oven to 350 degrees.

Stale or toasted French or wheat bread, enough to cover the pan in one layer

6 eggs

2 cups milk

1 cup chopped fire-roasted red peppers, fresh
   or from a jar

1 cup grated sharp cheddar (or pepper jack
   cheese, if you like spicy food)

Cube the stale bread and spread it in a single layer
at the bottom of a 9x13-inch pan.

Sprinkle the chopped pepper and the grated cheese
on the cubed bread.

Beat the eggs with the milk and pour the mixture
over the bread and cheese.

Cover the pan and refrigerate it overnight or for a
minimum of an hour.

Bake the casserole for 45 minutes.

Serves 6 for breakfast, brunch, or lunch.

For a meat version, brown and drain a pound of
bulk sausage (pork or turkey) as the first step. Then
follow the vegetarian recipe, but substitute sausage
for the peppers. If you're not hung up on using
only five ingredients, you can use both the meat
and peppers in the casserole. The recipe for the
meat casserole is similar to the strata recipe at the
end of *By Cook or by Crook*, the first *Five-Ingredient
Mystery*, but this version includes details that were
missing from that one and some variations.

With meat, the casserole serves 8.

NUTTY BUTTERY MINI MUFFINS

Even if you don't like breakfast muffins, you might like these. They're sweet enough to serve for dessert. They don't even have a lot of calories if you limit yourself to one. Good luck with that.

Preheat the oven to 350 degrees.

    ¾ cup light brown sugar, packed down
    ½ cup flour
    1 cup chopped pecans
    ⅔ cup melted butter
    2 beaten eggs

Grease and flour 18–24 mini muffin cups or line them with paper muffin liners. (The cups for small muffins vary in size and that's why the number of muffins varies.)

Beat the melted butter and eggs together. In a separate bowl, mix the sugar, flour, and pecans. Make a well in the center of the dry ingredients, pour the wet egg and butter mix into the well, and stir just enough to combine everything.

Spoon the mixture into muffin cups. The cups should be ⅔ full. If you have some unused cups in your muffin pan, put a teaspoon of water in the empty cups.

Bake for 20–25 minutes. They're done when a toothpick inserted into them comes out clean. Cool them on a wire rack for at least 10 minutes.

Yield: 18–24